Praise for The Rogues' Dynasty series

"Sweeps readers along at a lively pace in a lusciously spicy romp."

—*Library Journal*

"A sinfully delicious read... Completely beguiling and never misses a beat with memorable characters, sensual love scenes, and a lovely ending."

—*Book Junkie*

"A captivating mix of discreet intrigue and potent passion."

—*Booklist*

"Grey's Rogues' Dynasty mixes romance with a touch of mystery. Add in lively characters and a strong hero and heroine, and the result is one delightful novel."

—*RT Book Reviews*, 4 stars

"An intoxicating story meant to be savored... Amelia Grey entrances with this devilishly charming romance."

—*Fresh Fiction*

"An exotic tale of passion and mystery that will leave you breathless."

—*Best Romance Stories*

Praise for *A Gentleman Never Tells*

Grey combines wit and charm in another enchanting, delicious romance… This is a story to sit back and enjoy."

—*RT Book Reviews*, 4 stars

Delightful… charming characters… great chemistry… The dialogue was sharp and amusing and I found myself laughing during several of the escapades."

—*Night Owl Romance* Reviewer Top Pick

A stubborn heroine clashes with an equally determined hero in the latest well-crafted, canine-enhanced addition Grey's Regency-set Rogues' Dynasty series."

—*Booklist*

A beautifully written tale… Brimming with humor, sizzling hot love scenes, charismatic and compelling characters, a touch of mystery, terrific repartee, love, intriguing plot, and disappearing dogs, this book is delight."

—*Romance Junkies*

Funny and charming, sensual and compelling… a delightful Regency-era romance."

—*Long and Short Reviews*

Well written, it offers… touches of humor, mystery, and steaminess… Very refreshing."

—*Bookloons*

Praise for *Never A Bride*

"Lively pace, appealing protagonists, and sexual chemistry that almost visibly shimmers between them in a charming, lighthearted, and well-done Regency."

—*Library Journal*

"Witty dialogue and clever schemes... Both of Grey's vivid characters will charm readers."

—*Booklist*

"I absolutely adored this story. The characters are beautifully developed, their chemistry is unmatched, and the story is written so superbly that you fly through the pages and are swept away."

—*Long and Short Reviews*

"Captivating... a delightful tale full of mystery and intrigue."

—*Fresh Fiction*

"A delightful Regency romp. You'll have lots of fun with this one!"

—Kat Martin, author of *The Handmaiden's Necklace*

"Charming and delightful—a must-read! Fresh and original and destined to be a keeper."

—Joan Johnston, *New York Times* bestselling author of *Rebels*

A LITTLE MISCHIEF

AMELIA GREY

sourcebooks
casablanca

Published by Sourcebooks Casablanca, an imprint of Sourcebooks,
Inc.
P.O. Box 4410, Naperville, Illinois 60567-4410
(630) 961-3900
FAX: (630) 961-2168
www.sourcebooks.com

Originally published in 2003 by The Berkley Publishing Group, a
division of Penguin Group (USA) Inc., New York

Printed and bound in the United States of America
VP 10 9 8 7 6 5 4 3 2 1

One

The first week of the Season draws to a close with a flurry of elegant parties and delicious news. The dashing Lord Colebrooke has returned to London to attend the rest of the Season. Word has it he is determined to make a match before Season's end. There is news about a group of young ladies who meet in the home of Miss Isabella Winslowe. Hmm—can anyone report on what mischief those damsels might be up to?
—Lord Truefitt, *Society's Daily Column*

DANIEL FLETCHER COLEBROOKE, THE SEVENTH EARL OF Colebrooke, folded the broadsheet before letting it drop to the floor by his feet. He settled into the comfortable leather-covered wing chair in the book room of his London town house. Leaping flames flickered and crackled in the fireplace, casting pleasant shadows on the bookshelves, the furniture, and the lean face of his best friend.

The brandy in Daniel's glass, warmed by his hand, slid smoothly down his throat as he took a sip. It was an unusually cold spring afternoon. The brandy and the fire took the chill off the dreary gray day.

"You know, Chilton, I could not care less what the gossips say about me."

Sitting opposite Daniel, his impeccably dressed friend eyed him with unconcealed doubt. "Liar. I remember when you used to take great delight if any of the scandal sheets saw fit to mention your name."

When Daniel was second in line to the title, that used to be true, but things had changed. Back then he was young and restless and enjoyed the excitement of doing things that brought the eyes and ears of Society to him and away from his older brother.

"Those days were a lifetime ago," Daniel said, more to himself than to Chilton.

"Merely two and a half years. You used to be an adventurous friend and a sought-after rake by all the young ladies, Danny. Now you are as dull as a lamppost."

Daniel laughed and remained relaxed in his comfortable chair by the low-burning fire. The warmth of the familiar room and the banter with his close friend made him aware of how much he'd missed being in London and enjoying the company of his friends and family.

"That's what I call an endearing remark from a friend of more than a dozen years. No chance of a man feeling melancholy when you're around."

"Everyone in the *ton* was upset that you chose to skip all the parties last Season and make a pilgrimage to your lands and holdings throughout the country."

"Damnation," Daniel muttered with no real frustration in his voice. "I was in mourning for my father and my older brother as well as trying to comfort my distraught sister. I needed to get away from London and see to my estates. I hadn't exactly been groomed to take over managing the properties."

Chilton stretched his long legs out before him and crossed one booted foot over the other. "Not an excuse, Danny. Eight months had passed. As the new earl, Society thought you should have at least attended the parties and looked over their eligible young ladies."

Daniel gave his older, dark-eyed friend a knowing smile. "The way you do every year? You look whether or not you intend to take."

"It keeps the pushy mamas and eager fathers at bay."

"You would be a handsome catch for any lady," Daniel told him.

"If I were interested."

"And why aren't you?"

"I'm content."

Daniel couldn't help noticing that Chilton hesitated before he answered, and it wasn't contentment that Daniel heard in his voice. It was more like resignation. Daniel wondered what had happened in Chilton's life in the year he'd been gone.

"Has it escaped the *ton*'s notice that you look over the young ladies every Season, but at thirty-three you have yet to make a match?"

Reflections of the fire flashed in Chilton Cummerford's eyes as he warmed to the debate. "Ah—but don't let your memory fail you so quickly. The *ton* doesn't care as much about the second son of a title as it does a title."

"Oh, the title again."

"You can't escape it. Society considers it downright vulgar when an eligible earl leaves Town and doesn't attend even one party of the Season."

Daniel's smile turned to a grin. "It sounds as if someone is trying to intimidate me. Did anyone send you to speak to me about my neglected duties?"

Chilton shook his head, but the movement was so slight Daniel might have missed it in the dim firelight had he not been watching his friend so closely.

"Right now you are the most eligible gentleman on the market in London, and the *ton* wants you to attend the parties and act like you know it."

"What a wretched thought," Daniel muttered, and then took a deep breath.

"I understand that you don't want to be leg-shackled, but it's expected of you."

"I'm beginning to believe you are the one responsible for telling the gossips that I was returning to London to find a wife."

Chilton's lips curved in a roguish smile. "Why would I want to tell on my best friend?"

"Jealousy, of course."

"Right." Chilton huffed under his breath and stirred in his chair. "I'm filled with envy because you are now an earl with all the responsibilities the title carries, and I am still merely a second son with a generous income and absolutely no responsibilities whatsoever."

Daniel shrugged and wondered why he couldn't decide if Chilton was mocking him or himself. There was something about his friend that was different, but Daniel couldn't quite put his finger on what it was. Yet.

He chose to ignore Chilton's comment and said,

"No doubt Gretchen or Aunt Mattie let it slip to someone that I intended to come back to town for the purpose of making a match. It appears that my returning to claim a bride has made the *ton* happy."

"Deliriously so."

"If not myself."

"You don't matter. It's the title that is important. There's already a wager in the book at White's that you'll have your first offer from some young lady's father tomorrow morning before you've finished dressing."

Daniel inhaled the deep, satisfying aroma of the brandy before he sipped his drink. He then looked at Chilton and asked, "How much did you wager?"

"Danny, do you think I would bet on my oldest and dearest friend?"

"In an instant."

"Five pounds."

"Ouch. Why so little?"

"I expect to lose."

Daniel laughed again. He'd missed Chilton and the carefree days of their youth. In the past they had enjoyed spending their nights gaming at the private tables and drinking until dawn broke the sky. Most of their days had been spent gambling or racing horses. But Daniel knew those times of ignoring all the rules were behind him. His destiny was now to be a respectable, married member of the *ton*, not a rakish bachelor in search of debauchery.

"Back in Town, and in less than twenty-four hours, I'm in White's book? I'm flattered."

"Now, that sounds like the old Daniel."

"Damn, Chilton," Daniel said, letting his guard drop for a moment as he stared into the fire. "Life was so much easier before I came into the title. Back when I was merely the Honorable Daniel Colebrooke, with no thought of ever stepping into my father's shoes."

Chilton drained his glass before saying, "You're up to the task."

There were times over the past two years when he didn't think he was. Daniel had no idea of the magnitude of his father's wealth until the earl's death. Being the second son born, Daniel had no thoughts of ever becoming the Earl of Colebrooke. That honor should have fallen to his brother. Not Daniel. He had been content to live in London playing the carefree role of the gentleman rogue.

Daniel picked up the brandy decanter from the table beside him and passed it to Chilton. "I don't relish the idea of having a wife," Daniel said.

"What man does? It's just an easier life when you have no one depending on you."

"Well said."

"But you must choose a girl suitable to be your countess if you don't want the title to pass to your cousin and his son. You have no choice," his friend reminded.

Daniel's gaze met Chilton's. "I won't let that happen. Bradford would gamble the fortune away before a year had passed. No, I'm committed to marry before I'm thirty."

"By autumn, then?"

"By summer."

Chilton splashed a generous amount of the fine brandy into his glass and handed the decanter back to Daniel. "You have a late start."

"Now that I've set my mind to getting the job

done, it shouldn't take too long to find an acceptable lady to be my wife."

"I can tell you've never seriously considered marriage if an acceptable lady is all you're looking for."

"No, I haven't. Have you?"

Daniel didn't know what made him ask the question, but he wasn't prepared for the troubled expression that flashed briefly across Chilton's face.

Chilton didn't immediately answer but sipped his drink instead. The fire crackled and hissed as the silence stretched. "No, not seriously," he finally answered and immediately added, "Look on the bright side, there is always a chance you'll walk into a party and see the lady of your dreams and fall madly in love."

Daniel nodded. "And there is always a chance it will snow in July, but it doesn't. I need a wife to give me sons. Not love. Besides, if you haven't found anyone you want to marry this Season, I don't hold out much hope for finding the perfect lady for me."

"I'll take that as a compliment to my high standards." Chilton smiled a bit wickedly at Daniel and lifted his glass to him, the earlier sign of concern gone. "But as you know, my mistress serves me well. I have no need to look for a wife. You, on the other hand, need an heir."

Daniel groaned. "Perish the thought."

Chilton swirled his brandy in his glass and for a moment seemed mesmerized by the dark amber liquid. "I should get to the reason I'm here."

"I thought we had."

"Truly? You thought I came out on a dreadfully cold afternoon such as this just to talk about you?"

"Well, you did give me the scandal sheet to read as soon as I poured the brandy."

"Yes, but the reason I'm here is about the other bit of news written in the column."

"Really?" Daniel could see in Chilton's dark eyes that he was serious and tried to remember what he'd read. What was it—something about a lady and mischief?

"It's about Gretchen."

Daniel perked up. "My sister? I didn't see anything in the column about Gretchen." He bent to pick up the sheet of paper he'd dropped to the floor earlier.

"Don't bother looking at it again. Her name isn't there."

Leaving the paper where it lay, Daniel said, "Then what the devil are you talking about? I instructed Aunt Mattie to see to it Gretchen was invited to all the right parties and to secure her vouchers for Almack's."

"I'm sure your aunt has done a splendid job. I don't think the parties are the problem. It's whom she dances with at the parties and with whom she has tea."

"Who?"

"I'm not sure you'll be happy with one of the bachelors who might be pursuing her."

Daniel shifted forward to the edge of his chair. The fire and the brandy heated his face. "Tell me."

"Boswell Throckmorten."

"Damnation! That drunken wastrel. Are you sure?"

"Quite."

Daniel shook his head in disbelief. "Before they left for London, I instructed Aunt Mattie to make sure Gretchen was presented to acceptable fellows like Thomas Wright and Harry Pepperfield."

"I'm sure she was. I've seen her dance with both Tom and Harry."

"Then *what* the bloody hell is she doing dancing with a gambling scoundrel like Throckmorten?"

"Neither man is as handsome as Throckmorten. I'm sure she's flattered by his attention."

"What was Aunt Mattie thinking to allow Gretchen to know him?"

"She probably had no choice. You have to admit that Throckmorten is a charmer when it comes to ladies. I'm sure Gretchen prefers him to Pepperfield or Wright."

"But what would a man like Throckmorten see in a young lady like Gretchen?"

"Spoken like a true brother."

Daniel pulled on his tight collar and neckcloth. Suddenly the chill had gone out of the air. "Don't get grumpy, Chilton. You know I only meant that she's always been so shy, and she can't see a damn thing without her spectacles. She hates to wear them, but she trips over things and bumps into furniture when she doesn't."

"How long has it been since you've spent any time with your sister?"

Daniel thought back. "I saw her in the Cotswolds not more than a month ago, but only for a day or two. Why?"

"You look at her through a brother's eyes. I think you might be surprised at how she's changed."

"In what way?"

"She's no longer shy for one thing. She does wear her spectacles." Chilton paused and looked thoughtful a moment before adding, "But even when she has them on, it's clear she's blossomed into quite a lovely young lady."

Daniel had missed that. He had to admit that with his travels, he hadn't taken the time to really look at Gretchen, and certainly not the way another man would look at her.

"Do you really think Throckmorten is pursuing her?"

"Or her dowry," Chilton said without hesitation.

Daniel eased back into his chair. It had never crossed his mind that someone like Throckmorten would take an interest in Gretchen. The man usually went for the prettiest of the young ladies, but then Throckmorten would assume Gretchen's dowry would be substantial. And to a big gambler like him that would be important if he were seriously considering marriage.

"I think you may be right, Chilton."

"It's only a possibility, Danny. As I said, Gretchen is quite fetching."

Fetching? Gretchen? Daniel would take a closer look at his sister when she returned home.

To Chilton he said, "I want to see her married to a decent man—not some fancy-dressed dandy who lives off his winnings and can't stay out of his cups or the gaming hells."

"Yes, I saw Throckmorten at White's placing his bets only a short time before I came over here, and he was already quite foxed."

It appeared Daniel had come to town not a moment too soon. "No doubt Throckmorten wants the steady income a generous dowry would afford him."

"Could be, but he is only part of the problem."

There was more? "What do you mean? Just spit it out, Chilton. I don't have the patience to pull each word from you."

"Gretchen has also become part of a group of ladies who are being talked about in an…"

"What?"

"Unflattering way," he finished. "Some of the young bachelors are calling them the Wallflower Society. The group mentioned in the newspaper."

Daniel rose from his chair and stood before the fire. "Gretchen? In a group called Wallflowers and said to be up to mischief? Good Lord. First, Throckmorten, and now this. What is she thinking? And what is this group about?"

"The name only pokes fun at the ladies, of course. I think they call themselves a Reading Society or something like that. I really don't know any details. I just wanted to make you aware of everything that's going on since you've only just returned. I didn't want you to be caught off guard by any of this when you attend your first party. I don't think harm is intended by this group, but…"

"Say it."

"Some of the young ladies who visit with Miss Winslowe on Tuesdays and Thursday are, shall we say, considered the least likely ones to make a match their first Season."

"Hence the term *Wallflowers?*"

"Exactly. I can't help wondering if Miss Winslowe is a troublemaker."

"She's probably just some lady with nothing better

to do than befriend a few young ladies. What kind of trouble could a Reading Society get into?"

"Perhaps you're right."

"Who is this Miss Winslowe, and why does she have such a gathering?"

"I'll leave you to form your own opinion of the lady when you meet her, as no doubt you will when you attend your first party this evening. Suffice it to say her little gathering started last year with only a handful of ladies, but this year her group has grown to about a dozen. It appears the mothers don't seem to mind because it makes their daughters appear more sought after when they are part of a select group."

"How, if they are called Wallflowers?"

"That term is not widely known among the *ton*. Only a few of the confirmed bachelors are having a bit of fun with it. Somehow, once a part of the group, some of the ladies seem like anything but wallflowers."

"I wonder why Gretchen would want to be part of a group like that."

"Apparently whatever they do helps the young ladies overcome their shyness."

Daniel looked into the fire. He'd come back to London in the nick of time. "Well, that can't be all bad, but I agree about one thing. No mother should want her daughter associating with a group called Wallflowers. If that name got out, it could prevent Gretchen from making a good match."

"My thoughts exactly."

"I'll speak to her immediately when she returns. She won't be attending any more of Miss Winslowe's Wallflowers meetings."

Elizabeth's eyes opened to cold darkness and the eerie feeling of not knowing what disturbance had stirred her slumber.

She rose on her elbows and listened, trying to ascertain what had startled her. Her pale green eyes scanned the darkened corners of her bedchamber. Her sight slowly adjusted to the moonlit room. No one was there. Nothing appeared out of place.

This was the first time Elizabeth had spent the night in the drafty old house on Glenberry Hill.

Suddenly from the adjoining chamber came a noise—like someone thrashing in his sleep. Elizabeth's eyes widened in fear. Should she stay in her bed or pursue the noise? The decision was made quickly. She crept from her bed, tiptoed across the Turkey carpet, and peeked through the door that stood ajar between the rooms.

The shadowy figure of a man loomed toward her, his shoulders broad and rugged; his chiseled features visible even in the dim light.

Isabella Winslowe slammed the book shut. The young ladies sitting in her parlor jumped and gasped. Isabella smiled. "That's all for today, ladies. We will start a new chapter on Thursday."

"You can't stop now, Isabella," Abigail Waterstone moaned. "We *must* read on!"

"Oh, please read one more chapter," the soft-spoken Amanda Wright breathed.

Isabella looked over the room of eager ladies muttering and talking among themselves about the intriguing horrid novel. She had a delightful time every Tuesday and Thursday afternoon drinking tea and reading with the ladies. They were never ready to go home when the hour was up.

"Just one or two more pages, Isabella, please. I simply must know if Elizabeth sees a man or a ghost," Lady Lynette Knightington pleaded without shame.

"Oh, we know it's not a ghost," Abigail argued, looking at Lady Lynette. "But we want to know who the man is."

"How do you know the shadow is not Lord Pinkwater's ghost?" Lady Lynette said, taking umbrage at Abigail's claim.

Isabella remained quiet and let the ladies talk for a while. She enjoyed listening to their comments. Lady Lynette, who sat to her right, was a tall, buxom young lady who had a lovely face except for a dark brown birthmark that spilled down her cheek. She was not afraid to speak her mind. Beside the duke's daughter sat Miss Abigail Waterstone who was short and slightly built. She fell down a set of stairs when she was a young girl and was left with a bad limp.

Miss Beverly Smith, who occupied a small ottoman, was really rather pretty until she opened her mouth. Her two front teeth had been knocked out when she was younger and now even with her fake teeth, she never smiled or laughed when she was around gentlemen. Lady Gretchen Colebrooke had to wear spectacles to see anything. Completing the group were other young ladies like Miss Amanda Wright who were either plain in appearance or extremely shy.

Isabella liked to think she'd helped them all to feel more confident and to be more accepted in a Society that seemed to demand beauty above all else.

"Ladies," Isabella said, rising from her chair. "I suggest that you don't miss Thursday and we'll see what the author has to say about the shadow. Now, Aunt Pithany is standing at the door with Mrs. Dawson who has your cloaks and gloves. Your maids have had your carriages brought around front, and they are ready for you."

One by one, the elegantly clad young ladies strolled to the front door. Isabella and her aunt spoke with each of their guests as they donned their wraps and left. After a final wave to the last girl, Isabella closed the door against the chill and leaned against it with a shiver.

She looked at her aunt and smiled. "I do enjoy the group, but it seems to take longer and longer to get them out of the house."

"That's because they have such a delightful time, dear. They are in no hurry to leave. Remember one of the reasons they are here is because there is no pressure on them to please or impress anyone. They feel free to chat and be themselves."

Miss Pithany Winslowe was the best liked spinster in all of London. Tall and robust, she always had a twinkle in her eyes and a smile on her face for everyone she met. After more than two years living with her aunt, Isabella was still trying to attain Pithany's sunny disposition.

Isabella absently nodded to her aunt as something niggled her mind. Instinct told her something was wrong. Suddenly she realized what it was. Auntie Pith was still holding a dark blue cloak. She opened the door again and looked out. Cold air stung her face.

There were two carriages left on the front street. She watched Amanda Wright climb into one of them. The driver shut the door, jumped up on the driver's seat, and they left. The other carriage, a handsome landau, remained. Amanda was the last young lady out the door, so why was one carriage and one coat left behind?

Could one of the ladies from her reading group still be inside the house? That seemed unlikely.

She turned back to her aunt. "Did someone leave without taking her wrap?"

Auntie Pith looked down at the cloak in her hands. "Oh, my. I didn't realize I was holding this. I thought we said good-bye to everyone, but who left without their cloak and gloves?"

"I think one of the ladies must still be here. There's a carriage outside."

"Let me see." Auntie Pith hung the items on the hall stand and peeked around Isabella and out to the street. "That's odd. You stay here, I'll find out whose carriage it is. Maybe there's a reason the landau hasn't left."

Isabella watched as her aunt walked to the coach and spoke to the maid inside before returning.

Auntie Pith had a puzzled expression on her face. "It's Lady Gretchen Colebrooke's carriage. She must be somewhere inside the house. I told her maid to stay by the coach and we would see the young lady out."

"I suppose it's possible she wandered away from the group," Isabella said, refusing to be alarmed, but knowing something wasn't quite right. "You check the bedrooms. Perhaps she felt a bit faint and—"

"Without letting anyone know?" Auntie Pith said, aghast at such an idea.

"Perhaps she asked Mrs. Dawson. Just look and I'll check the rest of the house."

The four ground-floor rooms were empty and the kitchen held only the housekeeper and a scullery girl who was washing teacups.

"Have you seen anyone in the house, Mrs. Dawson?"

The stout Irish woman gave Isabella a curious look. "When, miss? Not five minutes ago there were a dozen ladies in the house."

Isabella smiled at her. "Yes, of course, but I meant since we've been standing at the door seeing them out."

"No, miss. I'm sure they are all gone," Mrs. Dawson said and moved to retrieve a kettle from the fire.

Auntie Pith called out, "No sign of her up here." Which meant there was only one other place to look. The back garden. Isabella opened the door and immediately saw Gretchen standing over to the side near a bench, her back to Isabella.

Curious about why she would be on the grounds without her cloak on such a cold afternoon, Isabella stepped outside and closed the door behind her.

"Gretchen," she called as she started down the four steps. When Gretchen turned toward her, Isabella's steps faltered. Gretchen's face was white, and her eyes wide with fear. She held a small marble cherub in her hand. A man lay sprawled at her feet.

A man in her aunt's garden? Where did he come from and why was he on the ground?

"Gretchen, what's wrong?" Isabella asked in a calm voice. "What happened?"

Gretchen's pale face registered shock. "I was angry with him." She looked down at the statuette in her hand and suddenly dropped it as if she'd been holding a hot poker. "I hit him, but I didn't mean to kill him."

Two

ISABELLA GASPED, THEN RUSHED DOWN THE STEPS AND stared at the man sprawled on the grass. He lay on his back with his arms and legs stretched wide.

"Sweet mercy! It's Mr. Boswell Throckmorten." Isabella looked back to Gretchen. "You say you struck him with the cherub?"

Gretchen nodded.

"Why?"

"I don't know."

"Did he accost you? I don't know how he could have gotten inside. The garden gate is always secure," she said as she glanced toward the alley that led to the stable block. "Good heavens!" she declared, spying the latch that was disengaged.

"I didn't mean to kill him," Gretchen said again, seeming oblivious to the unlocked gate.

"Piffle, Gretchen, get hold of yourself. Surely he's not dead," Isabella said, seeing no outward sign of a gash or swelling on the man's face or forehead. "Maybe he's just sleeping. Although why he would have chosen our garden, I have no idea. He's not bleeding, and I don't see a bruise."

"He's not moving."

"That much is obvious." Isabella bent forward and looked him over more closely. "Perhaps his neckcloth was too tight and he fainted. I've never seen one so elaborately tied. Mr. Throckmorten, wake up."

Not even an eyelash fluttered. Perhaps he needed a bit more stimulation.

Isabella took a deep, cold breath and lowered herself to her knees. Hesitantly she put her hands on the man's shoulder and shook him. There was no doubt from the smell of him that he'd been into the bottle. But if he'd just passed out from too much wine, surely she would have been able to rouse him.

"He's not waking up," Gretchen said.

"I can see that, but it doesn't mean he's dead." Isabella shook him again. Harder this time, and she called his name again louder.

The man remained unresponsive. Isabella glanced up at Gretchen. "Where did you hit him?"

She pointed with a shaky hand. "There on the side of his head above his ear."

Not a hair on his head seemed out of place, but there must have been a lump the size of a goose egg beneath all that thick brown hair because he was definitely unconscious. His lips had lost all color, too.

A sinking feeling attacked the bottom of her stomach. "Wake up, Mr. Throckmorten. You must wake up."

When there was still no reaction, Isabella laid her ear to his cold chest, but could detect no heartbeat nor any rise or fall of breath.

Isabella knew she had to keep a calm head as she got to her feet and faced Gretchen. This was horrible. This was madness. This was an impossible situation!

"Gretchen, do you know what he was doing in my garden? How did you happen upon him? Why did you hit him? Tell me, did he accost you?" she asked again.

Isabella felt she couldn't ask the questions fast enough. But Gretchen made no attempt to answer. She only looked at Isabella with pale, trembling lips and wild, teary eyes that were made even larger by her spectacles. Isabella was perceptive enough to know the answers to some of her questions without Gretchen saying a word.

Maybe she should be more specific. "Did you plan a rendezvous with Mr. Throckmorten in my garden?"

Gretchen nodded.

"Sweet mercies. This is scandalous. We will both be ruined if your brother doesn't kill us first. How could you do this? Why did you—?" Isabella stopped herself. She didn't want to make things worse.

She needed to think, but for the moment her mind seemed blank. Reluctantly she looked at Mr. Throckmorten again. His body appeared so lifeless. What was she going to do?

"Why did you strike him? Did he try to compromise you?"

That seemed a foolish question the moment she asked it. Just meeting the man in the garden would compromise Gretchen beyond saving if the right people found out about it.

"You must answer me," Isabella insisted firmly.

Gretchen's eyes remained wide with fear. "I don't know why I hit him."

"Of course you do," Isabella said, trying not to lose patience with Gretchen and trying not to panic. "Did he try to kiss you or… or force his attentions on you?"

"I just remember being so angry that I picked up the cherub and swung it. The next thing I knew, he was lying on the ground just like that."

Isabella saw she was getting nowhere with the young lady. She had obviously arranged a tryst with Mr. Throckmorten and for some reason had struck him. Why didn't matter right now. They had bigger concerns.

"What are we going to do?" Gretchen asked in a childlike voice.

We?

Yes, Isabella supposed she was a part of this misfortune whether or not she wanted to be. She had to concentrate on what they should do now.

She took another deep breath and rubbed her icy hands together against the chill. First, she should alert Auntie Pith, and then she must tell Gretchen's aunt, but both those ideas were frightening. What would she say to them? What would they think? Would she and Gretchen be thrown in Newgate?

No, Isabella wouldn't let that happen.

Gretchen was the sister of an earl. Best she let Gretchen's family handle this. They would want to be the first to know, and they would see to it not a word of it got out. Besides, Isabella was quite eager to turn this situation over to someone else. And on further thought, perhaps she should keep this from Auntie Pith, too, if possible.

"I must take you home immediately and tell your aunt what has happened."

"Not her," Gretchen said. "She won't know what to do. My brother arrived last night. We can tell him. Danny will know what to do."

Isabella hesitated. A dry lump swelled in her throat. She'd seen the impressive-looking Lord Colebrooke two years ago at a party, but she'd been much too shy to gain an introduction to him. This was not how she wanted to meet the new earl, but did she have a choice?

"All right, we'll go to your brother. Is he at your town house in Mayfair or does he have a house of his own?"

"He's with us now because he just arrived, but he is arranging for his own place."

"Good. Your aunt will be there in case he wants to tell her about this."

She had to think quickly. Should she try to cover the body or hide it? No, it would be easier to leave him be and to find a reason to send Mrs. Dawson, the other servants, and her aunt away from the house so they wouldn't happen upon the dead man lying in the garden.

"Let's go back inside and get our wraps. I'll ride with you to your home, and we'll tell the earl what happened."

"Danny will take care of everything," Gretchen said, as if she were trying to reassure herself.

They returned to the house, and as soon as they stepped inside, Isabella told Mrs. Dawson to take the rest of the afternoon off and to dismiss the servants as well as Isabella's maid. The housekeeper was surprised but pleased to do this because it gave her an opportunity to visit her ailing sister. Isabella met Auntie Pith as she was walking into the foyer.

"Oh, I see you found Gretchen." Auntie Pith glared at the young lady. "Dear girl, you shouldn't wander off that way. We've been searching the house for you. Why, you're pale as a ghost. And you're shivering. Are you unwell?"

"Yes, Auntie Pith, she is feeling poorly. I think I should see her safely home. If you don't mind, I need you to run an errand for me."

Auntie Pith questioned Isabella with her eyes. "What's that, dear?"

"I told Mrs. Hollyfield I'd collect the new gown she made for me today, and I forgot about it until just now. Would you take the coach and get it for me? I fear I won't have the time."

Her aunt hesitated. "Well, I'm not sure. I hadn't planned on going out this afternoon with it being so cold and so late in the day."

Using a ploy she'd learned from her aunt, Isabella walked over to the stand where Auntie Pith's cloak hung and took it down.

"Oh, I know, and I'm sorry to ask it of you on such a dreadful day, but I do so want to wear the gown to the parties tonight." She draped the cloak over her aunt's shoulders and began tying its ribbons into a bow under her chin.

"Mrs. Hollyfield is on the other side of Town, dear. It will take me the rest of the afternoon to get over there and back."

Isabella let go of the ribbons and stood back. She clasped her hands together under her chin. "Of course, you are right. It is too much trouble. I shouldn't have asked." She started to remove the cloak from her aunt's shoulders.

Auntie Pith touched Isabella's hand and hesitated

again. Suddenly she smiled. "I suppose if you have your heart set on the gown, I can go and get it for you."

"Thank you, Auntie Pith. You are such a dear to do this for me."

Isabella smiled at her aunt while taking a deep breath of relief. She disliked deceiving her only remaining relative, but what else could she do? The fewer people who knew about Mr. Throckmorten, the better. "Now, while Susan gets your bonnet and gloves, I'll summon Milton to bring the carriage around for you. It won't take that long, and you'll be home before you know it."

Isabella waited until her aunt was gone before she and Gretchen climbed into the Colebrooke coach. The earl's town house wasn't far away, but in the chilling silence it seemed to take forever for them to arrive.

The house was the largest and most impressive on its exclusive street in Mayfair. An elaborate iron arch framed the entrance. Isabella was not accustomed to succumbing to fits of the vapors, but that was exactly how she felt as she walked with Lady Gretchen and her maid up the limestone steps to the door of the earl's London town home. After all, it wasn't everyday she told an earl that his sister had struck a man and killed him.

Apparently Lord Colebrooke had just returned to London after more than a year's absence. Some of the gossip she'd heard about him characterized him as a dashing rogue who set out to break as many young ladies' hearts as possible. Others considered him devilishly handsome and charming, and put him at the top of their guest lists.

Everyone in the *ton* had been disappointed he hadn't stayed for any of last Season's parties. And that he hadn't returned for the first parties of this Season was an outrage. Isabella would find out for herself, in a matter of moments, what kind of man the earl of Colebrooke was.

From Gretchen she knew that their father and older brother had been killed two years ago in a carriage accident. Upon inheriting the title, Daniel had to prepare himself to take on the duties of being an earl and the first thing he'd wanted to do was visit all the properties and holdings entailed to the title. And, if the gossips were to be believed, he was returning to London from his travels to find a wife and produce an heir.

Isabella glanced at Gretchen as they waited at the front door. The girl's lips were gray and her eyes dull and vacant behind her spectacles. Isabella didn't know how Gretchen was holding herself together.

It was an impossible situation for anyone, let alone for a young lady of nineteen. Isabella was more than ready to turn this distressing state of affairs over to Gretchen's brother. Surely he would know what to do.

They continued to wait as Gretchen's maid hit the door knocker for the third time. Isabella had wanted to comfort Gretchen in the carriage but knew she couldn't alert the maid to what had happened. Instead she'd taken the time to shore up her own courage and formulate a way to tell Lord Colebrooke what had happened.

There was no easy way to say it.

Unfortunately, Isabella would have to take some

responsibility for this accident. After all, Gretchen was in her care when it happened. It could be considered Isabella's fault that Gretchen had slipped away into the garden to meet with Mr. Throckmorten. It was Isabella's Reading Society she had been attending.

And Isabella's aunt would be considered a terrible chaperone.

An older, well-dressed butler with an unusually small pinched nose opened the door. Isabella didn't wait for him to speak. Going against her natural inclination, she forced herself to be assertive and said, "Lady Gretchen isn't feeling well." Isabella pushed past him. "Please show us to the parlor at once."

"Yes, madam," the startled butler responded.

Isabella turned to Gretchen's maid and said, "Perhaps you should prepare her bed. I think she might need to lie down after she speaks with her brother."

The young maid looked at her mistress for approval. Gretchen nodded, and the maid headed up the stairs.

Isabella kept her hand on Gretchen's arm as the butler ushered them into the front parlor. He helped settle the trembling young lady on the tapestried settee. Gretchen immediately took off her spectacles and laid them none to steadily on the little satinwood table in front of her.

Taking charge again, Isabella commanded the butler, "Please summon the earl. If he isn't here, send someone to find him and say he is needed at home immediately."

The portly butler merely said, "Yes, madam, his lordship is home." He bowed and hurried from the room.

Looking around the luxuriously appointed room, Isabella spied two crystal decanters and some glasses on a gilt inlaid sideboard. Without a second thought, she walked over and poured a hasty splash of the amber liquid into a glass for Gretchen.

Isabella was surprised to see that her hand wasn't shaking, but she felt as if her stomach was quivering and her knees were terribly weak. On the carriage ride over, she had not allowed herself to think about what might happen to her or what would happen to Gretchen if this story hit the London *Times*.

Feeling wretched about the whole affair, Isabella sat down beside Gretchen and said, "Drink this. It will make you feel better. Your brother will be here shortly. I'm sure he will know exactly what to do."

Gretchen's hands trembled so badly that Isabella was afraid to let go of the glass, so she helped Gretchen to take a sip of the strong drink.

"Madam," came a firm masculine voice from the doorway. "What do you think you are doing?"

Isabella looked up and brought the glass down from Gretchen's lips. She rose from the settee and stared into the light-brown eyes of one of the finest-looking men she had ever seen. Not even the furrow on his broad brow could mar the handsomeness of the width of his cheekbones, his wide, well-defined mouth, and his narrow, high-bridged nose.

He stood tall, commanding, and powerful-looking. He was so imposing that Isabella was stricken with her old fearful shyness.

She couldn't move or speak. Her heart beat so wildly in her chest, she could only stare at the man advancing on her with unconcealed anger. All the self-confidence she had learned the past three years fell away like the skin from a peeled apple. Suddenly she was once again the timid child of her youth.

"Can you not answer me?" he challenged, stopping in front of the settee.

No, she couldn't.

"What's that you're giving my sister to drink?" he demanded as he swiped the glass from Isabella's hand and plunked it on the table by Gretchen's spectacles.

His shocking rudeness and his callous tone of voice cut through Isabella's fog of shyness and her shoulders edged up a notch. Resolve took hold and flourished inside her. He might be powerful-looking and easily the most handsome man she'd ever seen, but she would not let him intimidate her again.

She swallowed past a dry throat and calmly said, "I would think it obvious, my lord, that I was helping her to drink brandy from that glass."

His gaze pierced hers severely and held fast. "That much is obvious. I want to know why."

"Then it should also be obvious that she is too upset to hold it herself."

His eyes narrowed, and for a fleeting moment she thought she saw admiration in his sparkling eyes. And she'd never been so glad that she'd found her voice.

"You try my patience."

"It appears you have none, my lord," she countered quickly.

"Not when I'm talking to someone who can't answer an uncomplicated question."

"I responded to your questions. You simply didn't like the answers."

"Your impertinence is provoking."

She glared at him. "No more so than your antagonistic approach."

Not taking his imperious gaze off Isabella, he said to the butler who had followed him into the parlor, "Parker, bring Lady Gretchen tea at once." Then he looked down at his sister for the first time, and his expression softened.

Gretchen still wore her dark blue cloak and gloves. Her matching bonnet was askew. Her eyes were watery with tears, and her lips were still ashen.

In a tender voice Lord Colebrooke asked, "Gretchen, what has happened?"

Gretchen rose and fell into her brother's arms, weeping. She buried her face in the soft wool of his coat, crying all the harder.

Isabella was immediately struck by the gentle way Lord Colebrooke affectionately embraced his sister. One strong arm circled her waist and held her protectively against him. His large hand cupped the back of her neck and comforted her with caring movements. When her shoulders shook with despair, he slid his hand from her waist up to softly pat her back with a loving touch.

"I only meant to hurt him," Gretchen said between sobs.

"Calm down, Gretchy. Everything will be all right." He pulled on the ribbon under her chin and slipped her bonnet off and let it drop to the settee. "Stop crying and tell me who you hurt?"

The quiet, concerned tone of his voice stunned Isabella. She wouldn't have thought him capable of such compassionate treatment after his accusing tone and his brash behavior toward Isabella.

Isabella's gaze strolled up and past his high collar and perfectly tied neckcloth to his brown eyes that were so light they almost looked golden. She found them staring at her over Gretchen's shoulder. His gaze was so intense Isabella had to force herself not to take a step backward. She would not cower before him again.

"I'm afraid to tell you," Gretchen managed to mumble between broken sobs.

"What nonsense is this, Gretchy? You know you can tell me anything."

"Not this. It's too horrible."

Lord Colebrooke's burning gaze found Isabella's again. "Who are you and what the devil is she talking about?" he said, returning to the annoyed voice that was obviously reserved for Isabella.

"My name is Isabella Winslowe and—"

"I've heard of you," he interrupted in a heated tone. "You're the one who started that odd Wallflower Society."

Isabella gasped and stiffened with indignation. Wallflower Society? Her group of ladies? How dare he use that derogatory term in connection with *her* ladies' group? What nerve!

"I beg your pardon, sir. I will not allow you to besmirch my—"

"Never mind that right now, Miss Winslowe. What have you and your group of misfits done to Gretchen?"

Isabella's temper rose with her chin and her shoulders. This man was impossible to talk to. She should have insisted on taking Gretchen to her aunt, and would have if she had known that the earl was an ill-mannered ogre.

"We have done nothing, Lord Colebrooke. I've only tried to see to her best interest under extremely trying circumstances. Furthermore, I will gladly explain to you if you will see fit to let me finish a sentence without interrupting me."

Gretchen's sobs grew quieter, and her brother visibly relaxed, if only a little. "Finish your sentence," he commanded. "And be quick about it."

It was clear that the small concession was as close as she was going to get to an apology or politeness from him. Obviously the man was used to asking questions and then giving orders without waiting for answers.

"Thank you."

If this wasn't a most unusual of circumstance, Isabella would turn and walk out on this man and not say another word to him—ever. But she couldn't do that to Gretchen, and she did have Mr. Throckmorten to worry about.

Isabella moistened her lips and took a deep breath. There was no easy way to get the job done. She said, "I'm afraid I have some disturbing news."

"What could be more disturbing than Gretchen falling apart in my arms?"

"Your sister killed a man in my garden."

Three

HOT DENIAL FLASHED ACROSS LORD COLEBROOKE'S face. "That is an outrageous accusation, Miss Winslowe. What kind of trickery are you up to?"

"This is no trick, Lord Colebrooke. I'm quite serious."

"It's true, Danny," Gretchen whispered, looking up at him with red, tear-soaked eyes that pleaded for help. "I hit him with a marble statue and he fell dead to the ground. I didn't mean to kill him. What are we going to do?"

She started softly weeping again and tried to bury her face in his coat once more.

The earl gently forced her to face him. He picked up the glass he'd just taken from Isabella and said to her, "Here, stop crying and drink this, Gretchy. You are home now and everything will be all right. You must calm down so I can find out what the devil you and Miss Winslowe are talking about."

Gretchen would not be consoled or talked into drinking the brandy. Lord Colebrooke should know that there were times a lady just had to cry until there were no more tears.

Isabella disliked barging into what was really a family

situation, but unfortunately, she was already in the middle of this horrid affair. The dead man was in her garden. It was clear to her that the consoling earl wasn't going to get any more out of Gretchen this afternoon. She was overwrought.

At the risk of provoking further resentment, Isabella dared to offer, "Lord Colebrooke, may I suggest that perhaps Gretchen's maid should take her upstairs to lie down. There are things you and I need to discuss, and I don't believe we have much time."

He pierced her with another cold gaze before looking at Gretchen. "Very well, Miss Winslowe. Stay where you are," he ordered. "I'll be right back."

Isabella watched him walk out with his sister wrapped firmly in his arms. She heard him call for Gretchen's maid as he climbed the stairs. Lord Colebrooke was the most exasperating person she had ever had the misfortune to meet. He couldn't have been more unapproachable if he'd been a wild boar.

She realized again that her knees were shaking and her insides were trembling. Thank God she had managed to get over her initial fear of him and had not let him continue to intimidate her with his anger and condescension. If she hadn't seen how gently he spoke to Gretchen, she would have thought him a monster incapable of kindness.

Feeling chilled, Isabella hugged her arms to her chest. She picked up the untouched brandy and downed it all at once in a most unladylike fashion. It burned her lips, her mouth, her throat, and she winced as it settled like fire in her quaking stomach. Heat rose up her chest and neck to flame in her cheeks.

"Sweet mercies." She coughed and untied the
ribbon under her bonnet as the warmth of the liquor
settled low in her stomach.

Auntie Pith had told her there were times a lady
needed a little fortifying with a strong drink. If that
were true, this must be one of those times. Isabella
wasn't sure she would last through another stretch of
Lord Colebrooke's interrogation.

As she turned to place the empty glass on the table,
she saw the earl standing in the doorway looking at her
with unconcealed distrust.

Even with the apparent anger in his strong features,
she found there was something unusually compelling
in the way he looked over her face. She watched his
gaze glide down the length of her and back up again
to center on her eyes. It was as if he were assessing her
physical attributes as well as her sanity.

And Isabella felt an unexpected shiver of awareness.

Lord Colebrooke's wide shoulders tapered to a
flat stomach, slim hips and long powerful-looking
legs encased in black breeches that disappeared into
shiny top boots. He walked toward her with that
commanding presence that had intimidated her earlier.
Now she realized she no longer feared him at all. She
was intrigued by his intense dislike for her.

Amazed that she was no longer fearful of him, her
self-confidence soared. Isabella relaxed and waited for
the earl to speak.

"Gretchen is clearly talking out of her head, Miss
Winslowe, and I can't make any sense of her words or
yours. Tell me, what is this preposterous tale you and
my sister have concocted?"

"Concocted, indeed, sir. You sound as if you think I have nothing better to do with my time than go around and spit out stories."

"I'll reserve my judgment on that until after I hear what you have to say for yourself."

Isabella ignored his accusation and simply said, "Very well, would you like the short version or the long one, my lord?"

"Short."

Yes, she had a feeling he would pick that one.

She looked up into his troubled eyes and, after taking a deep breath, she said, "Your sister says she struck a man and killed him. As we stand here wasting time, his body is lying in my back garden."

"Impossible," he said coldly.

"I assure you, it's true. He was lying on the ground and Gretchen was standing over him with a statue of a cherub in her hand when I happened upon them."

Lord Colebrooke's brow furrowed so deeply she didn't know if it was caused by rage or disbelief.

He took a step closer to her. "If there is a man, as you say, in your garden, are you sure he is dead?"

"Yes."

"And how do you know that, Miss Winslowe?"

"It was really quite chilling." She folded her arms across her chest again as she remembered the way Mr. Throckmorten looked. "I shook him and tried to rouse some kind of response from him, but there was no life in him. I wanted to—"

"Perhaps you should give me the long story—but quickly."

Under his bold gaze, she found the courage to say,

"The time it takes me, sir, will depend on how many times you interrupt me."

"Talk, Miss Winslowe."

"Your arrogance knows no boundaries, my lord."

"You seem to be the one without boundaries, Miss Winslowe."

"Whatever have I said that made you come to that conclusion?"

"As if this bizarre tale of yours and Gretchen's isn't reason enough?"

Isabella would never get the story out if she continued to mince words with this unreasonable man. She skipped the angry retort she wanted to make and mentally braced herself for another bout with the earl.

As briefly as possible, she told him what had happened from when the ladies first arrived for their readings until she dismissed all the servants and sent her aunt to pick up a gown that could have waited until another day.

"We boarded Gretchen's carriage and came straight here," she finished.

His face hardened with suspicion. "I don't know what kind of chicanery you are up to by trying to pin this outrageous tale on my sister, but hear me now—I won't allow you to do it."

He took another unfriendly step toward her.

Isabella's muscles recoiled, her eyes flinched, but she stood her ground. "My lord, I swear to you, I would not do such a thing. You heard Gretchen admit she struck the man."

"Yes, but I don't know that you didn't somehow persuade her to say that."

"I wouldn't."

"What was she doing at your house?"

"I told you, I had ladies in for tea and readings, as I have done every Tuesday and Thursday afternoons for over a year."

His voice remained low but cold. "Then what in damnation was she doing in your back garden alone with a man?"

His insinuation left no doubt that he found her responsible and contemptible. Isabella couldn't allow that to bother her. She had to accept some of the responsibility because she wasn't prepared to tell him that Gretchen had admitted to arranging a meeting with Mr. Throckmorten in the garden. That piece of the puzzle would have to come from Gretchen.

"I have no answer for that, sir. You must get that information from your sister."

"Do you know who this supposed dead man is?"

"Yes, of course. I recognized him as Mr. Boswell Throckmorten."

A thick gasp blew from his throat as he whispered, "Good Lord. Are you certain of this?"

For a fleeting moment Isabella thought she saw alarm for his sister flash across his eyes, but she couldn't be sure. She wondered why knowing the name of the man made such a difference to him.

"Positive."

"Did you alert anyone?" he asked.

"No," Isabella said, thankful that his anger had been suddenly replaced by concern, and high time. Gretchen was in trouble.

"Good."

She could see the news of the man's name upset him, and he was trying desperately not to show it.

"How this is handled is up to you. I told you I immediately dismissed all the servants and sent my aunt on a fool's errand for the rest of the day so that no one would stumble upon Mr. Throckmorten. I left straightaway and came to deliver your sister and seek your instruction about what to do."

"I'll get my coat. We'll go to your house immediately." He looked around the room. "Where's your maid? In the kitchen? With your carriage?"

"No one traveled with me. I rode with Gretchen and her maid in your carriage."

"Then I'll get Gretchen's maid to act as your chaperone. Wait for me by the front door, Miss Winslowe."

He turned and left the room without further word. He did like to give orders. Isabella would be so glad when she passed the age of needing a chaperone and she was free to come and go as she pleased just like Auntie Pith.

A few minutes later Lord Colebrooke helped Isabella into a smart new phaeton pulled by a perfectly matched pair of horses. Even though both were wearing gloves, when she placed her hand in his, Isabella's skin tingled with pleasing warmth. Their clasp was a firm holding of hands, and it was enough to cause an unexpected leap in her breath.

She sank into the plush seat by Gretchen's pleasant-looking maid for the short ride. She hoped to feel relief once she turned this unfortunate incident over to Lord Colebrooke, but so far relief had eluded her.

They were silent on the ride to her house. Isabella

found herself glancing at the intriguing earl and wondering what he was thinking. She really couldn't blame him for looking at her with suspicion. The story was shocking, outrageous. She would react the same way had someone told her Auntie Pith had killed a man. Still—

The carriage stopped. Lord Colebrooke didn't wait for the footman to open the door. The earl stepped down and immediately turned back to reach for Isabella. "Wait here," he told the maid.

Isabella placed her hand in his. This time he clamped his fingers firmly around hers and Isabella's pulse quickened. Most men hardly touched a woman's hand when they helped them in or out of a carriage, but there was no such wariness in this man. He boldly took hold of her, leaving her no doubt she was—in his hands.

What was there about his touch that made her breath grow short and heat rise to her face? She didn't know. She only knew she had never felt that way with any other man's touch.

As they walked toward her front door, Isabella turned to him and said, "I wasn't aware that your sister knew Mr. Throckmorten."

"I don't intend to discuss my sister's private affairs with you."

"Must you be so unfriendly to a lady who's only trying to help your sister?"

"Gretchen was in your aunt's home, Miss Winslowe. I'll hold you and her responsible for any harm that comes to her. Besides that, I see no reason to be friendly to a lady I don't plan to ever talk to again after today."

He couldn't have made his feelings for her any plainer than that, and for some odd reason she didn't understand, his words bothered her. But he would never know that.

"I find that reassuring, sir."

"So do I, Miss Winslowe. I don't like receiving messages that my sister was alone in your garden with a man."

"It is not the kind of news I like to deliver. And I can assure you it did not make me happy that Gretchen chose my garden in which to strike Mr. Throckmorten."

"If you hadn't persuaded her to come to your reading group, this never would have happened."

"Persuade? I simply invited her. You, sir, cannot blame this on me. I had no idea your sister had such designing intentions or inclinations."

"She doesn't."

"I'll leave her to answer that."

"And so you should. Anyone else would have taken greater care for her safety and well-being."

His words stung, but Isabella would rather be stuck with sewing needles than let him know. "And I happily turn her over to your custody."

Isabella stomped through her front door with Lord Colebrooke right behind her. They went straight through the vestibule, their destination the rear garden. Isabella opened the door and looked out, but immediately saw that the body was not where she had left it.

This was unbelievable. She slowly walked down the four steps to the area to where Mr. Throckmorten had been and turned back to Lord Colebrooke.

Her eyes widened with shock as she whispered, "He's gone."

"Gone?"

"The body—Mr. Throckmorten is gone," Isabella said as relief washed across Lord Colebrooke's face.

❧

Chilton was right. Miss Winslowe was a troublemaker.

Daniel looked at the irritating lady standing before him stunningly dressed in her bold blue cloak with black braid trim and matching bonnet and gloves. Infuriating or not, she was incredibly beautiful. Not only was she not the old, unattractive spinster he imagined her to be when Chilton had mentioned her, she had almost convinced him that Gretchen had committed a horrible crime.

She was downright audacious.

He took in a deep breath of cold air and exhaled it quickly. He undoubtedly had a beautiful madwoman in front of him. But that, he admitted to himself, was preferable to a dead man.

What kind of game was Miss Winslowe playing and what had made her think she could play this devious game with him? She should be on stage, and perhaps she had been, for surely she was acting now with her beautiful, flashing green eyes so wide with shock.

She was taller than most women and, by far, more beautiful. Her clothing, her speech, the way she carried herself, and the fact of where her house was located told him she was not a young lady without considerable means. But who the hell was she and what was her purpose in this madcap tale?

"How about Mr. Throckmorten was never here?" Daniel said with a bit of a scoff in his tone.

She held cold eyes on his face and said, "Do not insult me or your sister, Lord Colebrooke."

"Then perhaps you were serving something stronger than tea at your meeting this afternoon," he said, remembering how she had downed the brandy in his parlor.

Her eyes rounded in heated denial before she said, "That's a vile accusation. I would never serve spirits to the young ladies who visit me."

"Then what is your explanation? I'm ready to hear something reasonable."

"He was lying right there on the ground." She pointed to the spot. "See the cherub. That's where Gretchen dropped it when I found her."

"The cherub, indeed, lies on the ground, Miss Winslowe, but not Mr. Throckmorten." He walked over to where she pointed and bent down for a closer inspection of the ground. Twilight was descending fast, but even in the waning light of day he saw no stains.

"I don't see any blood."

"He wasn't bleeding."

Daniel gave her a questioning look. "Yet she hit him on the head with a marble statuette?"

"Yes. I know it sounds preposterous."

Her eyes sparkled with indignation, and she showed no sign of wavering from her story.

"I'm glad we agree on something."

She took a ragged breath. "I can't explain his disappearance."

"Obviously."

"Nor do I understand his disappearance, but he was indeed here and dead. I saw him. I shook him and called his name many times."

Daniel was beginning to think his first inclination must be right. She had to be an actress to appear so shocked that the man was no longer in her garden dead or alive.

"Then where is he?"

Her gaze held fast to his and he was impressed with her audacity. "I just admitted that I don't know. I have no idea."

Daniel was in no mood to relent. "Dead men do not get up and walk off, Miss Winslowe."

She stiffened. "I know that. Someone must have stolen the body."

Despite his efforts to control it, a smile tugged at the corners of his mouth and he had to bite back a chuckle. She was not to be believed. A dead body stolen from her garden in the space of not more than half an hour? His shoulders shook with humor. What kind of fool did she take him for? If she wasn't up to mischief, he'd consider her downright charming.

Sparks of fire shot from her gleaming eyes, making her all the more attractive. For a brief moment his thoughts strayed to what she would look like with her golden hair spilling down her shoulders.

"This is not funny, Lord Colebrooke."

He cleared his throat and did his best to wipe the smile from his lips, difficult as it was. "I quite agree—in some respects."

"Then why are you smiling like Saint Peter on Judgment Day?"

"Perhaps because I don't know what kind of madcap game you're playing, Miss Winslowe. If it weren't so cruel a joke, it might be fascinating."

"This is no game, sir."

"I believe it is, and this one involving my sister is over here and now."

Her gloved hands made fists at her sides, and her eyes blazed with indignation.

"You are the most thickheaded man I have ever met. You heard your sister admit she struck Mr. Throckmorten and killed him. I don't know what happened to him after we left him. I only know he was here. I know a dead man when I see one, and he was dead."

Daniel hid a smile behind the pretext of clearing of his throat. "How many dead bodies have you seen, Miss Winslowe?"

She blinked rapidly and seemed to study his question a moment. "I'm not sure. I had an uncle who passed on, and then there was a neighbor a few years ago. Sweet mercies, I don't know how many. But Mr. Throckmorten was lifeless. There wasn't even the flutter of an eyelash."

"Well, it appears that if Mr. Throckmorten was here, he's gone now and that is all that matters."

"If?" she said imperiously. "There is no *if*."

"But there is. *If* he was here, I suggest he wasn't dead but had merely passed out. I've seen Throckmorten so smashed he had to crawl out of White's or be carried out by his friends."

"That doesn't mean he was overindulging in drink today."

"It just so happens only a short while ago a good friend of mine said he saw Throckmorten today at White's and he was already well into his cups. No doubt he was wandering around foxed and found your back gate unlocked as it is now. He stumbled in and passed out from too much wine. When he woke, he left the garden."

"Very well. How would you explain your sister standing over his body holding a statue, saying she had struck him?"

"It's simple really. She walked into your garden where she had every right to believe she would be safe and saw Mr. Throckmorten. She assumed he would accost her so she picked up the statue ready to defend herself when he approached her. Since there were no marks on him, I assume she missed when she struck out at him. He passed out and fell to the ground."

"Even if the situation happened as you stated, do you think one of our servants would leave our back gate unlocked where anyone could wander in? That wouldn't happen."

"I don't know what you would allow, Miss Winslowe, because I don't know you."

"Quite true, sir, and with your attitude, you are not someone I want to get to know."

"That statement pleases me. You could have lured me into your garden with this false story in hopes of someone finding us together in a compromising position so that you could catch me in parson's mousetrap."

The fire of righteous anger burned brightly in her eyes, and she advanced on him in anger. "Dupe you into marriage? That is a contemptible suggestion, sir. You flatter yourself. I would rather spend my life in chains at Newgate than with you!"

Her fury was undeniable but not daunting, and for some reason Daniel found that strangely appealing. He met her challenge by taking a step toward her. They stood so close he could have easily touched her simply by lifting his hand. And for one startling moment he thought he wanted to caress her creamy-soft cheek with the backs of his fingers.

He had a bewildering desire to pull her to his chest and kiss her. He wanted to feel her rosy lips soft and pliant beneath his.

Daniel shook off his straying, astonishing thoughts. "Fancy you should mention Newgate, Miss Winslowe, because that is exactly where you will find yourself if I hear of you concocting any more tales such as this. I'll personally see to it that your chicanery is stopped."

"You, sir, are the most disagreeable man I have ever met."

A slow confident smile spread across Daniel's lips. He expected her to move away from him, but she remained so close he heard her labored breathing, saw the rise and fall of her chest, and caught a wisp of the clean scent of a lady's perfumed soap. She was provoking, and in so many ways that wasn't bad.

"I wouldn't have you think of me any other way, Miss Winslowe."

She continued to stare boldly into his eyes, refusing to back down on her story or back away from his nearness. Her courage was impressive, her beauty undeniable, and her mischief troublesome.

She kept her hot gaze on his. "I believe it's time you took your leave," she said.

He nodded once. "Something else we agree on. I trust I can rely on you not to breathe a word of this outlandish story to your group or to anyone."

"If I had the forethought to send my aunt and servants away so they wouldn't see the body, do you really think I would tell this to a roomful of impressionable young ladies?"

"As I said, I don't know you. But hear me on this, Miss Winslowe, and hear me well." He moved in closer to her and caught the appealing scent of freshly washed hair and new cloth. "Stay away from my sister."

"You cannot intimidate me, Lord Colebrooke. I do not fear you. And I will not tell your sister she cannot come to our Reading Society."

"Then I will. Good day, Miss Winslowe, and good riddance."

Four

IT TOOK ALL OF ISABELLA'S WILLPOWER NOT TO SLAM the door behind the insufferable earl.

"Good riddance, indeed!" she muttered aloud. "I heartily agree, Lord Colebrooke."

Isabella was far too sensible a woman to stomp her foot in frustration, but, oh, how she could see the value in it right now.

She untied her bonnet with cold fingers and removed it as she continued talking to herself. "I shall be happy to never look upon your handsome face again.

"Handsome?" Isabella stopped and breathed in a heavy sigh of surprise. "Sweet mercies, where did that word come from? And how could such a man as he be favored with such captivating appeal?"

She took off her gloves, one finger at a time, as she mumbled to herself with each pull on the tip, "He is positively arrogant, scornful, impatient, judgmental, and formidable." She threw her gloves on a small table and took off her cloak, tossing it on top of the gloves and bonnet.

"I forgot *infuriating*," she continued her conversation

with herself. "Yes, he's most infuriating. How could that man possibly be the most eligible bachelor in London? Piffle!"

Having reached the ground floor parlor, she took a deep calming breath as she walked over to the window. She brushed aside the dark green drapery panel and watched as Lord Colebrooke climbed effortlessly into his phaeton and took the reins.

It was widely known that the earl was only looking for a wife to give him a child, not love and devotion from an intelligent young lady who would be his partner for life. What woman would want a man who thought like that?

There were other words to describe him that she'd forgotten. He was impressive with his tall, powerful-looking frame and she'd been oddly attracted to him when he'd stood so close to her she heard his breathing and smelled the clean scent of shaving soap. She'd felt a strange quaking in her lower stomach and her knees had suddenly felt watery.

That he was loyal to his sister and protective of her was thoroughly commendable. Maybe that was the part of him that appealed to Isabella. For surely something about him had. It certainly wasn't his overbearing self-confidence or his uncompromising and ill-mannered behavior toward her.

Yes, he was much too commanding for her taste. If she were to ever be interested in a man, it wouldn't be someone as disagreeable as Lord Colebrooke. He certainly wasn't the kind of beau she should get starry-eyed over.

She didn't plan to marry, but if she were ever to

reconsider, she wanted a husband who would love her and allow her to love him. She certainly couldn't be interested in a man who had openly admitted that he was only looking for a wife to bear his children.

A husband would be an impediment to what she wanted. Freedom to do as she pleased—within reason. No doubt a husband would want her to be as silent as her father had. A husband would restrict her and take away the liberty she'd enjoyed since coming to London.

Isabella sighed as the phaeton disappeared around the corner. It was no wonder Lord Colebrooke thought her up to some kind of trickery. And he probably thought her a lunatic, too. What on earth could have happened to Mr. Throckmorten? She had never been so shocked in her life as when she found the garden empty.

She supposed she was going to have to accept Lord Colebrooke's explanation about what happened. His assumption as to how the story worked out is the only one that made sense. Not that she would ever admit that to him. Surely no one came into her garden and stole Mr. Throckmorten's body while she was away.

Had she really suggested that possibility to the earl? And to think he had smiled at her. Smiled! Oh, what he must have been thinking. No doubt he thought her a madwoman in need of chains at Bedlam.

"Oh, good heavens!" Isabella almost groaned aloud as the drapery panel slipped from her fingers. She turned away from the window.

No wonder he didn't want his sister attending any more of her readings. He thought her a mischievous prankster up to no good.

But, now that Isabella thought about it, perhaps it was best for Gretchen to sacrifice their meetings. After all, the girl had admitted that she had made secret arrangements to meet Mr. Throckmorten in the garden. That was completely unacceptable behavior. Both she and Gretchen would be outcasts in Society if this story was repeated.

Certainly, Isabella wouldn't tell anyone about today's unsettling affair, having gone to such great lengths to keep it quiet from all her household. Lord Colebrooke made it clear he wouldn't breathe a word of this incident to anyone, either.

Nor did she have any fear that Mr. Throckmorten would say a word. Whether Gretchen struck him or he passed out cold from drinking too much, he wouldn't want anyone knowing he met Gretchen in the garden. Unless he wanted to find himself married to her.

"Well, it's over," she said to herself, reaching for her shawl that lay over the back of the wing chair. "I will dismiss the entire incident from my mind. Obviously Mr. Throckmorten was not dead and that is all that's important. It would have been tragic for him and Gretchen if that had been the case."

Wrapping the paisley silk around her arms, Isabella decided she would do a better job of watching after the young ladies at her home from now on. It had never occurred to her that one of the girls might use their meetings for a private assignation.

"Should I ever find myself in Lord Colebrooke's presence again, I shall ignore him." She sighed softly. "And if I tell myself that often enough, maybe I will be able to do it."

Isabella walked into the kitchen, hoping to find the kettle warm enough to make tea. She looked around her aunt's quiet, well-appointed house. Her aunt was such a dear sweetheart to have taken Isabella in when her father had all but abandoned her three years ago. An unusual pang of longing floated through her. It was unlike her to miss her father.

She allowed her thoughts to drift back to her life before coming to live with her aunt.

Isabella was the only child born to Sir Charles Winslowe and his wife Sharon. Because of Sharon's poor health, they had no social life outside their country estate south of London.

Charles adored his wife and spent most of his free time doting on her. There was little time left to spend with Isabella. As a child, she was seldom allowed in her mother's sickroom, and when she was, she had to be very quiet. Even the governesses she had over the years insisted she be quiet at all times.

Her mother died when Isabella was twelve. She was sad but never cried where anyone could see or hear her.

Isabella's father was devastated and mourned his wife until Isabella was fourteen. That spring he went to London and returned home married to a beautiful young lady only five years older than Isabella.

Her father was smitten by his new bride, Olivia, but she didn't take to Isabella. Olivia was never mean but simply ignored her step-daughter. This was nothing new to Isabella. She contented herself as she always had with reading books, taking walks, sewing, and riding.

When Isabella turned eighteen, Olivia told Charles she was certain if they could travel for a few months she would relax and conceive a son.

Her father knew it was time for Isabella to have a Season so she could make an acceptable match. But to please his wife, Charles sent Isabella to live with his maiden sister in London so he and his wife would be free to travel to Europe.

Isabella had been left with Aunt Pithany only two weeks before the opening party of Isabella's first Season. It was a complete disaster. Isabella was so shy she did nothing but stand against the walls party after party, seldom speaking to anyone and refusing occasional requests to dance.

Over the course of the Season, Isabella had noticed how capable and self-assured her aunt was. Auntie Pith was a contented spinster with a wide circle of friends and social projects to keep her busy. She was intelligent, well-read, and extremely popular among the *ton*.

Isabella, who had grown up an introverted child, admired the strength, confidence, and cheerfulness she saw in her aunt, and she became determined to become just like her auntie Pith.

Throughout the next year Isabella pushed herself to overcome the shyness that had plagued her all her life.

At the beginning of her second Season, Charles sent word that Olivia was with child, and they couldn't return home for Isabella's nineteenth birthday. She missed her father, but she understood how much it meant to him to have a son.

Isabella was a different young lady for her second Season. She was self-confident and engaging.

All the handsome young men who ignored her previously waited in line to dance with her. She enjoyed their attentions and accepted it graciously. After the first week of parties, she noticed the shy, quiet young ladies who stood on the perimeter of the room just as she had stood the year before. They were seldom asked to dance and never invited to the best parties.

Isabella decided if she could change, they could change, too. She would help them. She invited two of the young ladies for tea the very next day. They had a wonderful time reading poetry and a horrid novel with her. The next week Isabella added another lady to her guest list and the next week another.

By the end of the Season, Isabella's afternoon group had grown to a dozen. Isabella realized that what most of the ladies needed was to feel a part of a special group and not be treated as though they were not marriageable.

Her goal was to lift the confidence levels and social status of these young ladies who were more diamonds in the rough than diamonds of the first water.

Isabella poured weak tea into a cup and headed back to the parlor. Less than a month ago she received another letter from her father stating that his son wasn't well and he couldn't travel home for Isabella's third Season. She must remain with her aunt.

Isabella had expected something would come up to keep her father away and was fine with it. She was happy in London and didn't want to return to country life. She had made friends and had a full life where she didn't have to be quiet. Whenever her father returned, Isabella did not want to leave London and join him.

Everything was going well until this afternoon when she discovered Lady Gretchen Colebrooke standing over Mr. Throckmorten. Isabella thanked the saints that the man was able to get up and walk away. She didn't relish the thought of a man being killed in her aunt's back garden.

A few minutes later, while Isabella was drinking her tea, she heard the front door open. Auntie Pith and her maid walked into the parlor. Her aunt had an ivory-colored gown draped over her arms. A big smile spread across her round face.

"Here it is, dear. Look, you were so right to insist I go after it today. It's the most beautiful gown I've ever seen. I do believe it's the best work Mrs. Hollyfield has ever done."

Isabella touched the dress with fancy gold stitching around the scooped neckline and full capped sleeves. She smiled. "It's quite exquisite, Auntie, but I think it might be cut a little too low."

"Oh, botheration, Isabella, I don't know why you try so hard to be an old woman. You are young and beautiful and you should act like you are. It's perfectly acceptable to show a respectable amount of your bosom." Auntie Pith cleared her throat and smiled. "Especially when you are trying to catch the eye of a gentleman."

The face of Lord Colebrooke etched across Isabella's mind, and suddenly her undergarments felt too tight. She remembered his scent, the feel of his breath on her cheeks as he stood so close their noses almost touched. She remembered how charming he looked when he was trying to hold back a smile.

Isabella set her cup on the table and mentally shook herself. "But remember, I'm not trying to catch anyone's attention."

"Yes, you are, young lady. It's past time you married."

"You above all know I'm not interested in obtaining a husband."

"Balderdash." Auntie Pith beamed with pride as she gave the gown to her maid and said, "Susan, take this upstairs and place it on my niece's bed. We'll be up shortly to dress for the evening."

Auntie Pith turned back to Isabella. "There is no doubt that you will catch every young gentleman's eye tonight."

"Why would I want to do that?"

"Because you need a husband to take care of you, young lady. Lest you forget, dear girl, this is your third Season. This one does not need to end without a match."

"What will happen if it does? Will I then be considered a spinster? If so, let it happen quickly so I can be on my own, where I can finally be able to make some of my own decisions."

A hurt expression spread across her aunt's face. "Have I not given you plenty of room to make your own decisions about the parties we attend, your clothing, and your Reading Society?"

Isabella smiled and took hold of her aunt's hand. "Yes, and you have been so wonderful to me. You are a very special person. That's why I want to be like you."

Auntie Pith patted her cheek affectionately. "But you are not like me, Isabella. You are young and beautiful and you need a husband and children."

"You have done quite well without either."

"But we are not talking about me. We're discussing you. I know it is only that the right gentleman has not caught your fancy."

Suddenly Lord Colebrooke crossed her mind again. Why couldn't she get him out of her thoughts? Yes, he was handsome and his brashness made him intriguing, but he had the temperament of a wild boar.

Auntie Pith took off her cloak, gloves, and bonnet. "No doubt if your father were here, you would already be wed. I remember that during last Season, no less than three gentlemen expressed interest in making a match with you. Any one of them would have made you a perfectly charming husband."

"But I'm perfectly happy with my life as it is now." Why would she want a husband who would restrict her life? As a spinster she would answer to no one. But to her aunt she said, "I'm certain the three who offered were more interested in my dowry than me."

"That's not true. Viscount Traywick has no need of your dowry."

"Well, if I should fall in love with him, I'd be happy to marry him, but why would I want to marry without love?"

"Of course, falling in love would be better, but that usually comes with time, Isabella. You marry because it's expected of you. You should be looking forward to marriage."

"The only thing I'm looking forward to is being old enough to be off the marriage mart."

"Good heavens, I don't think your father would allow that to happen."

"Then it's my good fortune that Papa has not returned and insisted I marry."

"You shouldn't be so hard on your father."

"I'm much happier here with you than I ever was at home."

Auntie Pith opened her mouth as if she was going to reprimand Isabella, but what she said was, "Let's see what we have planned for tonight." She picked up a stack of invitations. "The first party we'll attend will be at the home of Sir Henry Vickery, and from there we'll go to Lord Gleningwold's. That should be a delicious affair with all the right people there." She looked up at Isabella. "Oh, I almost forgot. I've heard that the Earl of Colebrooke has returned to London to find a wife. No doubt he'll be there."

"Really," Isabella said, trying to sound calm, but just thinking about the man caused heat to rise in her cheeks.

"I'll be sure to see that introductions are made."

Don't bother. We've met.

"He's always been a bit of a rogue."

He still is.

"I met him once and he doesn't deserve the reputation he has. He's charming and the most pleasant gentleman you'll ever meet," Auntie Pith continued.

Surely you jest.

"Two years ago he was probably the most sought-after gentleman without a title."

You can't be serious.

"I've heard he's changed since his father and brother were killed and he became the earl. He's settled and ready to put his youth behind him."

You obviously don't know how much he's changed if you thought him charming and sought-after.

"I think you'll find him most attractive and suitable."

"Over my dead body."

"What was that you said, Isabella, I didn't quite understand you?"

Isabella realized she must have spoken aloud and quickly cleared her throat.

"I think we best get busy or we'll miss everyone at the first party."

"So right."

Auntie Pith turned away, but Isabella remained where she was for a moment.

Her aunt was probably right. Sooner or later she would be formally introduced to Lord Colebrooke. A more unpleasant man she had never met. And she'd never met one who intrigued her so much she couldn't get him off her mind.

❧

Daniel closed the door to the family's London home with more of a bang than he had intended. He removed his hat and gloves and left them on a table. He didn't believe he'd ever felt so duped, and he was certain he'd never met a lady as clever as Miss Winslowe.

What nerve the chit had to try to pull such a stunt with him. Did she think him witless? She must. Why else would she have concocted such an outlandish scheme? And he almost fell for it. What could she have hoped to gain from making him believe Gretchen had killed Throckmorten? What kind of sick game was Miss Winslowe playing?

All it would take was a word from him and no one in Society would have anything to do with her again. She should consider herself damned lucky if he decided not to mention her name to one or two of the dowagers in Town.

Parker appeared from around the corner, and Daniel handed the butler his coat. "Is my sister still in her room?"

"Yes, my lord. She hasn't been out of it since you left."

"Find her maid and have her tell Gretchen I'll be right up to see her."

"Yes, sir."

Daniel might as well inform Gretchen that she didn't kill anyone, and that she must never speak to Miss Winslowe again. But he wanted a drink first, so he headed for the parlor.

He couldn't believe he'd actually gone over to Miss Winslowe's house thinking he might find a dead man. The entire incident was absurd, and he had played right into the lovely lady's hands. She was probably passed out from laughing at him right now. He probably wouldn't have believed her if she hadn't had such a fetching face.

He poured himself a splash of brandy and downed it like a sea-drunk sailor downing ale. One thing was certain: Miss Winslowe needed to be watched. Carefully. There was no telling what she might come up with next.

Daniel's job was to see that whatever happened, it didn't involve his sister.

Miss Winslowe wouldn't have any trouble finding

a suitable husband. Aside from being a troublemaker, she had many desirable qualities. Gretchen's chances of making a match were slightly diminished because of the spectacles she had to wear, and it would be impossible if she became embroiled in scandal broth.

A few minutes later he went upstairs and entered Gretchen's room. She was sitting up in bed, pillows propped behind her head.

"Oh, Danny!" she cried when he rounded the doorway into her bedchamber. "Thank heavens you've returned. What's going to happen to me?"

He walked over to her and sat on the edge of the bed. He smiled at her, realizing he had not been much of a brother to her lately. With his father's and brother's deaths, she was his responsibility, and he'd left too much to his aunt. He wouldn't leave London again until Gretchen was properly wed.

"Nothing as serious as we were led to believe by Miss Winslowe."

"But I killed Mr. Throckmorten."

"No, no, Gretchy, you didn't. I don't want to hear any more talk like that come out of your mouth. Mr. Throckmorten was not in Miss Winslowe's garden, dead or otherwise."

Her eyes rounded in hopeful confusion and her sobs quieted. "Are you sure?"

"Very."

She wiped her eyes with her handkerchief and sniffed. "Where is he?"

"No doubt he's at the nearest pub or club continuing to drown himself in liquor."

"How do you know this?"

Daniel told Gretchen how the garden was empty when he arrived with Isabella and what he believed happened to Throckmorten. He insisted Gretchen failed to strike him and that he had just passed out from drinking too much. He left out the part that he planned to pay Boswell Throckmorten a visit as soon as he finished talking to her.

"Oh, Danny, I'm so glad he is not dead. I didn't want him to be dead." Gretchen threw her arms around her brother and hugged him tightly. "I'm so happy you're home. I told Isabella you would know what to do. Thank you."

"Don't thank me, young lady. We're not through. I want to know what were you doing in the garden alone with Mr. Throckmorten."

Gretchen lowered her head. "I arranged to meet him there."

"Did he try to harm you? Is that why you hit him?"

"No, I got scared after I saw him in the garden. I asked him to leave, and he didn't want to, so I picked up the statue and hit him."

Daniel took a deep breath. He wanted to be firm with Gretchen and he wanted to throttle Throckmorten, but it was difficult when over the years Daniel had asked many different young ladies to meet him in secret. He'd always considered it human nature to want to break the rules.

He didn't feel that way anymore. He was an earl now, and his sister's guardian, and with that came certain responsibilities. Instead of breaking the rules, he needed to enforce them.

"What you did was serious, Gretchen. Do you

realize that? If this got out I'm not sure we could repair your reputation."

She looked up at him. "I knew it was wrong. But Mr. Throckmorten was so handsome I was flattered when he noticed me."

"You will have plenty of handsome men noticing you. But they need to be the right young men. In the meantime you can't agree to meet alone with any of them. Do I make myself clear on that?"

She nodded. "I promise I won't do it again, Danny. I don't ever want to see him again."

"Good." He took her arms down and held her hands in his. "I'm glad that you have faith that I know what is best for you, because I must insist that you have nothing else to do with Mr. Throckmorten or Miss Winslowe."

Gretchen leaned back against her mountain of pillows. "Isabella? Why? I—"

"She and her aunt left you vulnerable to compromise, and I can't forgive that. You should have never been allowed to roam freely in their garden. Your reputation could have sustained irreparable damage."

Gretchen lowered her head. "It was my fault. Not theirs."

He lifted her chin with the tips of his fingers forcing her to look at him. "It's sweet of you to want to accept all the blame for this incident, but you can't. It was Miss Winslowe's group. You were in Miss Winslowe's care, and she failed in her responsibility to you."

"But I—"

"Shh," he said with growing solicitude. "Do not cross me on this, Gretchen. Aunt Mattie has obviously allowed you too much freedom to choose your own friends and make your own plans. I intend to be more particular about who you associate with now that I'm home. And that is especially true for men such as Mr. Throckmorten."

A contemptuous expression settled across Gretchen's pretty face. "Don't worry, Danny. I don't ever want to see him again."

He wanted that whole debacle over and done with.

"I need a promise that you'll stay away from Miss Winslowe as well."

"But I so enjoy our reading group. Please don't take that away from me," she pleaded.

"I must. I can't trust you in her care. Now I want your word."

Gretchen continued to hesitate for a moment but finally said, "I promise."

"Good. Now, do you feel like getting out of this bed and dressing for the parties?"

Her eyes brightened. "Yes, if I didn't kill Mr. Throckmorten, there's no reason why I can't go and enjoy the parties."

"No reason at all. Now up and get dressed for the evening. A dance or two with the right gentleman is just what you need."

Gretchen gave him a kiss on the cheek. "Thank you, Danny."

Daniel rose from the bed and looked down at his sister. "And I'll take care of Miss Winslowe."

Five

HE COULDN'T KEEP HIS EYES OFF HER. IT WAS INSANE, really. Miss Winslowe was the last woman he wanted to claim his attention, but for some strange reason he found himself looking for her among the gorgeously gowned women and faultlessly dressed gentlemen.

It was easy to tell himself that his only interest in her was to watch her and to make sure she stayed away from Gretchen. It was much harder to convince himself that was true.

The party had been a crush all evening with far too many people invited for Lord Gleningwold's house. Every time Daniel thought he'd move on to another party in search of Boswell Throckmorten, he'd spot Miss Winslowe again and thoughts of leaving fled. He'd gone to the man's house earlier, but he wasn't home. Daniel wanted to make sure the man stayed away from Gretchen.

Isabella was especially captivating tonight in her low-cut gown adorned with pearls, lace, and a cascade of golden-colored ribbons flowing from the high waist. When he'd met her earlier, she had looked very prim and proper in her afternoon dress, bonnet, and cloak.

Tonight she looked stunning with her honey-colored hair swept up in curls. And all the other gentlemen in attendance knew it, too. She was not without plenty of beaux at her side.

Daniel had been introduced to a bevy of lovely young ladies throughout the evening. He'd even danced with three or four of them before he stopped signing dance cards. Halfway into his second dance Daniel hung his head over the prospect of spending the next five weeks going from party to party searching for a young lady who would make a suitable match.

When it came to a wife, Daniel didn't even know what kind of lady he was looking for. How could he just consider appearance when they were all at least pretty if not downright lovely? Most of them seemed eager enough to secure his admiration and obtain his fancy, and some of them were pleasant to converse with.

How could he have known it would be so difficult to pick out a wife? No doubt an arranged marriage would have suited him fine. Not a one of the ladies he'd met so far tonight intrigued him like Miss Winslowe had.

She had captivated him. She was lovely with her blond hair threaded with ivory- and gold-colored ribbons and arranged neatly on top of her head. Her skin was a beautiful, tempting shade that made him think of lighted alabaster and it looked kissably soft.

He'd kept his distance from her all evening, but that hadn't kept him from seeing that her green eyes sparkled with laughter and confidence whenever she talked. She was poised and charming with everyone she talked to. After their chaotic encounter this afternoon, he was certain he never wanted to see her again, but his eyes kept searching the crowd for her.

Miss Winslowe was obviously intelligent and challenging. She was also trouble. Daniel had enough to manage right now without getting interested in a lovely menace.

Maybe he should put off finding a wife for himself and concentrate on finding a husband for Gretchen. Yes, that seemed to be the more sensible thing to do. Once he had her safely betrothed to an acceptable gentleman, he could then turn his attention back to finding a young lady to marry.

Too, it was Gretchen's first Season and he'd wanted to see her properly engaged before everyone started heading to their country homes to avoid the summer heat. He would have to do what his aunt Mattie had failed to do. He was going to see to it that Gretchen took calls from only the right gentlemen.

But at the back of Daniel's mind was the thought of what would happen to the Colebrooke lands if he should meet with an unfortunate accident as his brother, who died before having an heir. Daniel couldn't bear the thought of the estate going to his cousin Bradford Turnbury.

Daniel had no doubt Bradford would gamble away the family fortune and all the lands that weren't entailed before a year was up. If Bradford's father hadn't left him a sizable yearly allowance, Daniel was sure the man would be in debtor's prison by now.

Daniel's attention strayed back to Miss Winslowe.

She was talking to their host, Earl Gleningwold. She stood taller than the short and rotund man, but by the smile on the older man's face she had enthralled him with her charm.

Her smile was bright. Not once had he seen her use her fan or flutter her lashes. She was much too poised to rely on such feminine devices to gain or hold a man's attention.

It was no wonder she had a dozen young ladies in her Wallflower Club. He could see how she put everyone she talked to at ease. As he watched her, Daniel was struck by the realization that he was attracted to her the way a man was attracted to a woman he wanted in his bed.

Why was that? When the room was full of beautiful young ladies, why was his body telling him Miss Winslowe was the one he wanted?

"Have you met her?"

Daniel turned to see Chilton Cummerford standing beside him. "Who?"

"Don't feign innocence with me, Danny. It won't work. You haven't been able to take your eyes off her since you arrived."

"You lie."

Chilton gave him a devious smile. "Not by much."

"By enough."

It was one thing for Daniel to admit his attraction to Miss Winslowe to himself but quite another to admit it to his best friend. And there was no way in hell he'd tell Chilton about the debacle that happened with Miss Winslowe earlier in the afternoon. Daniel only wanted to forget about that.

"I should be happy to introduce you."

"To whom?" Daniel said with some smugness.

Chilton laughed. "All right, Danny. We'll play this your way. To the lady you are watching. Miss Winslowe, of course."

Daniel folded his arms across his chest and gave Chilton an annoyed look. "I think you deliberately misled me earlier in the day when you spoke of her."

"Truly? In what way?"

"From the way you talked about her, I thought her to be a shriveled-up old spinster who had nothing better to do than stir up mischief."

"Really? I don't remember saying anything about her age. I believe I said I'd leave it to you to form your own opinion of her. And by the way you've been watching her, I'd say you have and it's good."

Daniel looked out over the crowded dance floor again. It had always been a nuisance that Chilton knew him so well. In his younger days it hadn't bothered him, but now it did. Privacy was more important to him than it used to be.

"I'm not watching her specifically," Daniel lied to his friend and felt no guilt in doing so. "This is my first party in over a year, remember? I'm looking over all the young ladies tonight."

"In that case, come let me introduce you to Miss Winslowe."

Daniel looked at his friend. "We've met."

Chilton's eyebrows shot upward. "You don't say? When?"

"Earlier."

"Did you find her charming?"

"Not in the least."

Chilton grinned. "You lie."

Daniel turned to his friend and smiled. "Not by much."

"By enough."

Chilton and Daniel both laughed heartily at their mimic of their earlier conversation. "It's good to have you back in Town."

Daniel nodded. He was glad to be back in London, but he didn't look forward to the two tasks ahead of him. He needed to find a husband for Gretchen and a wife for himself before the Season ended. That didn't give him much time.

"How has she escaped marriage?" Daniel asked, searching the room for Miss Winslowe again.

"Who?"

"Are we going there again?"

Chilton chuckled. "No. I guess not. It's your first party, and already you've set your sights on the one lady you're not likely to get."

Daniel knew Chilton was issuing him a challenge that he fully expected Daniel would take him up on, but he wasn't falling for that.

"Believe me, Chilton, I do not have any designs on her, but if I did, what makes you think I couldn't entice her to marry me?"

"Miss Winslowe has made it clear to everyone she doesn't want to make a match."

It didn't surprise Daniel that the lady would rather play her games than get serious about finding a husband to take her off the mart.

Thinking back to how she'd tried to trick him

about Throckmorten, Daniel said, "My guess is that she's not married because she hasn't had any offers."

"Think again, my friend. She's had plenty of offers. At least three last year, maybe more."

"Maybe less?" Daniel questioned.

"No. I'm sure of the three."

"Suitable matches?"

"Yes. She even declined Viscount Traywick. She dances, smiles, and occasionally accepts calls but has shown no interest in making a match."

"Have you called on her?"

"Me? No." Chilton shook his head.

"Why?"

That same faraway expression that Daniel had noticed earlier eased across Chilton's face. "For now, I'm satisfied with the mistress I'm seeing. As I told you earlier, I have no need to marry."

That was Chilton's second reference to being content, yet his friend didn't have the look of a contented man. He didn't seem restless as he had in their youth, it was more a sad resignation. Daniel sensed something was wrong, but tonight wasn't the time to ask him about it. But Daniel would if Chilton didn't speak up soon.

"Perhaps there's a reason she hasn't married," Daniel said, thinking she must be up to all different kinds of trickery.

"There was a bit of a story about her father abandoning her for his new wife, but I have no idea how much of it is true."

"That could be part of the problem. She has no father or older brother or uncle to keep her in line? Who's her sponsor?"

"An aunt. Miss Pithany Winslowe."

"Yes, I've met her in the past. She's a well-respected lady."

"Lord Colebrooke, may I be so forward as to intrude for a moment?"

Daniel turned and looked into the long lean face of Thomas Wright. A tall, thin, brown-haired young lady stood beside him looking down at the floor.

"Of course, Tom, it's been a long time since I've seen you. How are you?"

"Good, my lord, and you?"

"Quite well."

"If it's convenient, I'd like to present my sister, Miss Amanda Wright."

Daniel assured him it was, and introductions, bows, and greetings were exchanged by all, including Chilton, who promptly excused himself shortly after Amanda Wright was introduced. Daniel couldn't help but notice that Amanda was comely enough with small brown eyes and shapely lips, but she barely opened her mouth when she talked and she wouldn't look at him.

He kept thinking she'd be so much prettier if she looked him in the eyes and smiled when she talked to him. He wondered why she acted so shy. She would do well to learn a few things from the confident Miss Winslowe.

"Lovely party," Tom said. "Lord Gleningwold and his countess always give a splendid affair."

"Indeed. I trust the rest of your family is well, Tom?"

"In good health, yes."

Daniel was certain Thomas had brought his sister over in hopes she would catch Daniel's eye. Daniel wondered if somehow Tom knew that he was interested in him for Gretchen. He wasn't the most handsome of men, but he came from a respectable family. He wasn't much of a drinker, and as far as Daniel knew he wasn't into gambling, either. That made him a far better catch for Gretchen than most of the acceptable men in London.

Daniel needed to make sure Thomas knew that a call on Gretchen would be not only acceptable but welcomed.

"Perhaps we can have a drink at White's later in the week."

Thomas's face reddened with excitement. "I should look forward to it, my lord."

"Good."

Over Tom's shoulder Daniel saw Miss Winslowe talking to Gretchen. He tensed. He'd told both of them to stay away from the other. He wasn't surprised that Miss Winslowe hadn't listened to him, but considering all the trouble Gretchen had been in, she should have heeded his warning.

"Excuse me, Tom, Miss Wright. I see someone I must speak to."

Daniel made his way over to where his sister and Miss Winslowe stood. He was stopped three times for introductions to young ladies before he managed to reach the other side of the room.

Gretchen looked up at him with a big smile. Looking at her tonight no one would ever know that only a few hours ago she'd thought she'd killed someone. Beneath her spectacles he could see that the redness and swelling had faded from her eyes, and the worried wrinkles were gone from her brow.

"Gretchen. Miss Winslowe," he said tightly, trying not to sound as adversarial as he felt when he stopped in front of them.

"Lord Colebrooke," Miss Winslowe said stiffly, but not without an appropriate smile. "I'm surprised to see you here."

"Why so?"

"I would have thought you'd be out slaying dragons for some damsel in distress."

"Distress no doubt caused by some pranks you've been up to, Miss Winslowe."

She gave him a dazzling smile, and Daniel's lower body reacted to her. Knowing what trickery she was capable of, it was unbelievable how attracted he was to her.

"Well, if it weren't for troublemakers like me... gallant gentlemen like you would have no dragons to slay."

"I should love for that day to arrive so I can concentrate on important matters."

"Are you two arguing?" Gretchen asked, confused.

"No," Daniel and Miss Winslowe said in unison.

"Gretchen, I want you to come with me," Daniel said. "I want to introduce you to Mr. Thomas Wright and his sister Amanda."

"Oh, Danny." Gretchen laughed with comfortable abandon. "I already know both of them quite well. Amanda is in our Reading Society that meets at Isabella's house. You are the one who's been away, not I."

"In that case, just come with me. We don't want to hold up, Miss Winslowe. I'm sure she has another ruse to attend to."

"Really, Daniel, I'm not a child who—" Suddenly Gretchen stopped and her eyes widened as if she'd seen a ghost.

Isabella and Daniel turned around to see what had caused Gretchen to turn so pale.

Mr. Boswell Throckmorten walked into the room looking more dapper than any man had the right to look.

Daniel couldn't help but smile, and his voice dripped with sarcasm as he said, "It doesn't appear as if anyone touched a hair on his head to me. Certainly not with a marble statuette of Cupid. In fact, I do believe Mr. Throckmorten is the healthiest-looking dead man I've ever seen." He looked specifically at Miss Winslowe and said, "Don't you think so?"

"Must you gloat with so much enthusiasm?" Isabella asked.

Daniel's smile turned to a satisfied grin. "It's not every day a man gets to witness a dead man walking."

"And it's not every day that a lady meets so arrogant a man who passed himself off as a gentleman."

"I'm so relieved he's not dead," Gretchen said.

"Yes. We all are," Isabella added, looking pointedly at Daniel.

"Some of us never believed he was dead in the first place," Daniel answered confidently.

Gretchen said, "I don't know why I thought I had killed him."

"You probably never even struck him, Gretchy," Daniel said. "But I think you've learned your lesson about walking alone in gardens where you're at risk. And what kind of people you need to associate with."

Gretchen nodded in answer to Daniel but didn't take her gaze off Mr. Throckmorten until he walked into another room.

"Good. I suggest we all put this matter out of our minds and forget it happened," he said, looking straight at Miss Winslowe. He wanted to leave no doubt that he was mainly talking to her. "Now, if you'll excuse me, I need to speak to Mr. Throckmorten to make sure he doesn't accidentally stroll into your back garden again."

"How kind of you to offer, sir," Isabella said as calmly as if she talked about the weather. "I'm quite capable of speaking to the gentleman myself. I don't need you to handle anything for me."

"Are you two arguing again?" Gretchen asked again.

"No," Daniel and Miss Winslowe answered.

"Then, if *you* two will excuse me, I need to go to the retiring room," Gretchen said and walked away.

At once Lord Colebrooke stepped closer to Miss Winslowe and in a low voice said, "I told you to stay away from my sister."

She didn't flinch but remained staring boldly into his eyes. "Or you'll do what, my lord?"

"A word or two from me and you will no longer be welcome in anyone's house in London."

"I do believe you have me shaking in fear, Lord Colebrooke," she snipped.

"You need to be. I will not let you ruin Gretchen's reputation with your Wallflowers Society."

Her shoulders lifted and her chin came up. "Are you always so boorish and ill-mannered to innocent ladies?"

"Just ladies like you, Miss Winslowe, are the only ones who need to fear me."

"Fear you, my lord? That won't happen."

He wasn't so sure he appreciated the fact he couldn't intimidate her, but it did spark a bit of admiration in him. "I don't care which way you take what I'm saying. Just stay away from my sister."

"Gretchen approached me tonight, and I am not as impolite as you are. You do what you must. I will not rebuff her if she speaks to me."

Someone clapped Daniel on the back. "Who's this? My long traveled cousin, the Earl of Colebrooke. How long have you been in Town?"

Daniel forced his gaze away from Miss Winslowe to look into the blurry eyes of Bradford Turnbury. It was just Daniel's luck that Bradford would show up while he was having a heated conversation with Miss Winslowe.

Daniel had never cared for his cousin. As a young lad he had been cruel to his animals, and he was always picking a fight with Daniel's older brother. Bradford had learned early that Daniel didn't have the passive personality of his older brother, so he made a point of not starting trouble when Daniel was around. On more than one occasion Daniel was forced to come to his brother's aid.

"I hope I haven't interrupted a serious conversation," Bradford said. "You both seem so intense."

"Bradford," Daniel said tightly, refusing to even acknowledge his inappropriate comments. "You haven't changed a bit, I see."

Bradford smiled broadly. "So true, Danny. You haven't bothered to write in over a year."

Daniel grimaced. He hated for Bradford to call him

Danny, but he had learned long ago that the more he tried to keep Bradford from using the name, the more he said it.

"I've been busy," Daniel said, noticing his cousin's flushed face, the puffiness and dark circles around his cousin's dark brown eyes. He was well-dressed but looked much too thin for his tall frame. It was clear he'd already had too much to drink.

"No doubt." Bradford bowed to Miss Winslowe. "How are you this evening, Miss Winslowe?"

"Well, Mr. Turnbury, and you?"

"Couldn't be better. You are looking beautiful tonight."

She smiled graciously. "Thank you, kind sir."

Daniel didn't like the expression on Bradford's face when he looked at Miss Winslowe. It reminded Daniel of a man who wanted to ravish a woman.

Bradford faced Daniel. "And might I add that my son is in excellent health, too."

"Good," Daniel said, knowing he was going to see that this man did not inherit the title Earl of Colebrooke. By the looks of him, he was drinking himself into an early grave.

"I had heard you were returning to London—and to claim a bride."

"I'm sure the thought chills you, Bradford, but it is time for me to marry."

"Couldn't agree more," his cousin said. "The sooner the better as they say. We never know what the future will bring, do we?"

It didn't surprise Daniel that Bradford referenced his brother's death. That was just another of his bad habits.

"I believe you two gentlemen have a lot of catching up to do," Isabella said. "Would you excuse me?"

"Don't go," Bradford said.

"I was…" Isabella said.

"She was…" Daniel said.

"Just leaving," they said in unison.

"What a coincidence," Bradford said. "So was I, but before I do—Miss Winslowe, I hear a dance about to start. Would you do me the honor of joining me, if you haven't already committed this dance to another?"

"I haven't promised, but I"—she hesitated a moment before smiling and saying—"I'd be delighted to be your partner. Thank you for asking."

"Wonderful. See you later, old chap," Bradford said to Daniel as he and Isabella walked away.

Daniel felt an unusual tightness in his chest as they disappeared into the crowd. He didn't want his cousin dancing with Miss Winslowe. He didn't want him touching her, smiling at her. And he didn't even want his cousin looking at her and wanting her in the way Daniel wanted her.

It was crazy what he was feeling for her. It was clear she didn't like him. Nor he her. Yet he wanted her. What kind of madness was this? Had she bewitched him in some way?

Daniel shook off those feelings. Enough of Miss Winslowe. He had to go find Throckmorten. Daniel wanted to make sure the scoundrel never approached Gretchen again.

Six

"HE WAS SO CHARMING WHEN I WAS PRESENTED TO him," Joanne Langley told the gathering of young ladies who stood around her in the retiring room. "Lord Colebrooke looked into my eyes and smiled at me with such delight in his face. I thought I was going to melt into the floor like spring snow."

"I was the first lady he asked to dance," Alice Eldridge said with a satisfied smile spreading her generous lips wide. "And I simply felt faint with heat when he looked at me."

"I felt the same way when he danced with me," Lady Katherine Spearmont announced as she fluttered her fan under her pointy chin. "He indicated he is going to ask to call on me later in the week."

"How did he indicate that?" Lady Lynette Knightington asked with more than a little interest in the earl.

"Yes, I want to hear this, too," Alice said. "Maybe he indicated he was going to call on me."

Isabella turned away from the young ladies' discussion. They were chatting and laughing about events of the evening as well as the dashing Earl of Colebrooke. From the sighs and mewling it appeared he'd stolen all their hearts with a few smiles and three or four dances.

What rubbish, she thought. It was clear to her that none of the ladies had seen the side of Lord Colebrooke that Isabella had seen. She was tempted to tell them he was the most arrogant man she'd ever had the misfortune to meet but decided they would think her insane.

She didn't know why she'd accepted the dance with Mr. Bradford Turnbury. She really didn't like the man. He always smelled of liquor. But when he'd asked her to dance in front of Lord Colebrooke, something unexplainable had come over her. She'd had this maddening feeling that she wanted to make the earl jealous. Where that had come from she had no idea. The very thought of it was ludicrous.

Lord Colebrooke had repeatedly let her know he had nothing but disdain for her. He couldn't care less who she talked to or with whom she danced. She had to get over this peculiar infatuation she had developed for him. It was disturbing her peace of mind and making her behave in the oddest manner.

And to make matters worse, now she had the headache. Too many perplexing things had happened today. Thinking Mr. Throckmorten was dead was bad enough, but then she was scorned unmercifully by Lord Colebrooke and later to see Mr. Throckmorten looking well-turned-out and charming as ever was just too much. She passed by the man not half an hour ago, and he smiled at her as if he'd never been found dead cold in her garden.

There was nothing to do now but go home and lie down. Tomorrow would be better. Yes, she would find Auntie Pith and make her excuses. They would go home and put an end to this most unusual day.

Isabella interrupted the ladies and said her good-byes. She lowered her forehead to her hand and rubbed it as she walked out the door. Not watching where she was going, she immediately bumped into someone. She looked up and found herself staring straight into the golden brown eyes of Lord Colebrooke.

"Oh, excuse me," she said, feeling that odd fluttering sensation in her stomach again. "I'm sorry I wasn't looking where I was going."

"Another bad habit, Miss Winslowe?" he asked.

She was not up to matching wits with him but neither could she let his rude comment pass without answer. She lifted her chin and her shoulders a notch and answered, "I'm just full of them, my lord, and no doubt you will see each one."

His eyes narrowed and he spoke slowly and low. "I'm ready for anything you have."

Isabella couldn't believe she'd said such an outlandish thing. What was she doing issuing a challenge to the most popular earl in London? This was no way to become as well-respected in Town as her aunt. She should learn to curb her tongue when this man was around.

She had all intentions of walking away without further comment, but as she made to brush past him, he touched her upper arm and stopped her. Even through the thickness of her evening gloves, Isabella felt as if a red hot heat had pierced her skin.

Isabella looked up into his eyes again, and something tangible passed between them. It made her tremble, but she didn't know what it was. The surprise she saw in his eyes let her know that he had felt it, too, and was just as shaken.

Lord Colebrooke dropped his arm to his side and cleared his throat before saying, "Excuse me, Miss Winslowe, but before you go, could you tell me if my sister is in there?" He pointed to the room that had been set aside for the ladies to have privacy and rest.

In order to break the spell of staring into the mesmerizing depths of his eyes, she looked away from him and to the room she'd just vacated.

She felt the need to clear her throat, too. "No," she answered. "Gretchen isn't in there."

Concern flashed across the earl's face.

"Is something wrong?" she asked.

"No. I'm sure not. I'm ready to go to another party, but I can't find Gretchen. I've looked the house over." His brows drew closer together. "Are you sure she isn't inside?"

Isabella watched him closely, feeling his distress. "I'm quite sure. Must I insist again that I would not lie to you regarding your sister or anything else?"

His brow softened a little. "All right, I'm sure I've just missed her. I'm worried about her after the afternoon's events."

A chill splintered through Isabella, and she didn't like where her thoughts were heading. Gretchen had admitted to her that she'd arranged the meeting with Mr. Throckmorten in her garden. The man was in attendance this evening. Could it be possible that

Gretchen had planned another secret rendezvous even after what had happened this afternoon in the garden?

Isabella didn't want to alarm Lord Colebrooke, but she had to ask, "As you looked for Gretchen, did you by chance see Mr. Throckmorten in any of the rooms?"

His worry faded into an angry scowl, and Isabella was sure she'd voiced what he'd been thinking.

"No, I've been looking for him all evening and I keep missing him."

"Well, then," Isabella said, taking charge, "perhaps we should take a walk outside and tour the gardens to see whom we may find."

She felt him tense more as he said, "What are you suggesting, Miss Winslowe?"

"I think you know what I'm saying, sir. Now, do you want to find Gretchen or do you want to pretend there is no way she would defy you and the rules of convention and take an unapproved walk with a gentleman?"

"I'm capable of looking in the garden. I don't need your help."

"But if she is indeed there, Gretchen might need the comfort of a lady when you find her. I'm going with or without your permission."

"Very well, but don't offer any comment. This really isn't any of your concern."

"I wouldn't dream of interfering."

Lord Colebrooke chuckled and Isabella felt her spirits lift. It was a beautiful sound that settled around her and made her feel wonderful all over. For a brief moment, in laughter, his face was completely free of concern and disdain, and she glimpsed the man all the young ladies had lost their hearts to. He was so magnificent she was left breathless.

Isabella was as captivated by him as the young ladies she'd just left.

"Come along, Miss Winslowe," he said. "We've no time to waste."

Side by side they worked their way through the crowded rooms toward the French windows that led to the back gardens. Their progress was delayed. Lord Colebrooke was stopped by a duchess, an earl, and three pushy mamas all wanting to make introductions. They finally stepped through the patio doors and outside.

Isabella saw the evening was heavy with a smoky gray mist. Several people were outside talking and laughing, while others milled around the abundant grounds of the house. The Earl of Gleningwold's house was famous for its gardens with its great walls of yew. His great-grandfather had purposefully made the house small so that he would have more area to plant his trees, shrubs, and flowers.

The grounds were noted for their nooks, crannies, and arbors that led into rooms of lush greenery. There were two lily ponds and a two-tiered fountain on the premises and three well-manicured knot gardens. It was a spectacular place to visit during the day, but on an evening like this the high yews and shrubs made it all appear ominous.

It was the perfect garden for a couple to wander the grounds and find a spot to hide so they could steal a few kisses. And tonight's low-lying mist added an extra unexpected cover.

Isabella stopped at the top of the limestone steps

and asked, "Should we part and you take one side and I the other?"

Lord Colebrooke shook his head as he carefully looked at the other couples who were outside. "No. I think the best way to handle this is for you and me to appear as though we are strolling through the gardens conversing."

She held back a smile that threatened her lips and said, "Oh, you mean you want us to walk around and talk as if we approve of each other?"

A half grin lifted one corner of his mouth. "That would be a stretch, wouldn't it?"

"Yes, I suppose it would, but for Gretchen, I'm willing to make the sacrifice."

Isabella let the cool air of night fill her lungs as she lifted the hem of her gown and started down the steps. Daniel stayed by her side on the crushed stone pathway that led into the center of the grounds.

"This is the perfect night for anyone who wanted to have an assignation in a garden," Lord Colebrooke said.

"It's impossible to see more than a few feet in front of us. Let's hope we don't find Gretchen out here."

"I can assure you that *is* my hope, Miss Winslowe. After our discussion this afternoon, I can't believe she would agree to meet anyone in the garden— especially Throckmorten."

The grass that had grown in between the footstones was moist, and it wasn't long before Isabella felt the wetness seep through her soft-soled shoes. The damp mist soon penetrated her thin gown, chilling her to the bone, but she would have rather gotten consumption than complain to the earl. Any other gentleman would have been aware of the chilly night and offered her his coat.

"Is there any chance she went home early with your aunt?" Isabella asked.

"No. Aunt Mattie didn't come when she found out that I would be escorting Gretchen. She's been out with Gretchen every night for a week and was relieved to have an evening at home."

They had wandered far enough away that they no longer heard the laughter and talking of the people on the patio, and they had lost all light from the house, too. Isabella could barely see Lord Colebrooke even though he was walking very close to her.

Just past one of the lily ponds they came to a fork in the garden. Isabella said, "You take the east and I'll take the west."

"I don't think so, Miss Winslowe. We will stay together."

"But we can cover so much more of the gardens looking separate."

"Yes, but what if I were to find Gretchen and you were still wandering out here somewhere in the dark? No, we stay together. We can walk much faster now that we are away from the house."

"All right. Let's continue."

They headed down the right side of the path and walked among the laurel hedges. Occasionally a wet limb would brush across Isabella's face. The dampness had penetrated the layers of the thin clothing she wore and she was cold and wet.

After several minutes of searching she was ready to call a halt to their pursuit when she noticed a vine-covered arbor near the back gate. She approached it and peeked inside. At first she didn't see anything. Mist wafted across the small area of garden but when she started to turn away the fog shifted and she saw the form of a woman standing alone.

"Lord Colebrooke, over here. I think I've found Gretchen."

He came up behind Isabella, and she felt his warm breath on her neck and it comforted her.

"It is Gretchen," he said, looking through the drifting mist. "What the devil is she doing out here alone?"

"I have no idea, but I'd say it a good thing that she isn't with anyone."

"I agree."

Their feet crushed on the loose stone as they left the pathway and ducked underneath the vine-tangled arbor. When they drew nearer, Isabella saw it was indeed Gretchen. At first Gretchen didn't acknowledge them but continued to look at the ground.

A chill that had nothing to do with the cold shook Isabella.

"Gretchen, what are you doing out here?" Lord Colebrooke asked as they approached.

Isabella stopped just short of Gretchen and turned to the earl and said, "Sweet, heavenly mercies. Look at her feet."

Daniel then saw what Isabella and Gretchen were looking at: the body of a man prone before them.

For a moment the silence lay as heavy as the mist.

"Damnation," Daniel cursed and quickly bent down to examine the man.

Even before Daniel rolled the man over to look

at his face, Isabella knew it was Mr. Throckmorten. The gray fog made it difficult to see, but there was no mistaking the presence of a gold-handled paper knife protruding from his chest.

Daniel swore under his breath again and pressed his ear to the area of the man's heart and listened. He then felt Mr. Throckmorten's pale, still face before looking at his wound again.

Finally Daniel rose and looked at Gretchen with a grimace. "What the hell happened?"

"I don't know."

"What do you mean, you don't know? How did you find him? Were you walking alone and stumbled upon him?"

Isabella could feel the tension in Lord Colebrooke, and she wanted to help. She knew exactly how he was feeling, having just gone through the same thing in her aunt's garden.

"Yes, Danny. He was just lying there when I got here. Is he dead?"

"Of course not," Isabella said, stepping up to join in, even though she'd promised the earl she would stay quiet. "He's just had too much to drink again and he's passed out cold."

"Damnation." Daniel paused only a second. "Miss Winslowe, the man has a knife buried deep in his chest and he's not breathing."

"That doesn't mean he's dead," she persisted stubbornly, wanting to keep Gretchen calm. It wouldn't do for her to go back to the house hysterical.

"I know a dead man when I see one, and this man is dead," Daniel insisted tightly.

"How many dead men have you seen?" she asked, remembering the exact questions he had thrown at her earlier.

"You try my patience," he said in an exasperated voice.

"Well, my lord, it was perfectly fine for him not to be dead when I saw him in my garden, but now that you've found him he must be dead."

"He wasn't bleeding when you found him," Daniel reminded her. "If you will look closely, you'll see his white shirt is now stained red with blood."

"Yes. I do see it," she answered, wishing she could make him understand that she was trying to be positive for Gretchen's sake. "But if he came back to life once before, he can do so again."

Daniel stepped closer to Isabella and said, "You are impossible to talk to."

"How convenient that I was just thinking the same thing about you."

"Will you two stop arguing and tell me what we are going to do?" Gretchen said in a trembly voice that sounded very much like a frightened child.

"We're not arguing," Lord Colebrooke said.

Even though Isabella could not see his face clearly, she knew Daniel wanted her to be quiet.

"The first thing we have to do is get you out of this garden. I can't have your name connected to a scandal like this. Miss Winslowe, take Gretchen back inside. I'll return in a few minutes and say I found him."

"That won't work," Isabella said. "Several people saw you and me walking together, and no doubt someone saw Gretchen leave alone. If I'm seen coming back with Gretchen, they'll assume you saw her with Mr. Throckmorten and that you became enraged and stabbed him. I must be with you when you report this to back up your claim of innocence."

"What anyone thinks of me doesn't matter right now. I won't have Gretchen's name involved in this."

"And we'll see that she isn't. She must return the way she came, alone. You and I will arrive back at the house shortly after her and say we stumbled—" Isabella stopped abruptly as Lord Colebrooke's hand landed softly, swiftly against her lips. His warm touch startled her so, she dropped her reticule.

"I hear laughter. Someone is heading this way," he whispered.

Isabella barely heard what he said for she was concentrating on the feel of his hand that spread delicious warmth through her all the way down to her wet toes. The heat of his body pressed close into hers was like a hot fire. His skin smelled of soap and—

"Come on, let's move away from here and get back on the path," he whispered. "Follow my lead." He grabbed Isabella and Gretchen by the hand and they headed back to the path.

There was no more time to dwell on his touch as she'd wanted to. The three of them quickly rushed back under the arbor and to the crushed stone path. Lord Colebrooke quickly stood between the two of them and held out his arms for them to slip their hands through just as they saw Viscount Stonehurst and his new bride coming down the trail.

They were all quite friendly except for Gretchen, who barely managed to say more than a greeting. They stood talking for what seemed like hours to

Isabella, but she was certain it was no more than five or six minutes before the viscount and his lady wife continued on their misty tour of the grounds.

Lord Colebrooke was the first to speak. In a husky voice he said, "Gretchen, I want you to go back to the house immediately, and I don't want you to speak about this incident to anyone. Do you understand?"

"I'm frightened, Danny. What if he's really dead this time?"

"Nonsense, Gretchen," Isabella said, butting in again. "Do as your brother said and go back inside the house and get a glass of punch. I assure you everything will be fine, just as it was earlier today."

"All right, if you're sure."

"I am. We'll find you shortly and you can go home. I'll see that your brother returns safely," Isabella said. "Now go."

Gretchen hurried away, and Isabella turned back to Daniel.

"You'll see that I'm safe?" he asked her in an annoyed tone.

She had a feeling he wouldn't like that. But he couldn't see that Gretchen was at the breaking point.

She cleared her throat. "Yes."

"You're incredible."

"I didn't mean to step on your masculine pride, Lord Colebrooke."

"I can assure you my pride didn't feel a thing," he answered a bit too quickly.

"Good. I only told Gretchen what she wanted to hear. She was worried about leaving you out here, and she needed reassurance that you would be safe."

"I find that I never know what you will say, Miss Winslowe."

"Well, a lady should know how to keep a man intrigued," she answered.

"You have done better than most so far, Miss Winslowe."

"Thank you for the compliment."

"Are you sure it was one?"

"No, but I'll take it that way."

"Are you trying to flirt with me?"

She gasped. "Certainly not."

He stepped closer to her and lowered his voice. "It feels as if you are."

"Don't be ridiculous. I'm merely explaining my indelicate reference to your capabilities of protecting yourself and my ability to help you. Now, do you want to stand here and banter or should we go back and pick up my reticule, which I dropped when you grabbed me?"

"I'm sorry about that, but we had to hurry. You're right, let's get your reticule and be on our way. I don't want Gretchen to arrive much before we do."

Isabella and Lord Colebrooke walked back underneath the arbor to where they had left Mr. Throckmorten. They looked around but didn't see him straightaway.

An eerie feeling stole over Isabella and she shivered. "Here is my reticule," she said, picking it up and fastening the drawstrings to her wrist so it wouldn't fall off again. She looked over to the earl. "But where is Mr. Throckmorten?"

"You must have dropped your purse when we were

on our way back to the pathway. He must be over in this direction."

Lord Colebrooke walked farther away, closer to the garden wall. Isabella was not wrong. She knew exactly where she was when she dropped her purse and that was when she was standing very close to Mr. Throckmorten.

Another shiver crawled up her back. Surely he didn't get up and walk away again.

Something strange was going on, and Isabella had no idea how she'd gotten caught up in it.

Isabella searched the ground again and saw something white. She reached down and picked it up. It was a lady's handkerchief. There was embroidery on it, but it was too dark for her to see the stitching. No doubt Gretchen had dropped it when they had to flee to the pathway.

Thankfully Isabella had found it. She slipped it into her reticule for safekeeping.

Lord Colebrooke walked back over to where Isabella stood. He was eerily quiet for a moment, and the only things she heard were night sounds and Lord Colebrooke's erratic breathing.

There were many things she wanted to say, but she had to let him speak first.

"He's gone," Lord Colebrooke said flatly. "Throckmorten's body is not here."

Seven

"Gone?" Miss Winslowe said to Daniel. "How about he was never here?"

"What are you saying?" he asked, but didn't give her time to answer before he continued. "That's insane. You were here. You saw him."

"Yes," she said calmly. "But remember that's what you said to me when he disappeared out of my garden earlier this afternoon."

"Will you forget about that?" Daniel said, exasperated, perplexed by this entire day. "Throckmorten wasn't dead when he was in your garden."

Daniel searched the darkened ground all around him. Throckmorten was here. What the bloody hell could have happened to him?

This was preposterous. Throckmorten had to be here somewhere. Daniel paced back and forth across the short space of grass. He looked near the hedge and around the bushes. It was just too damn difficult to see anything in the gloomy mist.

"Where the hell is he?" Daniel muttered aloud as he made his way back to where Miss Winslowe stood waiting.

"Dead men don't get up and walk away, Lord Colebrooke," she said with all the calm of a windless afternoon.

"I know that. Someone must have stolen the body while we were talking to Stonehurst."

Miss Winslowe laughed. A soft, seductive, playful sound that touched Daniel deep in his soul, and his lower body came to life. How could she excite him at a time like this? What kind of hold did she have on him? A dead man was missing, and he had thoughts of seducing this woman on his mind.

It was too misty to see her as clearly as he would have liked, but he saw enough to be enraptured by her loveliness. He was sane enough to know he had to fight the pull she had on him. His life had been nothing but trouble since she came into it. He moved closer so he could see more of her face in laughter.

He stopped just inches from her and lowered his voice as he said, "I fail to see the humor in the situation we are in, Miss Winslowe."

"Oh, really?"

Must she always challenge him? She was intoxicating. "Yes," he answered.

"Think back to this afternoon, my lord. You are saying the exact things that I said to you when I tried to make you believe that Mr. Throckmorten was in my garden. Dead."

There was a sudden break in the clouds, and faint moonlight brightened her face. Daniel saw her sparkling eyes filled with satisfaction and her beautifully soft skin that glistened in the pale glow from the moon. Her lips were moist, pink, and tempting. She looked so kissable he suddenly found it difficult to keep his mind on the problem at hand.

He swallowed the desire that rose up in him and threatened to overpower him. "That was different," he said, forcing his voice to remain firm but low.

"Oh, really, sir? In what way is it different? I fail to see any."

She smiled at him and his lower body tightened again. She was beautiful. How could he be so physically attracted to her when she challenged everything he said and played mischievous games that caused harm to others? She was not the kind of young lady he expected to desire so hotly that he ached to touch her.

"You said he had received a bump on the head. I saw a knife embedded in his chest."

"That's not proof he was dead."

"I know a dead man when I see one, Miss Winslowe, and Boswell Throckmorten was dead."

"How many dead men have you seen, Lord Colebrooke?"

Daniel opened his mouth to speak but stopped. He felt an unwelcome smile spreading across his face. Damnation, she was right. They were saying the exact things to each other that were said this afternoon, only their roles had been reversed.

He'd ridiculed her much the same way several hours ago. It rankled that she was right, but it didn't keep his admiration for her from growing. Or his attraction.

"Very well, Miss Winslowe. I admit you deserve an apology. I'm sorry for the way I treated you this afternoon. I should have been more understanding of your plight."

She looked directly into his eyes. "Does that mean I'm vindicated?"

Daniel felt his frustration easing away and his knotted muscles relax. Her games be damned. She was too engaging to ignore, and he didn't want to anymore.

He gave her a genuine smile. "Yes."

"Apology accepted."

"Good. Now can we get to the problem at hand?" Daniel asked.

"I suppose we must. Mr. Throckmorten has done it to us again."

"Gretchen was standing over a dead man when we found her. Now that man has disappeared."

"That he has, but I don't see it as a problem for us, my lord."

"You amaze me, Miss Winslowe."

"Thank you."

She never failed to say the unexpected. "Again, I'm not sure what I said was a compliment."

"It sounded like one to me."

"Take it however you wish, but I still have a problem."

"Lord Colebrooke, perhaps you should just have faith that Mr. Throckmorten will show up looking as healthy as he did when he arrived at the party tonight."

"That will not happen this time, Miss Winslowe."

"If that is indeed the case, then what will we do if his body shows up again?"

"I don't know because I don't know what is going on here, but I will get to the bottom of it." He paused. "I'm going to need your help, Miss Winslowe."

"Then call me Isabella."

He cleared his throat. He did not need to get any

more intimate with her. "I don't think that's necessary or appropriate."

"Nonsense. If you want my help, Daniel, it is. I refuse to continue calling you by the formal Lord Colebrooke when Daniel is much faster and, shall I say, will put us on friendlier terms."

She was in control. She was seducing him with her attractiveness, with her forthright manner. And he was letting her!

"Very well, Isabella." He paused. He liked the way her name tripped of his tongue so easily, so seductively. "I want to get Gretchen away from here as quickly as possible. Would you and your chaperone see to it that she gets home safely?"

"Of course we will. But what are you going to do? You cannot tell anyone you think Mr. Throckmorten is dead if you have no body. Everyone will treat you the way you treated me this afternoon."

"And the way you treated me just now. I realize that, Isabella."

"Then all we need to do is return to the party and say nothing."

"Yes, but after I see you back inside, I plan to go talk to the footmen and the coach drivers. There's only one way Throckmorten was able to get out of this garden tonight, and that was under someone else's strength."

"You think someone picked him up and carried him out to his carriage?"

"To someone's carriage, yes. Obviously Gretchen stumbled upon the body before whoever killed him could remove him. They must have been hiding in one of the tall shrubs. Then we came along."

"Whoever it was must have heard every word we said about the man."

"No doubt. The killer must have come out of hiding and taken the body away while we were talking to Stonehurst. He probably passed Throckmorten off as a man too deep in his cups to walk. He would have had to put him in a carriage. I want to see if anyone was seen carrying a drunken man to a coach."

"That seems the sensible thing to do tonight. Then I think we should go to Mr. Throckmorten's house tomorrow afternoon to see if he might have returned from the dead again."

Daniel smiled. Because she was so engaging, he remained tolerant.

"First, trust me, Miss Winslowe, the man is not alive. Second, there is no we. It's me. I will do these things alone. There is no reason for you to be further involved in this unsavory matter."

"The name is Isabella, remember. And I am involved in this up to my ears, Daniel."

And such beautiful ears.

"I've seen with my eyes Mr. Throckmorten dead twice now."

And such sparking eyes.

"My skin pebbles with gooseflesh whenever I think about that poor man."

And such lovely skin.

"I can't possibly bow out of this unfortunate situation until it concludes," she insisted.

Daniel was enchanted by her. She was the most unconventional young lady he'd ever met. She was as refreshing as she was enticing. He wondered if she knew her appeal.

Daniel wanted to remain firm, but it was getting harder to deny what he was feeling. "Don't be ridiculous. I can't possibly take you with me to Throckmorten's house."

"Why not?"

He gave her an incredulous stare. "Must I remind you, it's not proper for a young lady to call on a bachelor at his home?"

Her smile lingered and he felt as if she were casting a spell on him.

"Don't be so stuffy, Daniel. You will be my chaperone."

"Me?" He was enthralled by her fresh manner. He moved in closer to her. "I'm a bachelor, too. Don't be daft, Isabella. You know I can't possibly be considered a chaperone for you."

"Of course you can." She stepped closer to him, putting them dangerously close. "Do you have any romantic designs on me, sir?"

"Certainly not," he lied. He had to. He had to stop the magic she was working.

"Good. Then I'll be perfectly safe with you. What time shall I expect you to pick me up for our ride in the park?"

"The park?"

"But of course."

"What are you talking about?"

"I cannot possibly tell Auntie Pith that we're going to Mr. Throckmorten's house. While I'm quite happy to bend the rules of Society to suit my preference, my aunt is not. She would faint if she even thought I would do such a thing."

Daniel shook his head.

"You can't be serious about this, Isabella. If you were caught with me at his house your reputation would be in tatters."

"We won't be caught. I'll secretly borrow one of my aunt's old bonnets and a cloak. And I know where to find a wig. No one will recognize me."

She made him want to say yes to her precarious scheme. "We still can't risk it."

"It's a chance I'm willing to take."

He was too close to her. He felt her breath. He caught her scent of lavender. He needed to back away, but he didn't want to. She drew him much the way a drunkard was drawn to his ale.

Their eyes met and held in the shaded light of the gray-swept moon, and Daniel knew without a doubt that he wanted to kiss her.

"Why are you willing to risk your reputation for something like this?"

"Perhaps because it's not that important to me."

"It should be. A young lady's reputation is supposed to be her most prized possession."

"Perhaps if she wants to make a good match. I'm not interested in that."

He studied her face in the faint light. She seemed serious. "Why not?"

"I've thought about marriage, and some time ago I decided I'd rather stay unmarried like my aunt and one day be free to come and go as I please without the fetters of a demanding husband."

Not want to marry? She was a free-thinker. "It would be a shame if you didn't marry, Isabella."

"But it's what I want."

"You're much too beautiful and exciting to remain a spinster."

"And I've decided I'm much too headstrong to be married. I want to be free to do the things I want to do and not have to answer to a husband. Now, we need to find out what is going on with Mr. Throckmorten and what his connection is to your sister. This started in my garden. I can't let it rest until I find out what happened to the man."

Daniel realized he didn't want to refuse her, not tonight.

"All right, I will call for you around half past noon. We'll have a picnic lunch in the park and discuss this further."

A blissful expression of satisfaction softened her face. "Wonderful. I shall be ready with—" She stopped and her eyes searched his.

"Is something wrong?" he asked.

"Yes. Is there a reason you are standing so close to me, Daniel, that I feel the warmth of your breath touch my face?"

A heat of pleasure curled inside him, reminding him of long ago when youthful eagerness ruled his head and his body. He wanted Isabella. He wanted to lay her down in the wet grass and make her his lover.

Daniel shook his head. Where had those thoughts come from? She was a lady of quality. He was an earl, and with that came responsibilities he couldn't ignore. And he was no longer a callow youth. He was older and should be able to control his sexual urges, but he hadn't been this excited about a woman in years. She had him hungry for the taste of her.

He realized she was waiting for a response to her question, so he said, "Yes, there is a reason. I want to kiss you."

Eight

His breath grew low and deep. Was there any chance she was feeling the same things he felt?

"So you weren't truthful when you said you had no romantic inclination toward me?"

"No, not entirely. I don't want to be attracted to you, Isabella, but I find that I am. Does that frighten you?"

She moved her face closer to him and looked deeply into his eyes. His heart felt as if it was going to beat out of his chest. She was provoking and stimulating, and he didn't want to fight the way she was making him feel.

"Not at all, my lord. I suggest you go ahead and kiss me."

Her words didn't surprise him, they elated him. "I intend to."

Daniel slipped his arms around her waist and pulled her up to him. Instantly he realized she was cold. "You're chilled," he said.

"A little, but had I known how warm your arms were, I would have asked you to hold me earlier."

That was the wrong thing for her to say, and pulling

her so close to him was the wrong thing for him to do. He didn't want to let her go. He felt the length of her beneath the sheer gown she wore, and his lower body reacted to her softness.

"Why didn't you tell me you were cold? I would have given you my coat."

She stared into his eyes and said, "A gentleman should know when a lady needs his coat."

"You're right. I don't seem to act like a gentleman when I'm around you. And I shouldn't have said I didn't have romantic designs on you when I do."

"I know."

He bent his head and lowered his mouth to her lips. They were cold and unmoving. She made no attempt to respond to his kiss in any way. He raised his head and looked into her eyes again.

"Have you ever been kissed?" he asked.

"Of course."

He suspected as much. She was such a free spirit, defying convention at every turn and boldly admitting she wanted him to kiss her. Proper ladies didn't do that.

But whoever the blade was who had kissed her must have been an idiot. He hadn't taken the time to teach her how to respond to a man's kiss. Daniel might as well have been kissing a fish.

"How long has it been since you've been kissed?" he asked.

She laughed lightly. "This morning, of course."

He hadn't expected that answer. Who was she seeing that would have kissed her this morning? "Truly?" he asked, unable to hide his shock.

"Yes," she said without any guile. "Auntie Pith kisses my cheek every morning."

He smiled to himself. "Have you ever been kissed by a man?"

"Of course, my father always kissed my brow each morning and night when I was a child."

Her simple answer pleased him and made his heartbeat speed up. He asked, "Have you ever been kissed on the lips before I kissed you just now?"

"No."

Daniel felt his chest expand with relief and he felt like laughing. "Would you like me to teach you how to kiss properly?"

Her eyes widened, and then she seemed to cringe. "I didn't do it right?"

"It's not that it was wrong." His gaze drifted to her lips. "But there's a way to get more pleasure from a kiss."

"Then perhaps you should show me. In the name of learning, of course."

"Of course," he agreed.

His body tightened at the thought of being the first to awaken her to passion. He couldn't even remember the last time he'd been the first to kiss a young lady, but he knew it'd been years.

"Put your arms around my neck like this." Slowly he showed her how to wrap her hands behind his neck so that he could pull her tighter to his body and press his hardness against her softness. She felt so good, so right in his arms that he felt himself tremble.

He bent down and pressed his lips to hers again, only this time he really kissed her, moving his lips over hers, teaching her how to respond. He moved a hand up to her cheek and helped guide her lips against his. She relaxed against him. Her lips became soft, heated and active.

His body tightened even more and his shaft grew bigger, harder as she responded to his teaching. One kiss had his blood pumping with anticipation and his body hungry for more.

He lifted his head a little, giving her time to let the kiss settle on her lips. He didn't want to frighten her and it didn't appear he had. Her breath, like his, was short and shallow. Her hooded eyes were filled with wonderment.

"What did you think of your first real kiss?" he whispered.

She looked at him from beneath long, velvety lashes. "It was quite enjoyable, but it didn't last very long, did it?"

A low chuckle rumbled in his chest, and desire thickened in his trousers. "A kiss can last as long as you want it to."

"Then perhaps I should have another, longer one to see if I really enjoyed it as much as I thought I did."

"I was just about to suggest that."

Surrounded only by a pale gray mist, he lowered his mouth to hers again. The kiss was soft and gentle at first, but feeling her body so tightly against his own, he couldn't hold back his desire. He kissed her deeply, sensing her untapped passionate response, and suddenly Daniel was kissing her hungrily. He prompted her to part her lips, and he probed her mouth with his tongue. She tasted sweet and innocent and young.

She didn't resist his aggressiveness. He covered her mouth with his again, slipping his tongue gently inside, sipping her sweetness again and again, and increasing the ache that had consumed him. His groans of pleasure mixed with Isabella's soft feminine sounds, which heightened his own enjoyment.

His lips left hers and grazed along her cheeks, over her nose, and up to her eyes. He tasted the dampness that had settled on her skin from the heavy mist. His lips made a path down her cheek, over her jawbone to trickle down the slender column of her neck.

"How do you feel now?" he whispered without letting his lips leave her skin.

"Like something warm and fluttery is attacking my stomach and floating up in my chest."

"I hope that is a good feeling."

"Very good," she answered.

The touch of her soothed him while it provoked him to try things he never should try with such an innocent. He slipped the cap sleeves of her gown off her shoulders and kissed the soft skin along the crest of her collarbone and over to her naked shoulders, feeling any moment that she would tell him to stop.

He lifted his head and looked at her satiny skin in the gray moonlight. She was captivating. He placed the palm of his hands on her shoulders and caressed them gently before letting his fingers slide down her chest. He stopped when the tips of his fingers found the gentle swell of her breasts.

Daniel looked into her eyes and was relieved to see desire floating in their depths. Her breath came in short little gasps, indicating her pleasure at the new sensations he was creating in her. It pleased him that she had no fear about what they were doing.

"I shouldn't be touching you this way," he whispered in a tender voice.

"I know."

"But I find I can't stop myself."

Her eyes were swirling with emotions. "I don't want you to stop. It feels so delicious. I can hardly catch my breath and my knees are weak."

He laughed gently. She knew how to say what he wanted to hear. He had that same fathomless feeling.

"I don't want to pressure you into anything you don't want. Do you want to continue?"

"Oh, yes. Kiss me again, Daniel." And she lifted her lips up to his.

Daniel's breath fanned her cheeks as his lips pressed against hers once again in a deep drugging kiss. His fingers continued to caress the full supple flesh that pushed up and out of her gown while his palms dropped to the roundness of her breasts. Her skin softened and heated beneath his hands like velvet beneath a hot iron, leaving a burning sensation in their wake.

No woman had ever felt this good, this invigorating in his arms, and Daniel was lost to the sensual essence of Isabella. He let his tongue rake down her chin, her neck, and her chest all the way down to the rise of her bosom. He dipped his tongue below the cold fabric of her dress, searching for her nipple so that he could suck it into his mouth and sate his hunger.

With slow and deliberate movements of his hands he traced a path of passion from the nape of her neck, across the width of her shoulders, down to the small of her back until his hands reached the firmness of her buttocks. He fit her cheeks into the palms of his hands and lifted her bottom up against the thick, heavy hardness beneath his trousers.

Daniel moaned with need as Isabella gasped with pleasure. She felt so good. She made him feel good, and he couldn't get enough of her.

He didn't want to move his hands from her buttocks because she was pressed so tight against his thickening shaft. He couldn't bear the thought of taking away that gratifying sensation that helped ease the ache of wanting to be inside her.

The distant sound of laughter stilled him. He fought his natural impulse to continue even though he knew the danger in doing so. But finally he dragged his lips back up her chest to her lips and held her tightly against him.

Damnation, what was he doing? And what was he thinking? If they were caught like this, he'd be married to her before the week was out.

Daniel hastily set her away from him and stepped back. For a moment his breath was too shallow to speak, but he saw in her eyes that she didn't understand his abrupt change of heart.

Bloody hell! He was supposed to be a gentleman, a titled man of honor. He would be expected to right the wrong he committed against her. He should offer for her hand. Suddenly his head went light, and it was difficult to breathe. He didn't want to wed her.

He desired her yes, but marry her? She was too unconventional, too uncontrollable. He had expected to marry a quiet and demure young lady. But the fact that he didn't think she'd make a suitable wife shouldn't matter. If she demanded he marry her, he would.

"I'm sorry, Isabella. I shouldn't have let things go so far between us."

He watched as her eyes adjusted to the moonlight. She looked down at her dress where the bodice had fallen off one shoulder. Desire stirred inside him. A lump grew in his throat as hard as the one beneath his trousers. He still wanted her.

"Sweet merciful heavens!" she exclaimed. She spun around, pulling her dress up as she turned her back to him. "I don't know what came over me! What just happened between us?"

He cleared his throat and hoarsely whispered, "We were kissing. That's all."

"Nonsense. I might be an innocent young lady compared to your worldliness, but I know we were doing far more than kissing. Your hands were on my... body, and I... felt every inch of... I was very close to you."

"We were making love."

Isabella turned back to face him with an incredulous stare. "Love?" She straightened her sleeves on her shoulders and pulled up her gloves as far on her arms as they would go. "What are you talking about? We couldn't have. I don't love you and you don't love me."

No truer words had ever been spoken. Daniel would have laughed if he hadn't realized the serious-ness of how close they'd come to being lovers.

"Would it please you better if I said we were on the verge of copulating?"

She gasped and he saw a flaming red flush creep up her neck and settle in her cheeks. "Copulating?"

"Yes. After the way we just kissed, why do you sound so surprised?"

"It's just that I've never heard anyone actually say that word before. I've read it, but it sounds so different hearing it."

"That's because it's not a word anyone would usually say to a woman of quality, and I shouldn't have said it. But I find that rules of convention fly out the window when you are around."

"Obviously my good sense goes the same way when I am around you. I do believe we were headed for trouble, Daniel."

"That seems to be all I've had since meeting you this afternoon, Isabella. If I believed in such notions, I'd be thinking you had bewitched me."

"Funny you should say exactly what I was thinking about you. I can assure you, sir, I have never had an encounter such as we just had."

Daniel didn't understand why or how he had lost control so quickly, either, but his feelings shouldn't matter. He had an obligation to her, unless, of course, she released him.

"I'm quite aware of that, Isabella. If anyone had stumbled upon us, your father would have had us married before sunrise."

Daniel watched a fleeting sadness cross quickly and fade away.

"My father has more pressing concerns than me. It's always been that way. He's content to let my aunt handle my affairs. But I will soon turn twenty-one and have control of the allowance my mother left me."

"That day has not yet arrived, Isabella, and no doubt

your aunt would be just as disapproving as your father had anyone caught us."

"Thank goodness no one saw us. It would be dreadful to be forced to wed."

Daniel breathed a sigh of relief and looked into Isabella's eyes. There wasn't even a hint of the vulnerability he'd seen a glimpse of just moments ago when he'd mentioned her father. She was steady and in complete control of herself. Their close encounter hadn't upset her.

"So you don't intend to demand that I marry you?"

"Heavens, no. I plan to remain unmarried and declared a spinster so that I will be responsible for myself."

Daniel took a chance she was being truthful and said, "We were quite intimate just now. If you insist, I'll do the right thing and offer for your hand."

She scowled at him. "You'll do no such thing. I don't want to marry you, sir. I don't even know you. What we must do, Daniel, is make sure what just happened never happens again. I thank you for teaching me how to kiss, but I refuse to marry you because of it."

"I couldn't agree more, Isabella."

Laughter sounded again, and Daniel realized it was closer than it was before. Obviously someone else had decided to take a walk around the gardens.

He had let himself get so distracted by his desire for Isabella that he had forgotten all about Gretchen waiting for them at the house and Throckmorten's missing body.

What kind of brother was he that he could be so easily sidetracked by a woman? He would have to take greater care when he was with Isabella.

"Let's go find Gretchen," he said.

"Yes," Isabella agreed. "She's probably wondering what has happened to us."

Daniel had to remember that Gretchen was the one who needed his help right now, not the lady with him. Isabella had just proven she could take care of herself.

Nine

The elegant party at Lord Gleningwold's house was a smashing success. All the right people were in attendance, and none more sought after than the recently returned Earl of Colebrooke. He was seen dancing with Lady Katherine Spearmont and Miss Alice Eldridge. Rumor has it he stole a walk in the garden with Miss Isabella Winslowe. It appears the earl is not wasting a moment of time in his search for a countess.

—Lord Truefitt, *Society's Daily Column*

ISABELLA CRUMPLED THE SCANDAL SHEET IN HER HANDS and let it drop to the rose-colored settee she stood beside in the parlor of her aunt's home. She was mortified. Completely, totally, utterly mortified every time Lord Colebrooke crossed her mind. Which was at least three times a minute.

What had happened between her and Daniel in the garden last evening was shocking, and if that wasn't bad enough, she'd spent the entire night reliving each kiss, each touch, each shallow breath of desire they'd shared. Whatever had come over her had managed to eradicate every soupçon of common sense from her being, but what shocked her even more was that she was left with very little guilt.

She couldn't figure out what was wrong with her. She had never had such feelings for a man before. Daniel must have cast some sort of wicked spell on her. A wickedly delicious spell. What else would account for her sudden, unexpected wanton behavior? She was shocked she'd allowed Daniel such liberties.

Isabella might well have been Daniel's mistress with the way she did his bidding. She answered all his kisses and caresses with loving touches of her own. Her behavior was scandalous, but she wasn't sorry it happened.

Daniel was right. If anyone had caught them, her aunt would have either insisted she marry Daniel or she would have sent Isabella packing to the country to spend the rest of her days.

"Dreadful thoughts, both of them," Isabella mumbled to herself, shaking her head with displeasure.

She didn't want to think about the possibility of doing either. She was quite content to stay in London, as a spinster attending parties, riding in the park, and occasionally attending the opera. And she looked forward each week to the time she spent with her Reading Society.

London was busy and Isabella loved the city with its sights and sounds and even its smells. She never wanted to live in the quiet countryside again. She didn't want her father to return and insist she go back and live with him and his new family.

Her last coherent thought last night had been when she told Daniel his kiss wasn't long enough. That was true. It had been the most enjoyable experience of her life. And even though she told him it must not happen again, she wanted him to kiss her again.

The things that he'd made her feel were unbelievable and wonderful. His kisses had drugged her as surely as if she'd taken a dose of laudanum. She had done all manner of things with him from probing his mouth with her tongue to letting him fondle her breasts.

And she'd loved every moment of it.

Isabella squeezed her eyes shut and remembered his touch. She'd never experienced such shattering pleasure. Even now thinking about the sensations he created inside her made her legs turn weak again. Why should she be ashamed of the feelings that had made her feel so good, so womanly?

She wouldn't.

Isabella's eyes popped open, and she took a steadying breath. What was done was done. She had told Daniel it must not happen again and he agreed. That should be the end of it. She wasn't going to worry any more about it.

"Oh, there you are," Auntie Pith said, almost floating into the room with a big smile on her face.

Isabella put her hand up to her hair and smoothed it, trying to hide the heat that had crept into her cheeks while thinking about Daniel.

"I've been humming all morning, Isabella. We've already received three more invitations to parties next week. We must decide which ones to attend."

"How nice," Isabella said, hardly hearing her aunt. "I'll leave it to you to make the decisions."

Auntie Pith put a finger to her lips as she thought for a moment, and then said, "I think we shall accept them all. There is no substitute for being sought after." She stopped in front of the sofa and picked up the wadded gossip sheet. "What happened to this? I haven't had a chance to read it yet."

"Oh, I'm sorry; I'll pick up another one for you while I'm out."

"No, it doesn't matter," she said, laying the paper on the side table. "I'll get one later." Her small eyes twinkled brightly. "Imagine Lord Colebrooke's first party since his return, and he singled you out last night and asked you to a picnic in the park. And you agreed. This is the best news we've had in three Seasons, and we will not let this opportunity pass us by. I'm simply faint with happiness."

"Auntie, please don't get puffed up about this. Really, it's only an afternoon in the park."

"Nonsense. He saw how beautiful and charming you are, and he is interested in you. I'm sure of it. Oh, what a catch he would be. Your father would be so delighted."

"You must not read too much into this. I'm sure he will call on many ladies in his search for a wife. In fact, last night I heard Lady Katherine Spearmont mention that the earl was calling on her later in the week."

That wasn't exactly the way Lady Katherine had worded her statement, but it was close enough.

"Balderdash. She is not as lovely as you, nor is she

as intelligent. Besides, you are the first he's calling on, my dear, and that is very important."

Isabella must remember the stern Lord Colebrooke she first met rather than the desirable Daniel she kissed last night. "We really don't suit, Auntie."

"Oh, piffle, you say. You would suit with any titled gentleman." She looked at the clock on the mantel. "It is half past. Time for Lord Colebrooke to arrive. Where's your picnic basket?"

"On the table by the door along with my coat, my bonnet, and my gloves."

"Good. Perhaps I should check the basket for you and make sure Mrs. Duncan saw to it that the cook put in everything you need."

"Wait," Isabella said, wanting to stop her aunt from looking in her basket. "That's not necessary. I've already done that. Besides, I wanted to ask you a personal question," she said, thinking quickly. "Have you ever been kissed? On the lips? By a man? Who wasn't your father?"

"Oh, dear." A grim expression clouded her aunt's features.

Isabella felt the flush creeping back into her cheeks. She'd had no idea she was going to ask that question in such detail. Her thoughts of Daniel and their passionate embrace must have triggered her question.

"What made you ask that?" Auntie Pith studied her for a moment.

"I've been thinking about kissing recently," she answered honestly.

"Has Lord Colebrooke already made an overture toward you?" Auntie Pith didn't wait for an answer, but kept talking. "No, no. He's far too much a gentleman to do that. Perhaps someone else. But I can understand you wanting to know what you should do if any man is bold enough to ask for a kiss. You must give him a resounding no. If he does not accept your refusal, you are to box his ears and demand he bring you home immediately."

Isabella laughed lightly, thanking heaven her aunt didn't know about last night. "Thank you, Auntie Pith, I will certainly know how to take care of Lord Colebrooke if he steps out of line."

"Or any other man. Oh, there's the door. It must be the earl. Sit down and put this book of poetry in your hands. We must not seem too eager. We'll pretend not to notice that he is one minute late."

Half an hour later Isabella and Daniel were seated on a blanket in Hyde Park with two picnic baskets between them. The air was crisp but not cold and as still as midnight. A sprinkling of sunshine filtered between gray clouds.

The warmer weather had the park filled with magnificent horses, elaborately decorated carriages, and handsomely dressed couples strolling around the spacious grounds. Daniel and Isabella had been stopped three times by people wanting to welcome the earl home. They had finally found a quiet spot under a tree away from the busy walking paths.

Isabella thought Daniel looked positively dashing in his crisp white shirt, dark brown coat, and narrow striped waistcoat.

His hair was brushed stylishly back, and his neckcloth and collar were tied unfashionably low under his chin.

Isabella found herself constantly looking at the strength she saw in his neck and couldn't help being affected by it.

She found herself wanting to press a kiss on the throbbing pulse she saw beneath his skin. She wanted to lean over and feel the warmth of his skin on her lips and his taste on her tongue. She wanted to be close enough to breathe in the clean scent of his shaving soap as she had last night.

But she settled for taking a deep breath and asking, "How is Gretchen this morning?"

"Much better than I had hoped with all thanks to you."

"Me?"

"It seems you convinced her last night that there is a possibility Throckmorten will show up alive and well. She's going about her merry way to the luncheon she'd planned to attend and a tea later today."

"I'm glad to hear that since we don't yet know that the man is, indeed, dead."

His gaze stayed tightly on hers. "You might not, but I do."

"Did she tell you why or how she happened to be in the garden last night?"

"She swore to me that she just needed some fresh air and that she had not made arrangements to meet with Throckmorten."

"Hmm." Isabella didn't believe that, and by the look on Daniel's face he doubted his sister, too.

He leaned closer to her. "I'm not sure what you mean by that?"

"By what?" She feigned innocence.

"Your hmm. What do you know that Gretchen hasn't told me?"

"Nothing, really," she insisted. "I have taken walks alone in gardens, so I can understand her wanting to do so after the upsetting day she'd had."

"I hope she finally understands that she needs to stay out of all gardens unless she is chaperoned."

Isabella nodded sympathetically. "I'm sure she sees the wisdom in that now. Tell me what you found out from the coach drivers."

"Not much." Daniel released a heavy sigh. "It appears that because the night was so foggy, they were all huddled by a fire, and not a one of them would admit to seeing anything unusual."

"Do you suppose Mr. Throckmorten was playing a horrible trick on Gretchen?"

"No. Last night was no caper, but odd that you should mention the word *trick*, because that word has entered my mind, too." His eyes searched hers thoroughly. "I don't know how my sister fits into this, Isabella. And I don't know how you fit into it, yet."

"Me?" She studied him, surprised at how quickly he turned the conversation to her. "Sir, I have had nothing to do with these strange goings-on."

"I want to believe you, but I find it difficult considering you have managed to be around both times Gretchen has seen Throckmorten on the ground," he answered in a pondering tone.

"We have been victims, not participants. And remember that you were with me last night when we found Gretchen."

"I know. But I seem to remember that you were the one to mention that we might want to look in the garden."

Isabella suppressed her anger because he did have his sister's welfare at heart, but she didn't want to let him off the hook too easily. "I had no prior knowledge that Gretchen or Mr. Throckmorten would be there. It was merely an intuition."

"I'll accept that for now, but I'm not going to stop looking into this until I find out what's going on."

"I heartily agree that we should."

A couple strolled by, and Daniel and Isabella remained quiet for a moment while the man and woman passed.

When Daniel spoke again, his expression turned serious and his voice was low as he said, "Isabella, we need to talk about what happened last night."

"Which part? Finding Mr. Throckmorten's body or the copulation?"

"Damnation, Isabella." Daniel looked around to see if anyone was close enough to have heard what she said or his swearing. "Do not use that word. There was no copulation between us."

"You said we were on the verge."

"We had a few kisses."

"Passionate kisses, Daniel."

He nodded. "We got a little more intimate than we should have, but it won't happen again."

"Is that because you didn't enjoy it?"

His gaze swept softly over her face, and Isabella had the feeling that, like her, he was remembering the smallest details of their interlude.

"No, of course not. You know I did, but that doesn't make it the right thing for us to be doing. What we shared last night should be saved for your husband."

Isabella thought on that for a moment. "But I've

already told you I don't plan to marry, so no one need ever know that you and I were so intimate."

"It is my desire that no one ever know. I should have been more in control, and I will be from now on when I'm around you."

"Daniel, there are so many things about you that I don't understand. I don't know why I reacted to you the way I did. I don't understand the things you make me feel, but I know that just talking about our kisses makes me want to kiss you again."

"Bloody hell, Isabella." He glanced away from her. "Don't tell me things like that."

"I'm only speaking the truth."

"I don't doubt it, but it's not a subject that we can discuss. And you are the one who should be telling me not to talk so freely to you and not swear in front of you."

"But I want you to talk freely to me, and I don't mind if you swear."

"And that is part of your allure, Isabella, and that is what I have to fight. You are so honest with your feelings and so free with your attitude. I find it refreshing but dangerous for both of us."

"That's not my intention."

"I believe you. Now, let's see what cook prepared for us."

Daniel opened his basket and looked inside. "Let's see, we have bread, duck, cheese, and claret." He looked up at her. "What do you have in your basket?"

Isabella hesitated. She wasn't ready to quit their conversation, but Daniel made it clear he was. She opened her basket and said, "I have a white wig, an old black cloak, and a large bonnet."

Daniel grinned endearingly for a moment and then he started laughing. "It would be very foolish to let you go with me, Isabella."

"If I don't go with you, I shall go by myself and ask for Mr. Throckmorten."

"I believe you would, but I can't let you do that, either."

Isabella closed her basket lid. She leaned toward Daniel, smiled sweetly, and softly said, "Daniel, I go with you or without you. Your choice."

❦

Half an hour later Daniel was sitting by Isabella in the landau, though no one would recognize the lady in the carriage beside him. Daniel had his driver take them to an abandoned building on the east side of the park where Isabella had quickly donned the white wig, oversize bonnet, and large cloak.

Daniel trusted his driver not to say a word about Isabella's change in appearance or their detour to Throckmorten's house. But he didn't know what would happen if they passed anyone who knew either of them well. Up close, no one would believe Isabella was an old woman.

Daniel found it difficult to say no to Isabella, especially when it gave him the opportunity to spend more time with her. She held his attention like no other woman ever had.

He realized he was becoming much too attracted to her. Sometimes she seemed fiercely independent, and at other times she seemed abandoned like when he had mentioned her father. He was attracted to both sides of her.

He reasoned that his first concern had to be for Gretchen, and he still wasn't convinced Isabella didn't have a connection with whatever was going on with Throckmorten. His disappearance from the garden was the most baffling thing that had ever happened. And he intended to get to the bottom of it.

Isabella was a distraction he didn't need, but he was reluctant to give her up. Even now, sitting so close to her on the carriage seat, he found he wanted to move his leg over an inch or two and feel the warmth of her body beneath the mountains of cloak she wore. He wanted to move closer and tell her how dressed as an old lady didn't in any way take away from how she made him feel. He found her just as enticing as she was in the garden the night before.

He knew he was a fool for agreeing to this charade, but he had to admit that it held a strange, exciting appeal. He knew if they were caught he'd be forced to marry her. That had given him pause. But if she was courageous enough to risk her reputation to be caught with him in disguise, he had to be willing to risk his freedom to spend a few more minutes with her.

They pulled up in front of Throckmorten's house, and Daniel jumped down. He reached back up for Isabella and took her hand and helped her step down. Her fingers were warm beneath her glove, and a shiver of desire raced through him.

Daniel wanted to slide his hands around her small waist and pull her against him so that he could feel the length of her body against his. He wanted to cup her face in his hands and tenderly kiss her lips, but all he could do was let go of her and step away.

"I'll do all the talking," he said as they walked side by side up to the front door.

"I wouldn't dream of interfering."

He threw her a doubtful glance, and she gave him a smile that he felt all the way down in his groin. "Why don't I believe that?"

"Maybe because in the short time we've been acquainted, you know me too well."

"Perfect answer."

Daniel knocked on the door, and they waited for a short time before the butler appeared. Daniel introduced himself with his title as he had the afternoon before when he'd come looking for Throckmorten. The butler stepped aside and invited them into a small parlor.

"I'd like to see Mr. Throckmorten if he's available for guests," Daniel said.

The butler remained stiff and perfectly schooled as he answered, "I'm afraid he's not home at the moment, my lord. May I offer you refreshment?" He looked over at Isabella, but he didn't say anything to her. She kept her head low and the wide-brimmed bonnet shielded most of her face.

"No, thank you. Do you expect him to return soon?" Daniel asked and noticed that Isabella was slowly walking around the room looking at the paintings, porcelains, and fabrics of the furniture and draperies.

"I really can't say, my lord. Would you like to sit down?"

"No, not if your employer isn't here. I won't stay. Perhaps you can tell me when you do expect him."

"I'm sorry, I can't."

"Can you tell me if he's been home today?"

Daniel stole another quick glance in Isabella's direction. What was she doing snooping in Throckmorten's house? He knew women were naturally curious about households and how they were decorated, but she really shouldn't be looking Throckmorten's house over so thoroughly.

"No, my lord," the butler said. "He didn't come home last night."

"Did you find that odd?" Daniel asked.

"Not at all. Sometimes he'll be gone for days before returning."

"I see. Well, you will tell him that I'm sorry to have missed him."

"Yes, Lord Colebrooke. Would you like to leave your card?"

"I don't have one with me. I'm sure I'll run into him at White's or one of the clubs. Thank you."

Daniel remained quiet as they walked out to the carriage.

Suddenly Isabella said, "Daniel, stand right there at just that angle."

Isabella quickly reached into the carriage and grabbed her own bonnet. She knelt down, putting herself between Daniel's body and the wheel of the carriage.

"What in the bloody hell are you doing?" he asked.

"Changing back to Isabella."

"Don't do that here. Someone might happen by and see you."

"Not if you keep your voice down and stop looking down at me. I checked and no one is walking down either side of the street."

"What if someone is looking out a window?"

"I doubt they could see through you. So don't move."

"That's rather hard not to do when you are almost between my legs."

"Just look across the street at something," she offered.

"That's easier said than done," he mumbled as an excited thrill rushed through him as he watched her stooped in front of him, the top of her head moving back and forth as she swung the old cloak off her shoulders.

She looked up at him again, and her face was even with his crotch. Daniel's body reacted so quickly he was hard within seconds. He immediately envisioned placing his hands on each side of her head and pressing her lips to him.

"Pretend you are talking to your driver," she said before returning to her task.

Daniel couldn't move as long as she was kneeling in front of him so close the merest movement from him would have them touching.

Within moments she rose and dumped the old cloak, bonnet, and wig onto the floor of the carriage. Daniel swallowed hard. The bulge between his legs throbbed. His breath was short and labored, his control on the edge. For a wild second he wanted to say Society be damned and crush her to him to ease his aching need for her.

Isabella faced him, her own bonnet on her head but the ribbons not tied. Her face was flushed from her quick change, and her eyes full of excitement. No sunshine was needed when her eyes sparkled the way they did right now.

"Shall we go?" she asked and held out her hand for him to help her into the carriage.

Daniel was stunned she had no idea what she had just done to him. A labored breath whispered past his teeth, and he swallowed past a dry throat. Everything about her had become a sexual awareness for Daniel.

"By all means, let's get out of Throckmorten's neighborhood before someone sees us."

He helped her into the carriage and seated himself beside her. He motioned for the carriage driver to get them out of there.

"Well, now are you convinced that Throckmorten is dead?"

Isabella gave him an impish smile. "No, but I am convinced he wasn't home."

Daniel sat back in the carriage seat with his hands covering the fullness in his lap. What was he going to do with the lovely mischief maker?

Ten

DANIEL STOOD IN THE DOORWAY OF THE BILLIARDS room at White's watching Mr. Thomas Wright playing a game with a young man Daniel didn't recognize by name. It was clear they had a friendly wager riding on the outcome, and it looked as if Tom was going to beat his opponent with plenty of room for missed shots.

He liked the way Tom handled himself during the game. He was aggressive but not antagonistic as he played. He hadn't been offended or angered when his opponent tried to distract him with taunts and jokes. The more Daniel saw of Tom the more he considered him a good match for his sister. Now he had to let Tom know that he would like him to call on Gretchen.

Daniel had come to the club after seeing Isabella home. He wanted to find a card game going so he could get his mind off her. He'd played several hands, but she hadn't left his thoughts.

He shouldn't like the fact she was unconventional and not afraid to step outside the boundaries of Society, but he did.

A firm hand clapped down on Daniel's shoulder,

and he turned to see his cousin sporting a grin. Daniel shrugged off Bradford's offending hand. Seeing Bradford everywhere he went was one of the things Daniel hadn't missed about the time he spent away from London.

Bradford moved away from Daniel but didn't stop grinning. "You are a sly one, Danny."

"Is that right?" Daniel said, having no idea what his cousin was talking about and not caring. He turned his attention back to Tom and away from Bradford's bloodshot eyes.

"There's no way I would have intruded and asked Miss Winslowe to dance last night if I'd had any idea you had an interest in her."

Daniel glanced back at his cousin and wondered if he really expected him to believe that. "What makes you think I do?"

"You never were any good at lying, Danny."

"Neither were you. The difference is that I've never wanted to be good at it."

Bradford laughed, making his eyes seem puffier. He said, "According to what I read in the scandal sheets, you were seen with Miss Winslowe in Lord Gleningwold's garden and I'm told you were together on a ride in Hyde Park this afternoon. That sounds as if there might be something serious between the two of you."

"Does it?"

"Is it?"

Daniel wasn't about to discuss Isabella with Bradford, but he knew his cousin well enough that if he was too elusive, Bradford would latch on to the subject like a boar after a snared rabbit.

"Somehow it became known among the *ton* that

I'm looking to make a match, and every young lady I met last night was ready to hear a marriage proposal from me. No doubt Miss Winslowe was one of them."

Bradford laughed. "You've always thought highly of yourself, and obviously nothing happened while you were away to change that."

"And why haven't you been leg-shackled again? What's it now, three years since your wife's death?"

"About that, but all in good time, Danny. I have a son who is in good health, and I'm in no hurry to marry again."

"You are fortunate to have a child. I trust you are staying out of trouble for his sake."

"I believe you are really asking if I've stayed away from gambling. The answer to that, dear Cousin, is not on your life."

He laughed again, showing straight, white teeth. Daniel supposed most ladies would consider him a handsome man, but for the dark circles under red and swollen eyes.

"That's too bad."

"Not really. I'm not as careless as I used to be. I'm older, wiser, and I'm a much better player. Practice is what it takes."

"You've certainly had plenty of that over the years. You should be a master by now."

Bradford shrugged. "And patience. I win more than I lose of late. By the by, I hear you rented a house in St. James."

"It was easier for me to move into another place than to upset Aunt Mattie and Gretchen when I returned."

"Ah, yes, Gretchen. She's grown into a rather

fetching young lady even with those dreadful things she has to wear on her face, the poor dear. I almost didn't recognize her when the Season started. Has there been interest in her yet?"

Daniel shifted, his hackles rising. He was trying to hold on to his temper because he knew that Bradford liked nothing better than to get him riled.

"Nothing that I care to discuss," Daniel said without hesitation. "I expect to have a match by the end of the Season."

Bradford's eyebrows shot up in surprise. "That soon? That would be pleasant for you, wouldn't it? Gretchen married and the responsibility of a husband."

Daniel heard laughing and looked over to the billiards table. Tom and his friend had finished their game. He couldn't tell which had won because both men had the smiling faces of winners. That was a good way to end a game.

Tom saw Daniel watching him and said his good-byes to his friend and walked over to where Daniel and Bradford stood at the doorway.

Greetings were exchanged among the three men before Daniel said to Tom, "You play a good game."

Tom came very close to blushing and said, "Thank you, my lord. I can hold my own in most games."

He wasn't boastful. That was another excellent trait for Daniel to add to his growing list of reasons why Tom would be a good match for Gretchen.

"It was so kind of you to take the time to meet my sister last night," Tom said. "She was flattered by the attention you gave her."

Daniel paused in thought. Did Tom think Daniel

had an interest in Amanda? Daniel hardly remembered what she looked like. Best he let Tom know that his only interest in him was as a husband for Gretchen.

"I was just about to get a glass of port, Tom. Care to join me?"

Tom's eyes widened in surprise, which he quickly tried to cover. "Yes, thank you. I will."

"Sorry, Danny," Bradford said. "I cannot join you two for a drink. I think I'll see if I can get something going in the game room."

Bradford knew that he wasn't included in the invitation for a drink, but the remark was his way of wanting Tom to think he was.

"Good afternoon, gentlemen," Chilton said, joining the group before Bradford had time to walk away. "Am I interrupting anything?"

"Not at all," Daniel said.

Chilton coughed. "Good. Nasty weather out there, isn't it? I've had enough of the cold and the rain to last me for a dozen years. I'm convinced spring is not going to arrive this year. We'll be lucky to have warm days by summer."

"Let's hope that's not the case," Daniel said. "Bradford was just leaving us, and Tom and I were on our way to get a drink. Want to join us?"

"Don't mind if I do, but first, have any of you seen this today?"

All three men looked at the broadside he held up before them.

"Is that the tittle-tattle about Danny and Miss Winslowe walking in the garden?" Bradford asked. "I think everyone has seen it."

Daniel scowled at his cousin.

"Ah, no," Chilton said. "I'm afraid this is much more serious than that."

"What could be worse?" Daniel mumbled.

Chilton lowered the paper. "There's been a murder in London. It appears that Boswell Throckmorten was found floating in the Thames this morning with a paper knife wedged between his ribs."

The four men looked at one another.

The silence between them was deafening.

"I think the ghost is Elizabeth's father," Lady Lynette said to the group of young ladies who sat in Isabella's parlor for their Reading Society meeting. "He was the last one to die."

"No, no," Abigail argued. "Don't you remember her uncle the physician was murdered? I'm sure it is her uncle who's come back for revenge."

"Who do you think it is, Amanda?" Isabella asked, trying to draw out one of the shyest members of their group.

Amanda quickly looked down at her hands in her lap. In a quiet voice she answered, "Oh, if he is a spirit, I think it has to be that of Lord Pinkwater. He is the most famous ghost, isn't he?"

It was clear to Isabella that Amanda had not been listening to their discussion about the book.

"Perhaps it's Lord Pinkwater's ghost. He seems to show up everywhere," Lady Lynette said, and all the ladies in the room laughed.

Except Amanda and Isabella.

"But, ladies," Isabella said after they quieted. "What is the point of this portion of the story?"

"Don't send all the servants away on the same night," Abigail said, and the ladies laughed again.

Isabella sat back in her chair and watched the young ladies enjoying the discussion and the humor about the horrid novel they were reading. If only she could get them to be as self-confident and lively when they were at the parties and balls. It was her desire that no young lady be as shy and nervous as she was when she first came to London.

When they quieted down, Isabella continued with her thought and said, "The point of the story here is that Elizabeth confronted her fears. She heard a noise in the other room. She was frightened, but she didn't let the shadowy figure keep her from trying to find out what was going on just a few steps away."

"She was very brave," Beverly Smith said.

"Yes," Isabella agreed. "That is what we need to learn from this story. And we need to apply it to our daily lives. It's how we need to live. We need to know there is no reason to be frightened or shy if a handsome young man approaches us and asks us to dance. We are to stand tall, look him directly in the eyes, smile, and say, 'Yes, thank you.'"

"But a ghost is not as frightening as a handsome gentleman," Abigail said.

The ladies erupted into carefree laughter again. It pleased Isabella that they were having so much fun.

"Enough about ghosts," Beverly said. "I want to know what we should do if a gentleman asks for a kiss."

The room became very quiet. Everyone looked

at Isabella, including Auntie Pith, who sat beside the window, engrossed in her stitchery while listening to the ladies.

Isabella was unprepared for the question. It reminded her of Daniel and the kisses they had shared. She would never forget the feelings he stirred inside her. Would it be possible for her to ever feel that way again?

As she looked around the room, she realized they were waiting for her to answer. But how could she tell them that if they ever had the chance to kiss a handsome man, they should? She would be banished from Town if she said such a thing.

Out of the corner of her eye, Isabella noticed her maid standing in the doorway motioning for Isabella to join her.

"Ladies, this is not an area I'm comfortable discussing, so I'm going to turn this question over to Aunt Pithany, who is far wiser than I on matters such as this. You don't mind, Auntie Pith, do you?"

Her aunt rose from her chair. "Of course not. I'll tell them the same thing I told you."

"Good. Come sit here in my chair. I'm going to excuse myself for a few minutes."

Isabella rose and followed her maid out into the hallway.

"You have a gentleman here to see you, miss," her maid whispered.

That was not what Isabella expected to hear. She had told her maid to be on the watch so that none of the young ladies slipped into the garden.

"What is his name?" Isabella asked.

"He says he's the Earl of Colebrooke, miss."

Isabella's stomach tightened, and then fluttered in anticipation. "Oh, oh," she whispered, wondering what he could be doing here. Then it struck her. "He must think Gretchen is here for the Reading Society."

"I don't know, miss. He didn't say why he was here."

She looked at her maid. "No, of course he wouldn't. I'm merely talking to myself."

He would just have to take her word for it that Gretchen was not present.

"Where is he?" Isabella asked, wanting to get this over with.

"He's in the book room. I told him you had your Reading Society here, but he said it was urgent and he must speak to you."

"I'm sure he did."

"Did I do the wrong thing?"

"No," Isabella assured her. "You did the right thing. I'll go speak to him. Come with me. I'll leave the door ajar, and I want you to wait outside."

"Yes, miss."

Isabella and her maid walked to the book room at the back of the house. Isabella stopped outside the door and took a deep breath. There were still times she had to fight the shyness of her youth, and this was one of them.

She needed to heed her own words and remember there was no reason to be intimidated by Lord Colebrooke just because he made her knees weak, her lungs breathless, and her body taut with the ache to be held once again in his strong arms.

She walked inside. He stood by the unlit fireplace looking so handsome dressed all in black except for his white shirt and neckcloth. It was no wonder every young lady in London wanted to marry him.

"Daniel," she said, and he turned to face her as she walked into the room to join him where he stood.

"Isabella," he said. "Thank you for seeing me on short notice."

"I don't have much time. As you know, I have guests in the house, but Gretchen is not one of them."

"I know."

She hesitated. "You know?"

"Yes. I came to see you about another matter. That's why I asked your maid to be discreet about my presence. Should your aunt find out I'm here, you can tell her I was hoping to find Gretchen."

"What is so urgent that you had to interrupt my reading group?"

"If you have to ask that, it means you haven't heard." He paused. "Boswell Throckmorten was found floating in the Thames this morning."

Isabella gasped. "Dead? Are you certain?" she asked, not wanting to believe it was so.

"Very."

"Sweet blessed mercies," she whispered under her breath. "I was hoping this wasn't real."

"I knew it was not a ruse or a fake."

A little dazed at Daniel's confirmation about the man, she asked, "What are we going to do?"

"We? Isabella, *we* are not going to do anything but stay quiet."

"But we must. We have to make sure Gretchen is not implicated or even associated with this matter."

"Exactly." He moved closer to her. "That's why I

came to see you right away. I had to make sure that, now that Throckmorten's body has been discovered, you hold to your promise not to reveal your and Gretchen's involvement in this matter."

"My involvement?" Her voice rose and she immediately remembered her maid was right outside the door, so she lowered her voice and moved closer to him. "I have no involvement in this, sir. It's your sister that I have tried to protect from this at every turn."

"You are the only one who has seen her with Throckmorten. I want to make sure you don't breathe a word about this to anyone."

"If I implicated Gretchen, I would also implicate myself, considering she was first with him in my garden. I am not a simpleton, Daniel. I know that Gretchen had nothing to do with Mr. Throckmorten's demise, even though we found her standing over his body."

"We can forget an implication to you. I think it's clear he was not dead when in your garden."

"All right then, when she was with him in Lord Gleningwold's garden. We can assume we are the only ones who saw her, but we can't know that for sure. There was a crush of people at that party. And no doubt the real killer saw her."

His eyes searched her face. "Don't think I haven't thought about that."

"Daniel, we must find out who killed him, before someone discovers something that leads them to your sister."

"You are unbelievable."

"I believe you've told me that before."

"That's because it's true."

"Thank you."

He smiled a little. "Not everything I say to you is a compliment, Isabella."

"I'm aware of that." She would not let him change the subject. This was too important. "But back to our discussion. More than likely the killer is someone who was at Lord Gleningwold's party and someone who had recent dealings with Mr. Throckmorten."

"That is a fair assumption, but just how would we know who he has had recent dealings with?"

Isabella glanced toward the door before stepping closer to Daniel. "Well, I…" She paused.

"What have you done?" he demanded softly with no anger in his voice.

"It just so happens that while you were talking to Mr. Throckmorten's butler, I managed to read the calling cards that had been left on his table."

Surprise lit his eyes. "You snooped through his private correspondence in his home?"

"It wasn't as if it were his personal letters or invitations. It was calling cards. Besides, how private can something be if it is left lying out in the open for anyone to see?"

"Damn private. Especially if it's in his home," Daniel whispered loudly.

"I knew if Mr. Throckmorten's body was ever found, Gretchen could be at risk."

"This is more of your mischief. I should have known you had a specific reason for wanting to go to his house with me."

"And it's a good thing I did because we now have some clues."

He lowered his face dangerously close to hers. "Clues? We don't have anything, Isabella, because we're not going to get involved in this."

She held her ground and didn't back away. "We are already involved. I can't believe you are thinking of just letting this drop."

"Gretchen had nothing to do with the man's death. And as long as you remain quiet about what you know, there will not be any repercussions from this to damage her reputation."

"You know that I will remain quiet. I've promised it. Gretchen is a part of my group, and all the ladies are important to me. I will not see her harmed by this in any way. But we must have a contingency plan in case we are caught unawares by unknown facts."

"Once again I have the feeling you are not telling me all you know about this strange turn of events."

"I am not withholding anything of importance other than the names of Mr. Throckmorten's most recent visitors. Do you want to know who they were?"

"No," he said a bit gruffly.

She started to say all right and drop it but realized he said no too quickly, and there was almost a catch in his throat. As she looked in his golden brown eyes, something told her he wanted to know, and was only trying to do the right thing by saying no.

She remained quiet, giving him time to ponder.

After a moment he squared his shoulders and said, "All right, yes. I want to know."

She gave him an engaging smile. "Good. One of them was Sir William Peabody."

"I've met him, but can't say I know him. The

Peabodys are a highly respected family. I can't see him as the kind of man to stab another even in anger."

"Mr. Franklin Jackson."

"There's no way it would be him. He and Throckmorten have been friends since they wore short pants. He can't possibly be a suspect."

"Mr. Bradford Turnbury."

Daniel's eyes perked up. "Really? My cousin? It's no big surprise that he called on Throckmorten. They've been drinking and gambling friends for years." He stopped and rubbed his forehead in frustration. "Isabella, this is really getting us nowhere. I can't see any of these men harming Throckmorten for any reason."

"Not even over a gambling debt?"

"Especially not over a gambling debt. They've owed each other money for years. That's nothing new. I wouldn't be surprised to find out that Throckmorten owed half a dozen men."

"All right, that's a good point. Do you want to hear the last name that I saw?"

"I might as well."

"Mr. Chilton Cummerford. I believe I've heard the man is your best friend."

Eleven

SHOCK SNAPPED IN DANIEL'S EYES AND BURNED ACROSS his face. "Chilton? Are you sure?"

"Quite."

"Did you see the entire card? Perhaps it was a name similar to his."

She huffed with indignation. "I saw the entire card, my lord. And lest you have any other concerns, my reading capabilities are very good."

"I don't doubt that, Isabella." A deep frown wrinkled his brow. "It's just that I've never known Chilton to have anything much to do with Throckmorten." More thoughtfully he added, "I wonder what Chilton could have been doing at his house."

"Perhaps he is one of his gambling and drinking friends."

"No. Chilton has never been a part of Throckmorten's gaming friends. He didn't like the fellow any more than I did."

Isabella thought she saw uncertainty replace shock in his eyes, and she said, "Well, if Mr. Cummerford didn't like Mr. Throckmorten, then your friend is definitely a man we want to consider as a suspect."

"A suspect?"

"Yes."

He grimaced. "In Throckmorten's murder? That's impossible."

"Why? You have been gone more than a year, Daniel; perhaps there are things about Mr. Cummerford that you don't know."

He drew in a long uneven breath. Chilton had been different since Daniel returned, but he wasn't ready to believe his friend's reserve had anything to do with Throckmorten.

"I'm sure there are plenty of things I don't know about him, but there is one thing I do know and that is Chilton didn't have anything to do with Throckmorten's death any more than Gretchen did."

His last statement hung in the air too long. The truth was they didn't know how many people might be connected to the man's death.

Finally Isabella broke the silence by saying, "We are sure Gretchen didn't have anything to do with this, aren't we, my lord?"

"Yes, Isabella, we are," he answered without hesitation.

They stood so close that Isabella could sense the warmth of his body, feel the light fanning of his breath, and see the sparks of outrage about this entire affair in his eyes. Rare afternoon sunshine filtered through the windowpane and glimmered off his dark brown hair and shadowed half his face.

"Well, since you are convinced of his innocence, we'll forget about him for now, but I think the next thing we should do is talk to Gretchen again. We need to find out exactly what was going on between her and Mr. Throckmorten."

"Yes, *I* plan to do that as soon as *I* get home, and *I* don't need your help to question my sister."

"Perhaps not to question Gretchen, but you'll need my help when you search Mr. Throckmorten's home."

Surprise leaped into his eyes. "Search his home? Damnation, Isabella, what are you talking about?"

"Shhh, don't be so loud. Remember my maid is right outside the door."

Isabella placed two fingers against his lips. Her touch was so light his lips felt like gossamer against her fingers. Her heart started beating a little faster. Her skin tingled, her body prickled with desire. She felt his lips part beneath her gentle pressure, and she slowly removed her hand, she didn't step away.

She felt him take a shallow breath. He had been caught unaware by her touch, too. She wished she knew the meaning behind these strange feelings she had for this man. He didn't seem to like her any more now than he had their first meeting, but it was clear something was drawing the two of them together.

Isabella glanced toward the door. It didn't appear that her maid had heard them. She softly cleared her throat and offered, "I think it's time for us to admit the possibility that Gretchen had a secret liaison with Mr. Throckmorten in my garden. She must have been planning to meet him in Lord Gleningwold's garden, too."

"Yes." His expression immediately softened as it usually did when he talked about his sister. "She has told me that much concerning her meeting him in your garden, but I believe there is more that she hasn't said. I know she's young and I've tried to be gentle with her. I no longer can."

"Daniel, we also need to find out if her name or anything about her is written anywhere in his private papers. If it is, we need to expunge it."

He eyed her warily and leaned in closer to her. "Just where have you learned all these tricks, Isabella?"

"Tricks? I don't know what you're talking about, my lord."

"Reading calling cards, searching desks and private papers. You were not taught that at home. Where did you learn such stratagem?"

"From books."

"Books?"

"One can learn all sorts of things from reading, whether it be books on poetry, horrid novels, or the London *Times*."

He studied her closely. "I'm not sure I believe you, but if I did, it wouldn't matter. The authorities, his family, or someone will have already been through Throckmorten's personal papers."

It was difficult to concentrate on their conversation when he stood so close to her she could touch him again by merely lifting her hand. And she wanted to touch him.

"But they would not have been looking for anything with Gretchen's name on it, and it's quite possible they might have missed something. I think you should go home and question Gretchen, and then we'll make plans to meet tomorrow and go to his house again."

He shook his head with disbelief. "You never cease to amaze me, Isabella. What do you suppose we will do once we get there? I can't see the butler letting strangers rummage through his dead master's private papers."

She smiled easily. "Of course he won't. I will dress in the wig and the old cloak again. When we get inside, I'll pretend to faint and need a cup of tea."

"Did you read this in a book?"

"Well, not exactly. It was something similar. Anyway back to my point; while the butler is getting the tea, you can find the man's desk and search it."

"Me? Search his desk?" he whispered loudly. "Bloody hell, Isabella, I can't do anything like that. I'm an earl."

She put her fingers to his lips again to soften his voice, and once again they were both stunned by the sensations that passed between them.

Isabella forced herself to remain on subject. "You are a brother who must go to great lengths to protect his sister," she insisted.

His eyes narrowed as they searched hers, and for a moment she felt as if he were trying to look into her soul.

"You know I will do what I must to protect Gretchen, but why are you so willing to risk your reputation to help her?"

"I'm quite fond of your sister. I believe she has been someone's pawn in this terrible matter." She paused for a moment, wondering if she could make him understand if she told him all that she felt in her heart. "But mostly I think it's that I've been a part of this since I found Gretchen in my garden standing over his body. I have read about such adventures but never dreamed I would participate in a real intrigue. I know it's hard to understand, but it's too exciting. I can't let go of this mystery until it's solved, and I want to be a part of unraveling it and finding the answer."

"You would really go to Throckmorten's house and pretend to faint if I agreed, wouldn't you?"

She looked at him without blinking. "Yes, I thought it was settled that we would do it tomorrow."

His gaze held on her face. "I should have known that you were enjoying all this conspiracy."

"I do find it exhilarating, but I also want to see that neither Gretchen nor I are harmed by any of this."

Daniel's lips relaxed into a smile. "You are so beautiful when you are planning mischief, Isabella."

Isabella's chest tightened and she smiled at him. "Thank you."

With a slight unobtrusive movement of his hand, he reached up and rubbed the backs of his fingers down her cheek and across her lips before letting his hand fall away. Isabella's blood heated and she made no move to resist him even though she knew they were playing a dangerous game with their unexpected touching.

"Your father should have censored what you read. He obviously allowed you to read books that were not meant for young ladies' consumption."

Isabella expected the usual stiffness and that sudden feeling of emptiness in her stomach whenever her father was mentioned, but it didn't happen. Perhaps she had finally gotten over her father abandoning her.

With more ease than she expected she said, "My father didn't know what I read. As long as I was quiet and didn't disturb my mother or the household, he didn't know I was around."

Daniel grimaced. "That doesn't sound as if you had a very happy childhood."

She gave him a half smile. "I was happy. Maybe a

bit lonely at times. That is why I so enjoy the ladies coming here for our readings. I like having people around who aren't afraid to laugh and talk. I love the noise of the streets of London and its parties. I don't want to go back to the quiet life of the country."

His gaze swept up and down her face like butterfly wings in slow motion. "Sometimes you appear a green girl, and other times, like now, you are a fresh miss who flaunts convention."

"Daniel, I never stepped over the bounds of Society's rules until I met you," she admitted without any guile.

He grinned engagingly, but his gaze didn't leave hers. "Oh, so it's my fault that you have turned from an innocent miss to a lady who enjoys a mischievous game."

"Do you really think me that way?"

In a hushed whisper he answered, "You must be. Everything you say and do points to it."

"I am only trying to help you and your sister."

"I want to believe that, but there are so many things about you that make me wary of your intentions."

"You are standing very close to me again, Daniel."

"I know."

"I'm remembering what happened the last time we were close like this."

"So am I."

"One of us should move away," she said.

"Ladies first."

"I think perhaps I'll let you. I find my legs don't want to move. I feel if I should try to walk, they won't hold me up."

"Then perhaps I should hold you for a few moments until you regain your strength."

"Yes," she said, knowing that once again she had fallen under his spell. Why else would she agree to be alone with him in her own home?

Daniel cupped the side of her face with one hand while the other slipped around her waist and brought her up against him, settling her weight on him. Isabella's breath caught in her throat as she felt the hardness in his lower body press firmly against her.

He raked his thumb across her lips and down her chin to let it rest at the pulse in her neck. She felt the erratic beat of her heart in her ears. His hand lightly circled her throat. His thumb rested in the hollow, and his fingers made slow sensuous circles against the skin at her nape. He nudged his thigh gently between hers and lowered his face even closer to hers.

"I want to kiss you," he whispered.

Isabella's abdomen contracted deliciously. Shivers of expectancy tingled through her. She didn't want to deny him anything, but her freedom was at stake.

She managed to clear her thoughts enough to say, "There are a dozen ladies and my aunt right down the hallway from us."

With his open hand to her back he pressed her closer to his hardness and said, "I know."

"The door to this room is ajar and my maid is right outside."

"I know."

"We would have to marry if you were caught holding me like this."

His eyes held steady on hers as his fingertips drifted from her neck down her chest to the rapid rise and fall of her breasts. She tingled all over. Her heart felt as if it were going to beat out of her chest. She couldn't have moved away if she wanted to.

"I know," he said again.

"And yet, you have no fear?"

"Oh, yes, I do. All you say is true, and it gives me cause for alarm."

"But still you hold me and touch me like this? Why?"

He slipped his hand from her waist to her buttocks, lifting her up and fitting her perfectly against the hard bulge beneath his trousers.

"Holding you like this makes it worth the risk."

Isabella gasped from the sheer pleasure of feeling the warmth, the hardness, and the forbidding touch of his body next to hers.

She didn't know what made this man different from all the other men she'd met in her life, she only knew he was. "I have no power to resist you."

His lips were less than an inch from hers. He smiled as he said, "Ah, Isabella, I haven't even kissed you yet."

"I feel I will faint if you don't do so soon."

"Open your mouth for me," he whispered.

She parted her lips. Daniel met her lips and invaded her mouth with his tongue. He pressed deep with short fleeting strokes, retreating and then darting back inside. It roused her passion instantly, and they kissed over and over again. Long, hard and searing kisses that nibbled, enticed, and provoked.

His assault inflamed her, but yet she yielded to his silent demand for her to remain passive in his arms and let him devour her until he whispered, "Join me, Isabella."

She needed no tutelage this time as she gave herself entirely to the kiss. She slipped her hands beneath his coat and circled him, wanting to feel the power in the expanse of his back. She wanted this connection to him. She let her hands wander down to the firm muscles of his buttocks, and she fit her palms over them.

Daniel moaned softly. "Yes," he whispered. "Hold me against you."

She did.

Slowly he ran his hands up and down her back, over her shoulders, down the front of her dress. He flat-tened his hands on her breasts and pressed against their fullness. He gently squeezed and massaged her softly through the fabric of her dress and undergarments. His hand glided over and around each breast with the lightest of pressure, kneading them seductively.

Isabella closed her eyes and enjoyed the wonderful feelings of his exploration. A whispered sound of pleasure floated past her lips.

His thumbs and forefingers searched for her nipples beneath the layers of clothing and they rose and hardened to his touch. The constant rubbing over the tight peaks and his ravenous assault on her lips and in her mouth made her tighten her hold on his buttocks. She pushed her body against his and tried to sate the unbearable ache that had settled between her legs.

Isabella wasn't even sure her feet were touching the floor. She felt as if she stood on air. Nothing was real to her but his touch.

Suddenly Daniel slid both arms around her waist and squeezed her tighter than she had ever been held before abruptly breaking off the kiss. One moment their hot breaths mingled, and the next he was looking down at her with glassy eyes trying to catch his breath.

Isabella moistened her lips; inviting, willing Daniel to continue his possession of her. Looking deeply into the depths of his burning eyes she saw that he wanted to but wouldn't.

Their interlude was over.

She laid her cheek against the worsted wool of his coat. Her hands slid up his back once again to rest on the width of his broad shoulders. Over her own labored breathing she heard the rapid beat of his heart. She felt his breath stir her hair as he pressed his cheek on top of her head and softly whispered her name.

He turned her loose and stepped away from her. Isabella shivered as soon as his warmth left her.

She raked the back of her hand across her lips as she tried to regain her normal breathing.

"Something strange happens to me whenever you are near," she said.

"It's not strange. It's very normal for two people who are as attracted to each other as we are." He straightened his shirt in his trousers, pulled down his waistcoat, and checked his cuffs.

"Why do you suppose we are so attracted to each other when we seem to be so opposite in the way we think?"

"I don't know the answer to that because no two people have been less suited for each other than we are."

"Do you love me, Daniel?"

She saw that he swallowed hard just before he said, "No, but I do desire you."

She pondered that before saying, "Yes that must be what this strange feeling is that I have for you. Is there anything we can do to make it go away?"

He seemed to swallow hard again. "Nothing that I'm willing to do at this time."

"Oh. So we must find a way to control these urges we have."

"And the best way to do that is to stay away from each other." He stepped farther away from her.

"But we can't do that, can we, Daniel?"

His gaze held fast to hers. "No, I don't think we can." He stepped even farther away. "Thank you for seeing me today, Isabella. I'll have your maid show me out."

He turned and walked away.

Twelve

DANIEL STROLLED INTO THE FAMILY TOWN HOUSE IN Mayfair with only one thing on his mind. *Isabella.*

He handed his coat, hat, and gloves to the butler and asked him to get word to Gretchen right away that he wanted to see her in the garden. He needed to have another serious talk with his sister, and he didn't want the possibility of anyone overhearing their conversation.

With quick, determined steps he marched through the house to the back without stopping until he stepped outside and closed the door behind him. Maybe the fresh air would clear his head of thoughts of the tempting Isabella.

He looked over the barren garden that waited for some sign of the arrival of spring. The afternoon was chilly with the feel of more rain in the air. The sky was a smoky shade of gray and a thick mist was settling low on the ground. The dreariness of the day matched his mood.

Daniel needed to concentrate on Gretchen and the foul mess she'd gotten herself tangled in, but thoughts of Isabella consumed him. She was driving him insane with wanting her, and, as of yet, she had made no move to try to snare him in a parson's mousetrap as any other young lady would have done after their passionate embraces.

His return home wasn't going anything like he had planned. Instead of looking for a husband for Gretchen, a bride for himself, and making friends in Parliament as a new earl should be doing, his thoughts were on the lovely mischief-maker, and he was looking for a murderer.

So much for thinking he would find an acceptable young lady and make a match before Season's end. Isabella was the only lady who had appealed to him since his return. She had spoiled him for all others. Her unconventional manner made her an impossible choice for a wife, but it didn't keep him from desiring her. She created an excitement inside him whenever she was near.

Daniel smiled. To think she expected him to readily agree to rummage through Throckmorten's desk and look through his personal papers. What a daring and intriguing chit she was. She had definitely been reading too many novels. He would never admit it to her, but he did think the idea had merit.

A couple of years ago he would have done it without a moment's hesitation, but his brother's death had burdened him with the title of earl. He didn't want to bring any shame or disrespect to the legacy by stooping to such foolish activities.

"You asked to see me?"

Daniel looked up and saw Gretchen walking down

the steps toward him, her gray wool shawl wrapped tightly around her shoulders against the chill.

"Yes. Come sit down here on the bench beside me."

He took the time to really look at her as she made her way toward him. She was a bit taller than most young ladies her age, but she wasn't too thin or too large. Most men would consider her shapely. She had a lovely smile that showed off white straight teeth. Her lips were full and expressive.

Beneath the spectacles she wore, her brown eyes were big, round, and bright. There was a light shade of healthy pink color in her cheeks and lips. Now that he really looked at her, he could see why the gentlemen of the *ton* were attracted to her.

When he'd left London last year, Gretchen was too shy to look at anyone, let alone speak to them. He had always assumed it was because of the spectacles. Now he could see that they in no way took away from her loveliness, and he feared it was obvious she didn't have a shy bone left in her body. No doubt Miss Winslowe deserved the gratitude for that.

"Did you come by just to make sure I hadn't gone to my Reading Society at Isabella's house?" she asked as she took a seat on the bench.

Daniel sat beside her and made himself comfortable by putting his arm across the back of the bench. "No, that's not the reason I'm here. It's another more important matter that we must discuss, and this time you must tell me all the truth. Not just part of it."

"This sounds as if it's going to be another of our serious conversations."

"It is."

She took a deep breath and folded her hands in her lap. "All right," she said in a bored tone. "Let's get started."

"I need to know about everything that happened between you and Boswell Throckmorten," Daniel said, getting right to the point.

"You already know all about that, Daniel. It's over. Why must you bring it up again?"

"Because the man is really dead this time, Gretchen."

"Daniel, Isabella said for me not to worry about Mr. Throckmorten."

Daniel touched her shoulder and said, "Forget what she told you." He looked directly into her eyes. "Contrary to everything Miss Winslowe said last night in Lord Gleningwold's garden, Mr. Throckmorten is dead."

Her brown eyes widened and immediately tears pooled along the lower lid. Her mouth dropped open. "How can you be sure?"

"He was found in the Thames this morning. It's been confirmed by the authorities. There is no question this time, and there is no doubt that he was already dead when we saw him on the ground. I told you this was serious and I meant it. I must have the truth from you. All of it."

Her bottom lip trembled, and she stared straight into his eyes as she said, "I didn't do it, Danny. I agreed to meet him in Lord Gleningwold's garden, but I swear I didn't kill him."

Anger knotted in Daniel's chest, and he swore under his breath before saying, "Gretchen, why would you agree to meet the scoundrel again after what happened in Isabella's garden?"

She answered him with a sniffle and tears spilling over her lids to run down her cheeks. If she started crying, he'd never get anything out of her.

Daniel tamped down his anger and lowered his voice as he said, "Don't get upset, Gretchy. You're not in any trouble, and everything's going to be all right. Just start at the beginning and tell me everything from when you first talked to him until you found him last night in the garden."

She removed her spectacles and rubbed her eyes with the back of her hand, smearing tears across her cheeks. "He asked me to dance twice at the first party of the Season." Her face softened. "He told me I was beautiful, Danny. No one's ever told me that before. And when he looked at me, I felt beautiful for the first time in my life."

Daniel felt a twinge of guilt. He should have told his sister how lovely she was. He knew that it was the kind of thing all young ladies wanted to hear. "He was right, Gretchy. You are very beautiful, and he's not the only gentleman who thinks so."

She sniffled and wiped her eyes again. "He's not?"

"No. I know that Thomas Wright thinks you're beautiful. And Chilton."

"Chilton?" Her eyes turned as bright as sunshine after a spring rain. "Do you really think he does?"

"I'm sure of it."

"He's never told me."

"That's because he looks at you as a sister. And I know Tom thinks you are beautiful," he said, knowing he'd just finished talking to Thomas Wright about calling on her. "Now, finish telling me about Throckmorten."

She rubbed the wetness from her cheek. "When he asked me to dance, I looked him in the eyes and spoke confidently to him the way Isabella told us to."

Daniel pulled his arm from the back of the bench and sat forward. His brows drew together in concern. "What do you mean?"

"At our reading group Isabella tells us not to be shy around handsome gentlemen. She says they are attracted to young ladies who look them in the eyes and never to look down at our feet or our hands. She told us to appear confident when we talk to them and answer their questions intelligently. She said men really don't like for us to flutter our eyelashes or our fans."

So he was right. Isabella was responsible for the change in Gretchen. Why didn't that surprise him? "Mmm. That sounds like something Miss Winslowe would say. At these meetings has she ever suggested you meet a man in a garden?"

"Oh, no, Daniel. She's never suggested we do anything that's considered improper."

"But you did."

"Yes, but my actions had nothing to do with Isabella. She only asks the young ladies who are seldom sought after at parties or for special teas to join our group. She helps us to know how to be more poised so we'll have a better chance at making a match. And we always read from a book of poetry or a horrid novel."

"I see," he said. This confirmed what Chilton had told him about Isabella's Wallflowers Society. But he'd have to get back to that subject later.

"So start at the beginning and tell me how you managed to meet Throckmorten in Isabella's garden."

"One night, when we were dancing, he asked me to walk outside with him." Her eyes turned dreamy. "We stood under the stars and it was so lovely. He wanted to kiss me, but I wouldn't let him. Then he said he wanted to meet me somewhere we could be alone. I knew it was wrong, but I mentioned that Isabella and her aunt had a dozen ladies over for tea. I told him I could slip into their garden while they were reading and meet him for a few minutes and no one would miss me."

"Was that the first time you'd met him?"

"Yes. I thought he must love me, and he was so handsome I—I let him kiss me. I thought he was going to ask me to marry him. When he didn't mention making a match, I asked him about his intentions."

Good for you.

"He—he told me he wasn't planning to make a match any time soon and that all he wanted was to kiss me. I knew by that he had no intentions of marrying me. I was angry with him. I had risked my reputation to be with him only to find that he didn't want to marry me. I picked up a statue and hit him. I really thought I'd killed him."

"All right, was the next time you saw him at Lord Gleningwold's?"

"Yes. He brushed by me and whispered for me to meet him in the garden by the back arbor in half an hour."

The rage that he'd swallowed rose again in Daniel's throat and chest. "Why did you agree to meet him again after he made it clear he had no intention of marrying you?"

"I thought—I was hoping he had changed his mind." She sniffled before continuing. "And maybe he had and was going to tell me. I don't know because he was lying on the ground when I got there. I didn't know what to do. I called to him, but he didn't move. I know I shouldn't have agreed to meet him again, but—"

Tears spilled onto her cheeks. He pulled her into his arms and gave her a brotherly hug. "You're right about that, Gretchy, but everything's going to be all right now. I'm sure you're going to meet someone else and make the perfect match real soon."

"Do you really think someone will love me and want to marry me? Someone strong and handsome like Chilton?"

"I'm sure of it," he answered. Tom Wright had been very interested in calling on Gretchen once he knew Daniel was in favor of it. The poor fellow had no hopes of ever courting the daughter of an earl until Daniel approached him.

Daniel took a deep breath. Since Gretchen met secretly with Throckmorten, he might have very well written their meeting down in some kind of an appointment book. That would never do.

Daniel had already made plans to ride with Chilton the first thing tomorrow morning, and he wouldn't cancel that. But he would send a note to Isabella tonight and tell her what time he'd be by to pick her up tomorrow for their second visit to Throckmorten's house.

Daniel didn't know when he'd seen the sky so blue or the sun so bright. At last it looked and felt like spring had arrived. Just yesterday had been dreary, cold, and gray. Daniel and Chilton had chosen a fine day to ride their horses outside the streets of London and take pleasure in the clean air of the countryside.

The midday sunshine warmed their backs. Daniel had enjoyed the morning with his friend, talking about old times when they were in school together and later when they had toured France and Portugal with two other friends. Daniel also filled Chilton's head with stories about his pilgrimage to visit all the estates in his holdings.

They had ridden their mounts hard for a short while, and then let their horses rest and graze while they ate a meal of cheese, bread, pork, and wine. Now they were letting the geldings walk back to Town.

Daniel had deliberately avoided the two subjects that were most on his mind, Isabella and Throckmorten. He didn't plan to discuss Isabella with Chilton, which signaled a big change in his relationship with his friend. Before he became the earl, Daniel always confided everything to Chilton. He no longer felt the need to tell his friend about the latest lady to catch his fancy. Throckmorten was a different matter. He had every intention of talking to Chilton about him.

Daniel had sensed that something troubled Chilton the first time they talked. And even today while they joked and had their fun, his friend seemed more reserved than usual, but Daniel couldn't put his finger on why. Chilton had warned him about Throckmorten his very first day back in London. And Isabella had been certain she'd seen his card. Now

Daniel wanted to know what was going on between Throckmorten and his friend.

As the sun beat against the back of his neck, Daniel said, "Do you have any idea what happened to Boswell Throckmorten?"

Chilton threw Daniel a curious glance. "You mean other than he was stabbed in the chest and thrown in the river?"

Daniel nodded.

"Not a thing," Chilton said as calmly as if they were talking about the beautiful weather. "How about you? Have you heard anything more?"

Daniel took it as a good sign that Chilton didn't seem reluctant to talk about the man. "No. Did you see much of him this past year?"

"No more than usual."

Daniel couldn't help but wonder what amount of time had been usual of late. "I assume you've seen him at White's, a house party, or maybe at a private game of cards?"

"Could be," Chilton said, eyeing Daniel curiously. "Why the hell are you so interested in a dead man you hardly knew?"

Daniel wasn't sure how much he wanted to tell Chilton, so he only said, "As you told me, Gretchen had a few dances with him this past week and naturally she was upset to hear of his death."

"Right. I remember telling you about that your first day back in Town. His violent death proves that he was not the kind of man you wanted calling on Gretchen. Did you have the opportunity to speak to him about her?"

"No. I had tried to, but the chap was killed before I

had the chance. Obviously the man had dealings with the wrong people."

"He was known to gamble with men in the hells as well as with gentlemen of the *ton*. No doubt he got around Town with ease."

Daniel closely watched Chilton's face as he asked, "So I've heard. Any idea who might want to do the poor fellow in?"

"Probably a few, but I don't think any of them did. I assumed he met his unlucky fate by a common footpad out to steal his purse, didn't you?"

"I don't know. As you said, he had dealings with many different people. Perhaps he owed someone a gambling debt and couldn't pay."

Chilton shifted in his saddle, and the leather creaked beneath his weight. "Or maybe someone owed him and didn't want to pay up."

"True."

"Well, no one needs to be worried about the man anymore," Chilton said. "I'd say he's played his last game."

"No doubt about that," Daniel agreed.

It was clear Chilton wasn't going to mention his visit to Throckmorten. Daniel had given him ample opportunities. Daniel would like to just ask his friend what his card was doing at Throckmorten's house, but for now he had to be careful. He didn't think for a minute Chilton had anything to do with the murder, but he might know something more about the man's liaison with Gretchen.

He'd wait until after he'd paid his second visit to Throckmorten's house later this afternoon, and if need be, he'd question Chilton again.

Three hours later Daniel stood on the front steps of Throckmorten's house with Isabella by his side. He knocked on the door where a black crepe ribbon had been placed, before turning to look at her. She smiled innocently at him, but that didn't keep a knot of desire from tightening his lower body.

Daniel stuck a finger down his tight collar and tried to loosen it. He didn't know if it was Isabella or the sun that suddenly had him hot.

The day was really too warm for her to be dressed in the wig, oversize cloak, and bonnet, but it didn't seem to be affecting her at all. She looked cool, calm, comfortable, and tempting as ever while his collar and trousers felt too tight for his skin. He wondered if she were truly innocent to the effect she had on him. At times it seemed that she had complete control over him.

He chuckled as he looked at her. "I must be a crazy fool. I can't believe I'm doing this."

"There are some things a brother must do to protect his sister."

"I keep telling myself that."

"If we don't find any kind of appointment book or day record that mentions Gretchen's name, we should feel better about this whole dreadful affair and can be done with it. Besides," she added, "it's not as if you want to steal anything. And any information we find out is not going to hurt Mr. Throckmorten at this point. He is beyond being hurt."

"Exactly. That is the only reason I'm agreeing to this wild scheme of yours. Once I know Gretchen is in no danger of having her reputation ruined by the circumstances of this man's demise, I'm forgetting all about him."

The door opened and once again they looked into the stiff face of the butler. His eyes rounded in surprise. "Lord Colebrooke," he said, looking from Daniel to Isabella. "I didn't expect to see you here. I can only assume you have heard what happened to my employer."

"Yes, I'm… we… That is, Mrs. Vanlandingham and I were very sorry to hear about Mr. Throckmorten's untimely death."

"Thank you, my lord."

"I know it's an upsetting turn of events. Do you mind if we come in?"

The butler looked puzzled but said, "Not at all."

They followed the servant into the same parlor where they had been shown before. "Would you like to sit down, my lord?"

"No. Again, we won't stay that long. I was hoping that I might in some way be of assistance."

"I believe Mr. Throckmorten's brother has been notified by now and should arrive in London within the next few days. Perhaps you should come back after he arrives."

"Yes, perhaps that would be the thing to do."

"Oh, oh." Isabella put the back of her hand to her forehead and let her eyelashes flutter rapidly.

"Mrs. Vanlandingham, what's wrong?" Daniel asked with as much fake concern as he could muster.

"Suddenly I don't feel so well. I think I might need to lie down." With that, Isabella crumpled to the floor at Daniel's feet.

Daniel couldn't believe she actually hit the floor. Was she trying to hurt herself?

"My heavens!" the butler exclaimed.

"Mrs. Vanlandingham, are you all right?" Daniel said as both men dropped to their knees beside her.

Isabella kept her eyes closed, her breathing shallow. Daniel looked at the butler and said, "I think she's fainted. Do you mind if I lay her on the settee for a few minutes?"

"By all means, my lord."

Daniel slid one arm around her shoulders, and the other he hooked under the backs of her knees, and he lifted Isabella without effort and placed her on the settee in the drawing room. The butler placed a pillow behind her head.

Isabella pretended to flutter her eyelashes again as if she were trying to wake up. She moved her head back and forth and moaned softly. Daniel remembered that the first time he saw her he wondered if she might be an actress. That could still be true. He would have sworn to anyone that she had really fainted.

"Perhaps you could see to getting her a cup of tea," Daniel said to the butler.

"Of course," the man said and immediately left the room.

As soon as he was out of sight, Daniel whispered, "He's gone."

Isabella's eyes popped open. "Then go. Find the room with his desk in it and search it thoroughly. If the butler gets back before you do, I'll tell him that you have gone in search of him to let him know I'm feeling better."

Looking down at her lying on the settee, Daniel knew all he really wanted to do was kiss her. She must have realized that, too, for she said, "You're wasting time, Daniel, go."

Daniel strode to the hallway and looked in both directions. It was clear. He stole down the corridor, carefully peeking in every room, except the kitchen.

He took a left turn that led to a closed door. He quietly opened it. The room was dark, but he saw enough to know it was the room he sought. He crept over to Throckmorten's desk. He couldn't risk lighting a lamp or parting the draperies.

He quickly scanned several sheets of vellum that lay on the desk, but nothing implicated Gretchen. He opened each drawer of the desk one at a time and quickly looked through the papers searching for anything that looked like an appointment book, a journal, or even a sheet of vellum with names on it.

There was something different about the last drawer he opened. It didn't look right. He studied it for a moment and realized that it wasn't as deep as all the others had been. He looked it over carefully and discovered that it had a false bottom. He emptied it of the foolscap it contained, and using the paper knife that lay on top of the desk, he took out the fake bottom. Underneath it lay a black leather journal.

He picked it up and fanned the pages. It was filled with names, dates, and amounts of money.

Daniel's heartbeat raced like a Thoroughbred horse nearing the finish line. No doubt the book contained information about Throckmorten's gambling. Those who owed him money and those he was indebted to.

Daniel hesitated.

He doubted Gretchen's name would be in there. He should put it back, but instead he slipped it into the pocket of his coat.

Daniel quickly replaced the bottom of the drawer and put the loose sheets back inside. He eased out of the room and quietly closed the door. He took a deep breath and walked back in the parlor to see a puzzled butler staring at Isabella.

"Oh, there you are," he said with all the confidence of an earl but feeling very much like a thief. "I was trying to find you to tell you that Mrs. Vanlandingham is feeling better."

"Yes, I just told him so," Isabella said, rising. "I feel I must have become overheated. I'm not used to so much sunshine." She placed the teacup on the table in front of her.

"Here, let me take your arm and walk with you." He helped Isabella to the door.

He turned back to the butler and said, "If you think of anything I can do, don't hesitate to call on me. Good day."

Daniel let go of Isabella as soon as the door was shut behind them. They walked quietly and swiftly away from the house. Isabella reached into the carriage for her own cloak, but Daniel stopped her.

"No, you don't. Not this time, my dear Isabella. We will go to the same spot to take off this disguise as we did for you to put it on."

She questioned him with her eyes as she said, "It only takes a moment."

"I know," he said impatiently, knowing he couldn't withstand her kneeling before him again. "We need to get away from here as soon as possible. Now up you go."

When they were seated on the cushion and the team was under way, Isabella turned to him and asked, "Did you find anything?"

Daniel's heartbeat raced. Should he tell her? He could easily keep what he had done a secret. No one need know but him.

"I had very little time and couldn't possibly look at all the documents and papers the man had in his desk, but I didn't see Gretchen's name on anything."

"Oh," she said, sounding a bit disappointed. "Well, it would have been better if we had found her name somewhere, and then we wouldn't worry that there was something we missed." She looked up at him. "I suppose you feel that it was a wasted trip?"

"Not at all." He patted his jacket pocket. "I found his private gambling journal."

Thirteen

STUNNED, ISABELLA LOOKED INTO DANIEL'S GOLDEN brown eyes. Late afternoon sunshine beat down on her from a clear blue sky. For a moment, wrapped in her aunt's heavy cloak, she felt as if she might really faint. The carriage rumbled and bumped along the street under the clear blue sky at an easy pace, but Isabella's gaze didn't waver from Daniel's.

"His gambling journal?" she managed to say. "You took it from his desk?"

Daniel drew in a deep breath but remained calm as he said, "Yes."

"Why?"

"He's not going to need it again."

"Daniel!" she exclaimed.

He shrugged off her shock and answered, "I know that was an irreverent remark about a dead man, but you just looked so astonished that I had taken the journal when this entire escapade was your idea."

He was still the most unbelievable man she had ever met. And to think he had called her a mischief-maker.

He was ten times worse than she was and he seemed almost pleased with himself.

"It was my idea to look at his appointment book, a sheet of vellum, or anything that might have Gretchen's name on it and take that. I in no way indicated you should avail yourself of his private, ill-gotten-gains book." She stopped and took a huffing breath before she asked, "Is your sister's name in there?"

Daniel gave her a placating smile. "I haven't looked, but I would hope not. She's in enough trouble without adding a gambling debt."

She looked at him warily. "Then what do you plan to do with the journal?"

"You mean, after I read it?"

"Yes."

"I'll probably find a way to return it without anyone knowing I had it."

There had to be a reason he took the book that had nothing to do with Gretchen, so she asked, "What exactly do you plan to do with the information that is in the journal?"

"I'm not sure. Taking it just seemed like the right thing to do at the time. We know that Throckmorten was killed in Lord Gleningwold's garden and later dumped in the river. Everyone else, except the killer, of course, assumes he was killed somewhere on the streets by a footpad and then thrown in the water."

"That must be what the killer wanted everyone to believe, or why would he move the body from the garden?" Isabella said.

"Right."

Isabella found herself warming to the idea that

Daniel had taken the book. It was true after all that Mr. Throckmorten had no further use of it, and there was a good possibility it might help them solve the mystery of who killed the poor man.

"I think I see where you're going with this. It was obviously a member of the *ton* who killed Mr. Throckmorten. There were no others at the party." Isabella paused. "Unless, of course, a footpad made his way into Lord Gleningwold's garden."

"That's unlikely given the number of people in attendance. Someone would have noticed him before he made it to the garden."

"Or a gate was left unlocked."

"That's always a possibility. It's my guess that Throckmorten was probably killed by someone at the party who owed him money and couldn't pay up."

"Or maybe it could be that he owed money to someone and couldn't or wouldn't pay the debt."

Daniel nodded. "Yes, that's another possibility I've thought about."

"And you want to know if any of the men whose names are written in that book were also at Lord Gleningwold's party?"

"Yes. The only thing we know for sure is that Gretchen didn't kill him."

"And that journal," Isabella pointed to his pocket, "might help us determine who the likely suspects are. Let's look at it," she said, feeling a sudden excitement rising inside her.

"We can't look at it here on the streets." He motioned to the rows of town homes they were passing at an easy clip. "Someone might see us."

"Oh, heavens, Daniel, no one will know what we are looking at."

"I will know. Reading through this will be done in private."

Isabella leaned against the back of the seat cushion and laughed lightly. His gaze swept up and down her face like a feather-soft caress, and the way he looked at her made her even hotter.

"What amuses you?"

"You do."

He gave her a nonchalant grin. "Me? I'm not sure I like being the source of your entertainment. What is there about me that you find comical?"

"How you have pretended such innocence with me."

He relaxed against the cushion back with her. "Innocent? Me? What are you talking about?"

Isabella should have known that no man would want to be associated with the word *innocent*, so she explained. "I do believe you have been reading the same books I've read, and you wouldn't admit it."

"Trust me, I haven't read many books since leaving Oxford."

He chuckled softly, easily, and Isabella liked seeing his face in laughter. His eyes sparkled and looked lighter and brighter. She liked the way the wind blew his hair back, showing his strong forehead, making him look younger and even more handsome. His lips were full and tempting, making her desperate to press her own against his and to once again experience the passion she'd found in his arms.

As she watched him she couldn't help but wonder why Society said kisses were not proper when they felt so good. No doubt someone who didn't like kisses started that rule. And Isabella believed some rules needed to be broken. Not kissing until you were married was one of them.

Isabella smiled at him. "I'm not so sure you are telling the truth about your reading habits. You've come up with a very good clue about finding out who the killer might be."

"That is because I catch on quick about how your game is played."

Isabella's excitement ebbed, and she realized again how uncomfortably hot she was in the cloak. She wished for a chilling breeze to cool her cheeks.

Her expression turned questioning, and she said, "My game? I'm not playing a game, Daniel."

"That remains to be seen."

Isabella didn't know why it bothered her that Daniel thought she was making a game out of this. She truly wanted to see that Gretchen wasn't implicated in Throckmorten's murder, but she couldn't deny that there was an excitement in wanting to help find out who the killer might be.

Maybe she couldn't blame Daniel for not trusting her. Here she was sitting beside him disguised as an old woman. She'd been the one to suggest he search Mr. Throckmorten's desk for incriminating papers. Worst of all, she had failed in her duty to keep Gretchen away from Mr. Throckmorten, which started all this intrigue.

Isabella felt the heat not only from the sun but from her conversation with Daniel. She looked around the row of houses they were passing and didn't see anyone walking the streets. They were clear.

She reached up and untied her aunt's bonnet. In one fluid movement she swept the bonnet and wig off her head at the same time and let them drop to the carriage floor. Just as quickly, she plopped her own dark blue bonnet over her mussed hair and settled it on her head.

"What are you doing?" Daniel whispered as he looked around the streets to see if anyone was watching them. "You could get caught."

"It's so hot I couldn't possibly wear that thing another moment," she said as she tied the ribbons under her chin. "It seems as if it was winter yesterday and spring came to London overnight."

"Don't make light of your disguise, Isabella. That was a dangerous thing for you to do. Someone could have seen you."

"I checked the streets to make sure they were empty. I think I've made it clear that I don't want to get caught doing something I shouldn't do." She gave him a quick but winning smile. "You worry too much, Daniel."

"Obviously one of us needs to. I'm trying to keep your reputation from being ruined."

"I do appreciate that. I'm doing the same for Gretchen. As long as her name doesn't appear on any of Mr. Throckmorten's papers, we will assume she's safe from the gossips and the authorities."

Isabella unbuttoned the cloak and Daniel helped her to take it off. She let it fall on top of the bonnet and wig. Daniel told the driver not to make the planned detour, but to go directly to Isabella's house.

When Daniel turned back to her, he said, "Just

because I didn't see anything that looked like an appointment book anywhere on Throckmorten's desk, I'm not sure we can assume my sister is in the clear yet."

"I suppose you're right. We can assume that whoever killed the man saw her."

"I don't think we have to worry about him coming forward. But to be on the safe side, I will go to Bow Street and hire a runner to look into Throckmorten's death."

Abruptly Isabella's heart lurched, and then started beating rapidly. She glanced away from Daniel to the tall shrubs and a couple of pedestrians they passed. If there was no intrigue to settle, there would be no reason for him to see her again. If she never saw him alone again, there wouldn't be any more kisses. That thought caused an unexpected pain deep in her chest.

Isabella didn't want to stop seeing him. She enjoyed their banter and being with him. She wanted to work with him on solving this crime. She had even hoped he would kiss her again. He was a challenge to be sure but a welcome challenge.

Suddenly the sunshine didn't seem nearly so bright or feel so warm. In fact, she suddenly felt quite chilled. And once again she was having feelings for Daniel that she didn't understand.

Why did the thought of not seeing him again squeeze all the joy out of her heart? Why did it suddenly make her feel lonely? It had to be that without him there would be no adventure or intrigue for her to help resolve.

She turned her attention back to him. Isabella didn't

want him forsaking her and going to a runner. She wanted to continue to help him on this quest, but how could she convince him of that?

"I'm not sure that a runner is a good idea. If anyone in the *ton* hears about you hiring someone to look into this matter, they might wonder why you have such an interest in Mr. Throckmorten."

"I would make sure the runner was discreet and that my name would never be made known."

Isabella decided just to say what was on her mind and be done with it. "But if you turn this matter over to a runner, there would be no reason for me to help you with the names in the journal."

His expression turned serious, and he hesitated a moment before speaking. "Gambling debts and murder are not the kinds of things that a young lady like you should be involved in, Isabella. I think it's best that only one of us knows what's written in the book."

That sinking feeling settled in her stomach. He was telling her he didn't want her help? He was right. This wasn't something most young ladies should be involved in, but she was different. She had been a part of this from the beginning, but she knew it would do no good to argue with Lord Colebrooke.

"Yes, perhaps you're right," she said with no conviction in her voice. "There's no reason for both of us to know these men's private affairs." She took a painfully deep breath and looked directly into his eyes. "And if I don't need to help you protect Gretchen's reputation, I don't suppose there is any reason for us to continue to see each other."

He hesitated for a moment before he answered,

giving her a dash of hope that he might reconsider, but finally he said, "I don't see any reason."

He said it so flatly she had no recourse but to believe him no matter how much that reality wounded her heart and filled her with sadness. But she couldn't let him know that.

"Good," she said, keeping her voice as light as possible, not wanting him to know how deeply his words affected her. "It's settled then. Should we meet at a party, we will greet each other as acquaintances with a smile and continue on our way."

"I think that's best, Isabella. Our times alone have been too intense."

She knew she should let the conversation drop. They were near her home, but she couldn't let him go so easily. Keeping her gaze on his she said, "Daniel?"

"Yes?"

"I want to thank you for kissing me."

"Isabella. Don't thank me for something I shouldn't have done. I was just lecturing Gretchen for being involved in inappropriate behavior with a man and felt like the worst kind of scoundrel doing so when I've been just as guilty."

"How so?" she asked innocently.

He gave a short laugh. "Have you forgotten so quickly our passionate embrace in Gleningwold's garden or what we shared in your own home? We've shared a bit more than kisses."

"But you didn't do anything I didn't want you to do," she insisted defiantly. "And don't forget there is a big difference between your sister and me."

"And what is that?"

"One, I am three years older and, therefore, more worldly and wiser."

He laughed. "Ah, well now, three years. That does make a difference."

She gave him an impatient sigh. "I'm serious. Don't tease me about this, Daniel."

"Don't give me reason to make fun of you. Three years older is hardly a reason. In a lot of ways, the most important ways, you are still as innocent as Gretchen. You are going to have to come up with something better than that."

"And I have something more for you," she said, adding indignation to all the other things she was currently feeling because of him. "Gretchen wants to make a match and I don't."

"That doesn't make our passionate kisses the right thing to have done."

"If you hadn't kissed me, I might have never been kissed. And I'm glad I will now have that memory for the rest of my life."

"What do you mean, you might never have been kissed? Of course you would have and you will be again once you are properly wed."

"I don't plan to marry," she said, even though she knew she'd told him that before. It somehow seemed important to tell him again.

"Perhaps you should rethink your vow to remain a spinster."

"Why should I?"

"Because you are a very passionate woman, Isabella, and your passion should be shared with a man—your husband."

The only thing she heard him say was that she was a passionate woman, and for some reason that made her feel delicious inside. "You think so? You think I am passionate?"

"Oh, yes. No doubt about that."

"But as a spinster my aunt has more freedom than a married woman who has to answer to a husband about where she goes and what she does. Very much like a father controls a child's life. I don't think I would like that very much."

"Yes, but a spinster does not get kisses at night or in the mornings," he countered.

"Hmm. The mornings, too?"

Daniel laughed. "When you are wed you can kiss your husband anytime that you want to."

Isabella's brows drew together in contemplation. She had really enjoyed his kisses and caresses. "That is something to think about. Daniel, do all men's kisses feel the same?"

He cleared his throat and thought for a moment. "I don't know. Probably not. No, I'm sure not," he said looking as if he didn't know which of the answers he gave was the correct one. "Why do you ask?"

"I've never had trouble rebuffing a man until I met you, and I find it difficult to resist you. I never wanted to kiss a man until I met you."

"This is not a conversation we should be having, Isabella, and this is one of the reasons we must not see each other again. We talk too freely with each other."

"Why can't we have this conversation? Why is honesty not allowed between us?"

He looked away for a moment before turning to

study her face again. "It's not that. I want only honesty between us. It's Society's rules, and to live in Society we must obey their rules. We are to behave in a certain way, and you and I have not been following the rules. I take full responsibility for that."

"I accept my own responsibility."

The carriage stopped in front of her house, but if Daniel noticed, he didn't indicate it.

"Fine, but I don't want you hurt by anything I might talk you into doing." He leaned in closer to her and softly said, "I can assure you that I want to kiss you much more than you want me to, but the way I want to kiss you should only be done if we are wed."

"Marriage between us is not in the plans," she assured him.

"No, Isabella. It's not."

Fourteen

HE BROKE ALL THE RULES FOR HER.

Daniel Colebrooke, Earl of Colebrooke, had turned into a thief and a marauder of innocent young ladies' respectability. What the hell had happened to him? He was an earl. And that title demanded certain responsibilities, which he promptly ignored every time he was with the delectable Isabella.

Daniel sat at a table in a darkened corner of White's hoping no one would see him. He wanted to be alone with his decanter of claret and his thoughts before he had to go to the first party of the evening.

He'd come to the club hoping to ponder what he'd learned from Throckmorten's journal, but he'd spent more time thinking about Isabella than about the dead man's gambling habits.

There had been no surprise when he'd found his cousin's name in the book. Bradford was probably in everyone's gambling book, including the establishment where Daniel was sitting.

He downed the rest of the claret in his glass and poured himself another drink. There were names he'd found in Throckmorten's journal that he hadn't expected, like Thomas Wright's. Although Tom didn't owe the man a large amount, he was still indebted to him.

It was a bit of a surprise to see Lord Gleningwold's name in there, too, considering Throckmorten was killed in his garden. And it was Throckmorten who owed the earl a substantial sum. Daniel just couldn't picture the jovial earl as a killer.

Chilton Cummerford was also listed in the book. He'd been paying Throckmorten once a month for the better part of a year. He must have lost a great deal of money to the man in a card game. No doubt that was the reason that Chilton had visited Throckmorten's.

He'd like to know why Chilton had kept that information from him when Daniel had questioned him about Throckmorten.

Daniel really didn't know what to make of it all. He'd sat down and made a list of all the men who were in the journal who were present at Gleningwold's party the night Throckmorten was killed. The number was less than a dozen, but that seemed like too many when you were trying to narrow it down to one.

He'd made up his mind to seek the help of a runner from Bow Street. He knew that Isabella was caught up in the intrigue of Throckmorten's death, but Daniel's only concern was that Gretchen's name not be connected to the dead man's.

A couple of gentlemen walked by laughing, and Daniel looked up from his drink. He should probably be going. He picked up his glass and took another sip. Isabella returned to his mind.

He remembered the way Isabella looked earlier in the afternoon when she took off her disguise. She was stunning. Her face had been flushed from the sun, her golden blond hair was tangled attractively, and her eyes shone like gemstones.

He'd been so tempted to take her in his arms and kiss her that he thought he was going to have to sit on his hands to keep from embracing her right in front of anyone who might be on the street. He'd wanted more than anything in the world at that moment to show Society that he didn't give a damn about their rules. The only problem with doing that was that he did care.

At times like this, Daniel wished he was still just a second son. He hadn't wanted to become the earl. He wished his brother were still alive and taking care of Gretchen and all the affairs of the title. But fate had made him an earl, and he had to take his responsibilities seriously.

Isabella was charming and he liked the way she made him feel. He enjoyed being with her, but how could he continue to see her? One day she was helping him plan devious acts, and the next day she was entertaining her Wallflowers Society. He couldn't allow her to continue to be involved in such unsavory situations as gambling debts and a murder even though she seemed more than capable of taking care of herself.

Most young ladies he'd known over the years would have fainted or acted as Gretchen had if they saw a dead man, but Isabella had been completely in control and had immediately seen to Gretchen. He liked that she spoke intelligently. She'd impressed him earlier today when she wanted honesty between them.

Daniel had never worried that she'd hide anything from him concerning her feelings for him. He no longer thought she was up to mischief with her free thinking. She was merely caught up in the excitement and suspense of wanting to know who killed Throckmorten.

The only thing he was sure of was that he wanted her. He'd wanted her for days now. He wanted to take her in his arms and once again feel the shape of her body beneath his hands. He wanted to taste the depth of her mouth and her satiny smooth skin.

He remembered the way his body responded when he'd held her, the way her mouth responded to his, the way her softness rose up to meet his hardness. He thought of the pleasurable sigh that had floated past his lips at how she made him feel.

Still, he'd had no choice but to tell her she couldn't continue helping him look into Throckmorten's murder. Every time he saw her, he wanted to kiss her, and she was unconventional enough to let him. He didn't know how to treat a young lady of quality who had no fear of losing her reputation.

Daniel sipped his drink again. Isabella was driving him insane with wanting her. He hadn't planned to take a new mistress when he came to London. His plan was to find a wife, but it looked as if he was going to have to seek out a mistress because Isabella had him so tied up in knots he couldn't keep his hands off her. And that could only lead to disaster.

Society was made up of two kinds of women. Those you married and those you didn't. He had to make sure that Isabella remained one of the first and find a mistress for the latter.

Isabella and her aunt stepped out of the carriage at the home of the first party they were attending for the evening. The sky was clear of clouds, and there was a breezy crispness to the air that made the night feel springtime beautiful.

"Are you sure you are all right, Isabella?" her aunt questioned as they made their way to the front door of the house. "You don't have that glow you've had the past several days."

"I'm certain I'm fine, Auntie," Isabella said in a voice as light as she could make it.

She hated fibbing to her aunt, but she couldn't possibly tell her the truth. She wasn't fine. She wanted to be a part of Daniel's life and the adventure of looking for a murderer.

"Are you unhappy with the gown I picked out for you to wear?"

Isabella looked down at her pearl-white gown with three banded satin flounces. It was a bit overdone for Isabella, but she really didn't mind wearing it since her aunt had been so happy with her choice.

"No, it's lovely. Perhaps it's just that attending two and three parties every night is getting to be too much even for me."

"Yes. Perhaps we should start being more selective in which events we accept from now own. Especially if you continue to have afternoon rides in the park with Lord Colebrooke."

That empty feeling settled in Isabella's stomach again. "Auntie Pith, I've asked you not to read too much into my outings with him. Dan—Lord Colebrooke, has been calling on other young ladies, and I'm not certain he will call on me again."

"I know, I know," Auntie Pith said. She held up her hand to stop Isabella from saying more. "Of course he needs to consider everyone and he should. But when he is finished looking over all the young ladies, he will no doubt return to you."

Isabella couldn't very well tell her aunt that just this afternoon Daniel told her they no longer had a reason to see each other. Isabella understood that, she just hadn't expected it to make her feel so dreadful. And was it the intrigue she was going to miss or was it Daniel that she would miss? Perhaps it was both.

They entered the house, and their cloaks were handed over to one of the servants. The house glowed from brightly lit candles and was filled with fashionably dressed ladies and handsomely garbed gentlemen. Music played in the distance, laughter and chatter rumbled throughout the crowded room.

Isabella held her chin and shoulders high, but not even the gaiety of the event could lift her spirits or the feeling that she'd lost something very dear to her. She hadn't wanted Daniel or any man to become so important to her.

After they made their way through the receiving line Aunt Pithany said, "I see Mrs. Manchester, Isabella. Come with me and say hello to her."

"You go ahead and speak to her, Auntie. I'll join you in a moment. I want to make sure I have a dance card with me."

Isabella made her way to the side of the room. It wasn't like her to feel so melancholy. What on earth was wrong with her? She hadn't felt this way since her father first left for Europe. She was over those feelings of loss, and she didn't plan on letting them return to spoil the happiness she'd found in London.

She opened her drawstring reticule, and the first thing she saw was a white handkerchief. How could she have forgotten that she'd put Gretchen's hand-kerchief in her purse when she'd found it near Mr. Throckmorten's body? Probably because she had been so caught up in the intrigue of it all.

She pulled the handkerchief from her purse and folded it neatly so she could return it to Gretchen. Her thumb raked over the embroidered initials, and she took a moment to look at the finely stitched handi-work. All of a sudden her breathing became short and shallow. The three letters jumped out at her.

The initials weren't Gretchen's.

The last letter was a *W*, the same as Isabella's. But the first was an *A*. She had picked up a handkerchief that wasn't hers or Gretchen's.

A spark of hope roared to life inside Isabella.

The intrigue with Daniel wasn't over.

Another lady was in the garden with Mr. Throckmorten. She put the folded handkerchief back into her reticule and turned quickly to go find Daniel to tell him and bumped right into Mr. Thomas Wright.

"Oh, I'm sorry."

"Excuse me, Miss Winslowe, it's my fault," he said quickly. "I was about to announce myself when you suddenly turned into me."

She smiled at the tall, slightly built man staring

down at her. "No harm done at all, Mr. Wright. How are you this evening?"

"Quite well and you?"

"Good, thank you."

He gave her a nervous smile. "Might I say you're looking lovely this evening, Miss Winslowe."

"What a nice compliment, Mr. Wright, and you are dashing as always."

A faint blush added color to his pale cheeks. He hesitated for a moment before saying, "I wanted to thank you for inviting Amanda to be a part of your afternoon teas. She is so shy and has never received many invitations. Despite what some people say, I think it has been good for her to join your Reading Society."

"Thank you, Mr. Wright. I think so, too. She's a delightful addition," Isabella said, thinking that all of the ladies in her group had made progress in being more confident at the parties and balls. "We're happy to have her join us. Is she here tonight?"

"Yes. She's just left for the refreshment table with some of her friends."

"Good. I'll see her later."

Isabella smiled but didn't offer another sentence. She was anxious to excuse herself from him and find Daniel, but before she could say her good-byes, Bradford Turnbury stopped beside her.

"Good evening, Miss Winslowe. Tom," Mr. Turnbury said, but he only looked at Isabella.

They both returned his greetings.

"I hope I'm not interrupting anything important," Mr. Turnbury said.

"Not at all," Isabella managed to say with a smile

on her face, but it was getting harder to maintain. "I was just inquiring about Mr. Wright's sister Amanda. Do you know her, Mr. Turnbury?"

"Yes. Lovely young lady. I'm sure you're quite proud of her, as a brother should be." He glanced at Mr. Wright before returning his attention to Isabella. "Miss Winslowe, I was hoping you would be free for a dance later in the evening. That is, if Tom hasn't filled up your card?"

"Oh."

It was on the tip of her tongue to decline when out of the corner of her eye Isabella saw Daniel and Gretchen walking her way. He was so fine-looking dressed in his black evening coat, white brocade waistcoat, and perfectly tied neckcloth.

Her heart tripped.

All of a sudden Isabella had an inkling of why she felt the way she did about Daniel. Could it be she was falling in love with him?

Love?

Where did that idea come from? No, no, she wouldn't believe that.

Isabella had made up her mind two years ago about that when she realized she loved living in London and had no desire to go back to the quiet life of the country. She didn't want or need to love a man. She wanted to be free to come and go as she wished, like her aunt. She was very happy with her life just as it was. The last thing she needed was the Earl of Colebrooke interfering with her plans.

It must be that she felt the soar in her heart when she looked at him only because of the intrigue they had been involved in. It had been exciting, and it didn't appear that the suspense was over.

Isabella hesitated a moment longer before answering Mr. Turnbury so that Daniel would hear when she said, "I'd be delighted to dance with you later in the evening, Mr. Turnbury."

"Splendid, Miss Winslowe. I shall look forward to it."

When Daniel looked at her, his eyes were hot and demanding, and Isabella had no doubt that he'd heard every word she'd said to Mr. Turnbury.

As greetings and pleasantries were exchanged all around once again, Isabella mulled over the reasons why she once again accepted a dance with Mr. Turnbury. She had no desire to dance with the man, but that same ridiculous feeling of wanting to make Daniel jealous had come over her.

She didn't know what made her behave that way when Daniel had made it more than clear he had no long-term interest in her. And she certainly didn't want to have a romantic interest in him. But she did have romantic interests in him.

Isabella pushed the illogical and childish thoughts away. She wasn't a young miss to be swept away by a handsome earl. She needed to concentrate on how she was going to get Daniel alone so she could tell him about the handkerchief. She offered little to the conversation as the five of them chatted but managed to make an intelligent comment or two.

It seemed to her that Daniel was purposely avoiding looking at her, and she felt rebuffed even though they had just that afternoon agreed that if they met at a party they would be polite but not overly friendly. They had planned never to meet alone again.

But that was before she'd discovered this new evidence. Now she had to speak to him alone, and she really didn't want to wait until later in the evening.

Mr. Turnbury and Mr. Wright were between her and Daniel on one side, and Gretchen was between them on the other side.

Isabella hardly knew what was being said until she heard Mr. Wright ask Gretchen to dance. Gretchen looked him in the eyes, smiled, and said yes. Isabella smiled, too. Gretchen handled Mr. Wright perfectly.

They walked away and Isabella was left standing with Daniel and Mr. Turnbury. She certainly couldn't say anything in front of his cousin. It was best to take her leave and try to see Daniel again later in the evening. Finding the handkerchief certainly put a different twist on who might have killed Mr. Throckmorten.

Just as she was about to take her leave for the third time, Lord Gleningwold approached them and once again greetings were said all around. Isabella had had enough bows and curtsies, good-evenings and how-are-yous. At this rate she would be standing in this one spot the entire evening.

Lord Gleningwold asked Mr. Turnbury a question, and Isabella saw it as her chance to inch closer to Daniel.

Keeping her lips and teeth closed and her gaze on Mr. Turnbury, Isabella mumbled to Daniel, "Ask me to dance."

Daniel looked down at her and in a normal voice asked, "I'm sorry, I didn't hear you."

"Shh," she whispered tight-lipped and tried to tell him with her eyes to talk softer.

Daniel caught on immediately and mimicked her by speaking softly with his lips closed. "Why are we whispering? I can hardly hear you."

She moved a bit closer to him, hoping Mr. Turnbury would not turn his attention to them. "Ask me to dance. I must talk to you alone."

"Have you forgotten we've already discussed that and decided not to do it?" he said.

"I haven't forgotten. How could I? But things have changed. I have something important to tell you."

His eyes narrowed. "What?" he asked beneath his breath.

"I have evidence that a woman killed Mr. Throckmorten."

Fifteen

DANIEL STARED DOWN INTO THE MOST BEAUTIFUL EYES he'd ever seen. Despite his best efforts, a grin tugged at his lips.

Isabella was priceless.

Just when he was trying to talk himself into believing he didn't desire her, she charmed him all over again. There was no denying the heat that thickened his loins whenever he looked into her vibrant eyes.

But this was no place for such feelings. Half the *ton* was present tonight, and his obnoxious cousin was standing right in front of him.

Denying the delicious heady warmth that stirred through him, Daniel turned away from Isabella. He cleared his throat to get the attention of the two men standing with him.

He waited until they acknowledged him before saying, "Excuse me, gentlemen, but I believe this conversation has become too indelicate for Miss Winslowe. I'm going to escort her to the punch table."

Bradford gave him an infuriating glare that didn't bother Daniel at all, but what his cousin said did.

"What nonsense are you talking about, Danny? We

were discussing the new gardens that are being planted at Buckingham Palace."

Bloody hell.

"Right, I know," Daniel said, stalling for time, wondering what the devil he was going to say to get out of this blunder.

"But you see, Mr. Turnbury," Isabella spoke up quickly, "I'm one of those rare ladies who have an aversion to flowers, and it just so happens that Lord Colebrooke knows that."

"Yes," Daniel said, amazed at how easily Isabella came to his rescue with a made-up story, but nonetheless grateful she did.

"I had no idea you or any other lady disliked flowers," Bradford said with a doubtful expression on his face.

"Oh," Isabella said in her charming way. "I think it's quite common, but mostly it affects ladies who grow up in the country, as I did. Perhaps it's because most of the gardens are so expansive."

Not wanting Bradford to take her to task any further, Daniel said, "Now, if you two gentlemen will excuse us, we'll be on our way."

"Wait, Miss Winslowe." Bradford stopped her. "I'll see you later in the evening for our dance."

Isabella gave him a smile. "Of course. I'll be waiting, Mr. Turnbury."

Daniel couldn't believe how tightly his stomach knotted when Isabella smiled so sweetly at his cousin. He wasn't surprised that Bradford was interested in Isabella. She was the most poised and resourceful young lady he'd ever met. Her beauty was reserved and classic. What was he thinking?

Oh, hell. Everything about her was charming. And Daniel could only assume she found Bradford a polite and handsome fellow, or why else would she continue to accept his overtures?

As Daniel and Isabella left the two men, he said, "An aversion to flowers? Where did you come up with that idea?"

"From thin air, Lord Colebrooke, and it worked."

Daniel grunted his appreciation as they made their way toward the room where the buffet was set.

It was impossible for them to talk in the crush of people that filled the house. They were stopped several times for greetings and introductions before they waded through the crowd and into the less packed dining room.

Daniel stopped at the table, and a servant poured Isabella a glass of punch. He picked up a glass of champagne for himself. He then escorted Isabella to a corner of the room where they would have a small measure of privacy to discuss her latest revelation.

When they were far enough away from listening ears, Daniel stepped as close to her as he dared without raising the eyebrows of the dowager he'd spotted in the room. He said, "Now, what's this new evidence you have about Gretchen?"

Isabella's expression turned quizzical. "I don't have any about her," she assured him.

"Damnation, Isabella, you had me on edge. What mad scheme have you come up with now?"

"What are you talking about, sir?" she challenged him. "I am not scheming anything. I told you I have evidence of *a* woman. Not Gretchen."

Daniel hadn't meant to sound so irritated. He knew

it was a reaction to the way Isabella responded to Turnbury. It was illogical and not understandable, but Daniel didn't want any other man dancing with her. He didn't want anyone touching her hand, her waist, or even the tips of her fingers.

He tried to look contrite but wasn't sure he'd managed. "Oh. You were whispering so softly I wasn't sure what you said."

"I believe you owe me an apology."

"I don't mean to swear in front of you, but you exasperate me sometimes. Most of the time."

"I'm not offended by your language. What insults me is that you continue to think that I am up to mischief. I can't believe that by now you don't trust that I only want to help Gretchen."

He wanted to believe her, but at times like this he still had reservations. "Very well," he said. "Now, tell me what you are talking about."

Her accusing gaze held firmly on his, and she refused to back down by saying, "An apology first, my lord, if you don't mind."

He saw her resolve not to go further until he'd said the words. Damnation, she tried his patience. "All right. I'm sorry."

"Thank you."

"Now will you tell me what the devil you're talking about?"

Without further sparring she sat her punch cup on a nearby table and opened her reticule and pulled out the handkerchief. "This."

Daniel looked at the little square of material that was more lace than anything else. "A lady's handkerchief?"

She smiled confidently. "Yes."

Daniel swallowed his irritation. He was irritated and he knew why. He'd much rather be kissing Isabella than talking to her about this. His lower body kept telling him he wanted to pull her to him and kiss her madly.

She was so tempting tonight with her hair swept away from her face and sprinkled with tiny white flowers. The waist of her gown was high and the neckline was cut low. It was an odd color that had the look of aged stone and it made her skin glow.

"Isabella, you had me on edge thinking you had evidence on Gretchen, and all you had was a wrinkled handkerchief?"

"No, my lord. You assumed that about Gretchen. And this happens to be a very important handkerchief. Do you remember the night we found Mr. Throckmorten in Lord Gleningwold's garden?"

Daniel pulled in a deep breath, and then took a sip of his champagne. "I'll never forget it."

"While you were searching the ground for his body, I was looking around and I found this."

They weren't getting anywhere. Daniel remembered the first time they met and how she took so long to tell him the story of Gretchen standing over Throckmorten in her garden. He had that same feeling now.

He summoned his patience and answered, "All right. Gretchen dropped it and you found it. I'm grateful, Miss Winslowe."

"We're alone now, Daniel, you can call me Isabella. This is not Gretchen's." She held the handkerchief out in front of him. "It belongs to someone else."

Daniel paused as the implications of her words soaked in. "How do you know this?"

"That's what I've been trying to tell you. Mr. Throckmorten must have been in the garden with another lady before Gretchen showed up. That lady must have stabbed him. Gretchen was angry enough with him to hit him when they were in my garden. Perhaps another woman was angry enough to stab him."

Isabella could very well be on to something with this angle, and, if what she suspected was true, this would put a different light on Throckmorten's murder.

"Why didn't you tell me this before now?" Daniel asked.

"Like you, I assumed it was Gretchen's and put it here in my reticule. I forgot about it until tonight when I opened my purse to search for a dance card. I noticed the handkerchief and remembered when and where I'd picked it up. I took it out to fold so I could return it to her this evening, and that's when I realized the initials aren't Gretchen's."

"Whose handkerchief is it?"

"That I don't know. Yet. It has three initials, but I haven't taken the time to try and figure out who it might belong to."

Daniel pondered this new information. Thinking out loud, he said, "But if a woman had stabbed him, how would she have carried his body out of the garden?"

"I supposed it would have been difficult for a lady to have carried him out of the garden."

"Isabella, that would have been impossible."

"Well, there are some ladies who might be strong enough to have accomplished such a task."

"No, there aren't, but she could have left him there and gone for help. That could have been when Gretchen came upon him, and then we showed up."

"Yes. And whoever did this dastardly deed moved the body while we were talking to Lord Stonehurst and his lady wife."

"That seems a logical way for things to have happened. This will be more information for the runner. Let me have the handkerchief."

Daniel reached to take the handkerchief, but Isabella snatched it back before his hand closed around the white square of cloth, and it slipped through his fingers.

"Not so quick, my lord," she said, eyeing him with a bold stare.

There was something compelling about her when she looked up at him with such defiance, and it made Daniel want her all the more.

For a brief moment he fantasized about gently shoving her against the wall and pinioning her with his body while he playfully wrestled the handkerchief from her hands in a mischievous tug-of-war that ended in her total surrender to him. As the victor he received a passionate kiss.

"Daniel Colebrooke, what's this?" Chilton called from behind him.

"What next?" Daniel muttered under his breath as his fantasy faded.

"Are you trying to steal this young lady's handkerchief? What a villain you are! Did you lose all your manners while you were traipsing the countryside in search of your holdings?"

"Chilton, what perfect timing," Daniel said at his friend's ill-timing.

"Indeed. How do you do, Miss Winslowe?" Chilton bowed after he stopped beside her.

Isabella curtsied and smiled. "Very well, Mr. Cummerford, and you?"

"Very well, until I saw this scoundrel trying to accost you and take, of all things, your handkerchief. What an oaf."

"Thankfully, you came by just in time, and now I can safely put it away with no fear that Lord Colebrooke will take it from me."

Isabella made a great show of dropping the handkerchief into her reticule and pulling the drawstrings tight before slipping it back onto her wrist.

"Are you two finished?" Daniel asked, finding no amusement in their good-humored banter.

Chilton looked at Isabella and grinned mischievously. "I don't know. Are we, fair lady?" he asked her.

"Not if we can make him suffer a little longer. He's been such a brute. Should we try?"

"I would enjoy that, but alas, I have a young lady who is waiting for me to bring her a glass of punch."

"Don't keep her waiting. She might find another, less handsome, and less charming gentleman to bring refreshment to her."

"Well said, Miss Winslowe."

"Should we pick up our conversation another time, Mr. Cummerford?"

"I'll look forward to it," Chilton said and finally looked back to Daniel. "Are we still on for tomorrow morning?"

"Yes, my house." Daniel all but growled the words. He didn't like the way Chilton was flirting with Isabella and she with him.

Chilton bid Isabella farewell and walked away. Daniel said, "You two seemed very congenial."

"Really?" she asked innocently.

"Yes."

"I don't know him well, but Mr. Cummerford is always a pleasant man."

"What changed? Not two days ago you seemed to think him capable of killing Throckmorten."

"Nonsense, I was merely pointing out that he had visited Mr. Throckmorten's home. However, I agree with what you said at the time. He's not the type of gentleman to lose his temper and stab someone, neither over money nor over a lady."

She was damned intuitive. Daniel liked that about her, too. Chilton was a calm and patient man and always had been, even in their youth.

"And how do you know this about him?" Daniel asked.

"I've noticed that he watches a certain lady, but I've never seen him approach her at any of the parties."

"Chilton watching a lady? Are you sure?"

"Reasonably."

What young lady could Chilton be interested in? And why hadn't he mentioned her to Daniel? Probably for the same reason Daniel hadn't mentioned his attraction to Isabella to Chilton. They no longer had the need to tell each other everything about their lives.

It was best to leave this conversation for another day

and return to the one he and Isabella were discussing before Chilton interrupted them.

"I was about to tell you, that is to ask you," Daniel corrected himself before she had the chance, "to let me have the handkerchief. I'll hand it over to the Bow Street runner I've hired. He will find out who it belongs to."

Isabella smiled cunningly and shook her head. "I don't think so, my lord."

"Why?" he argued. "It might help him find Throckmorten's killer so that we will have no need to worry that anyone will find out about his liaison with Gretchen."

"Oh, I believe it will help."

He stepped dangerously close to her. "So why not let me give it to him?"

"You are in control of Mr. Throckmorten's journal, and you may choose to do with it as you wish. I am in control of the handkerchief found near his body, and I choose to handle it myself."

"Isabella," he said, wanting to explain again. "I don't want you involved in this unsavory, madcap situation. We're talking about a murder. This is not the kind of thing a lady becomes involved with."

"Then call me improper. I keep telling you I was drawn into this the afternoon I found him in my garden. Say whatever you will, I don't intend to bow out of this now."

That she argued with him no longer surprised him, but what she said did. "That's the first time you've admitted he wasn't dead the first time you found him."

"Really?" She smiled impishly. "I thought that was

assumed when we saw him walk into the room at Lord Gleningwold's party."

Daniel placed his champagne glass on the table beside her untouched punch. He had to fold his arms across his chest to keep from pulling her in his arms and kissing her. Everything she said made him want her more.

"You are enjoying this search for Throckmorten's killer, aren't you?"

"The suspense and finding the clues, very much so. I'm truly sorry Mr. Throckmorten is dead, but everything that has happened since we found him has been fascinating. I feel like I am helping to put together a large puzzle of events."

"Tell me, what are you going to do with the handkerchief?"

"The same thing you will or have done with the journal. Study it. I'll sit down and make a list of all the ladies I know who have the same initials as the ones on the handkerchief. I'll compare them to the ladies who were in attendance at Lord Gleningwold's party. From there I will research the ladies and try to establish a connection to the deceased."

Daniel was silent for a moment as he digested what she said. From the determined expression on her face, he could see she was fully committed to what she'd just proposed. Daniel was once again drawn to her inner strength, her adventurous spirit, and her open-mindedness. How had a quiet girl from the country become so enchanting?

He stepped a bit closer to her and softly asked, "And will you share that list with me when you have it, Isabella?"

"That depends, my lord."

She made everything a challenge, and though it was inexplicable to him, he loved it. He not only found her exciting and enterprising, he enjoyed spending time with her and trying to outwit her.

"On what?"

Her voice was breathy as she said, "Whether you share your list from the journal with me."

He smiled and then chuckled. They were back in business together.

He chuckled lightly and took a step back. "I suppose I'll have to."

"Don't make it sound so dreary."

"Nothing involving you could ever be dreary."

Daniel looked down into her eyes and yearned to hold her. He wanted to taste the sweetness in her mouth. He wanted to feel the warmth of her skin beneath his hands. He wanted to caress her cheek, kiss her lips, and fondle her breasts. He wanted to explore every intimate part of her.

Daniel cleared his throat and whispered, "You are bright as sunshine and tempting as a glass of the finest brandy."

"I think that is the nicest compliment you have paid me. Thank you. So, shall we meet in a day or two and compare notes?"

How could he wait that long to see her again when he was already remembering how perfectly their bodies fit together when he'd held her in his arms and how sweet the depths of her mouth when he plundered it with his tongue? How she had desired him as much as he wanted her?

"I'll send a note letting you know when I will pick you up for an afternoon ride in the park so we can compare notes."

"I will look forward to that. Now, perhaps we should bid each other good evening. We've been standing here so long, it looks as if everyone has left the room but us."

Daniel glanced around the refreshment room. He couldn't believe it. At the moment the room *was* empty of guests and servants.

"Maybe we should part," he said, "but we're not."

Without conscious thought, without really knowing what he was going to do or where he was going, Daniel grabbed Isabella's hand and pulled her through a nearby doorway.

Sixteen

DANIEL FOLLOWED THE DIMLY LIT HALLWAY TO THE END and darted into a room where trays of food were lined on tables waiting to be carried into the dining room. He knew there was a chance someone might see them, but right now that was a risk he was willing to take.

The next door he opened took them outside to a small open space. It was dark, secret, and welcoming. They walked down two steps to a stone terrace that was enclosed by a tall yew hedge. A pale shaft of lamplight filtered from inside the house through a small window lighting on a brief section of ground that looked like an herb garden.

Unable to wait, Daniel dipped his head low and covered Isabella's mouth with his. Her lips were supple, moist, and responsive to his burning hunger. Her warm body leaned into him, meeting him, letting him know that she wanted this, too.

For a moment he let his mouth devour hers, relishing the feel of her lips against his. He sucked her sweetness with fervor before finally lifting his head so that he could look into her lovely face. Starlight

glistened brightly in her eyes, making her more beautiful than ever. Her lips were full, lush, and a tempting
rose-colored pink.

He whispered, "If you don't want this, now is the
time to tell me."

Without hesitating she said, "Does this answer
your question?"

She reached up and curled her arms around his
neck. She let her lips brush lazily, deliciously over his
for a moment before pulling his bottom lip gently into
her mouth, then letting it go.

Daniel's heart skipped a beat. He was enraptured
by her.

They both knew the danger, the price they would
pay if they were caught. But not even that fear could
force him to let go of her.

He had hoped to stay away from her. It would have
been better if he could have, but he couldn't deny the
gripping attraction, the inexplicable desire that he had
to be with her, to touch her, and to possess her. He
only knew that the time he spent alone with her was
worth any risk he had to take.

Daniel moved Isabella to the darkest area of the
garden and drew her into his arms, once again bringing
her softness against his hardness. Throughout the night
he had been sexually stimulated by her beauty, their
challenging banter, and his out-of-control craving to
be with her like this.

His hands tightened on her waist for a moment
before he let them slide up her side to the peaks of her
breasts, which he easily felt beneath the thin fabric of
her clothing. He looked deeply into her desire-bright

eyes as his hands fondled and massaged the fullness of her breasts.

Daniel slid his hands up her chest to lightly caress the base of her throat, and then he slipped her dress off the crest of her shoulders, exposing to his view more of her beautifully soft skin that glowed like alabaster when heated by candlelight.

"You enchant me, Isabella."

"That is good."

"Mmm. Your skin feels like satin." He gently rubbed the tops of her shoulders to keep her warm.

"I'm glad you think so, my lord."

Daniel let his fingertips creep up to her face. He cupped her cheeks between his hands as his lips once again found hers in a ravishing kiss that stole his breath. She sighed with pleasure and Daniel grew hard. His lips molded to hers with insistent pressure as the urgency of wanting built inside him.

As they kissed, the flick of his tongue once again moistened the silky inner surface of her lips. He explored the depth, the corners, and the top of her mouth enjoying every stroke, every taste, and every soft breath she took.

Isabella leaned into his embrace, pressing her body closer to his, letting him know that she didn't want him to let her go. He listened to the soft sounds of satisfaction that wafted past her lips as he awakened her to the sweet, fulfilling stirrings of womanly passion.

On a husky whisper he said into her mouth, "I've wanted to do this all evening."

"I thought you'd never find a way for us to be alone so you could kiss me again."

Daniel shuddered and the tightness in his groin grew, torturing him to madness.

"I don't know how I've denied us this pleasure."

"I don't know why you wanted to," she answered without her lips ever leaving his, and her body rose to meet his.

Daniel knew. It was wrong. Society said so, but right now he didn't care. He had Isabella in his arms. He wanted it. She wanted it. Right now that was all he intended to concentrate on.

Their breaths and lips met in a long hungry kiss that stirred already heated passions. He liked that she didn't shy away from his aggressiveness, but responded by matching him kiss for kiss, touch for touch.

His lips left hers, and he kissed the soft skin underneath her jawline and over to that soft sensitive spot behind her ear that he'd wanted so much to kiss and taste. His tongue stroked skin, and he felt her shiver with anticipation.

Daniel pressed his nose to the edge of her hair at her nape. She was warm. He breathed in the heady scent of fresh-washed hair and soap that clung to her. He gently blew his hot breath into her ear, and it thrilled him to hear her delicious gasps of enjoyment.

Daniel chuckled lightly. "Did that please you, Isabella?"

"Oh, yes. It gave me chills of pleasure, my lord."

A shiver of satisfaction coiled inside him. "Then I'm doing it right. Shall I do it again?"

"Yes, please don't stop."

"I don't intend to. Not yet. I need a few more kisses to see me through the night before I let you go."

Isabella arched her head back to give him access to wherever his lips wanted to go. He gently blew in her ear again and again while he ran his hands down her spine to her buttocks and back up again. With his tongue he left moist kisses up and down her neck and across her exposed chest and shoulders.

"I love the way you smell, the way you taste, and the way you respond to me as a woman should respond to a man."

"You have shown me how, Daniel."

"I know." Daniel's voice was so husky with desire he barely got the words out to finish what he wanted to say. "You are so desirable, Isabella, and you tempt me beyond my control."

"Is that a good thing, my lord?"

"Yes and no," he murmured.

Daniel moved his open hands down to the swell of her breasts beneath her dress. With eager fingers he slipped her dress farther down her arms, which exposed the front of her undergarments. He worked on the tiny buttons that ran down the front of her undergarment while his lips caressed her neck and shoulders with fervent kisses meant to keep their pleasure high.

He wanted her badly.

"Lift your breasts out of your corset for me," Daniel said, "and let me kiss them."

Isabella leaned away from him, not questioning him at all. He watched as her white gloved hand reached beneath her undergarments and gown and pulled out the most beautiful breasts he'd ever seen.

Daniel felt as if his heart tumbled over. Her nipples

were a tempting brownish-rose color. They were hard and pointing right at him. Her skin appeared as creamy as the finest alabaster.

He bent his head and quickly suckled first one and then the other, trying to keep both warm with his mouth while he pressed her soft womanhood against his hard, burning need.

Daniel wanted to feel the weight of her breasts but knew if he moved his hands, her softness would fall away from his throbbing shaft, so he settled for giving his attention to her breasts as she cupped his head to her chest and answered him with soft feminine sounds of pleasure that were a lover's delight.

He held her securely, possessively, thinking he would never let her go, wondering how he could get her skirt up and his trousers down.

"You are so responsive," he whispered hotly against her skin. "I'm so glad no man has touched you before now, before me."

"I've never wanted any man to touch me like this, Daniel. Only you," she answered. "I can't believe how I'm feeling. It's all so new. Just a few moments ago I was cold, and now I'm so hot I feel flushed."

Daniel listened to her heavy breathing and knew she was as caught up in their passion as he was. Sucking gently, he savored the exquisite taste of her breast while his hands continued to press her buttocks to his throbbing hardness.

A soft moan of pleasure wafted past his ear, and Daniel became more desperate to plunge inside her. He couldn't believe how she came alive under his touch, how much she enjoyed how he could make her feel. When he touched her he was powerless to bank the fires she'd started inside him.

They kissed and caressed over and over again, enjoying the taste, the feel of each other, relishing this time together. Daniel let his hands leave her backside and move to fondle and softly squeeze her breasts while his thumb skimmed the nipples, pushing him further and further over the edge.

He kissed her forehead, her eyes, and her lips with wild abandonment. All thought of where they were and who she was left his mind. He wanted her. Nothing else mattered.

He dragged his lips away from hers and frantically searched around him for a place to lie down so he could enter her and ease the hard excruciating ache in his loins. He saw nothing but the cold stone floor and the damp, leafy herb garden.

Through the fog of sensual desire, Daniel looked at his options, and then he took a deep aching breath and came to his senses.

Oh, bloody hell.

What was he doing? He couldn't treat Isabella this way. She wasn't a trollop to be taken in the kitchen garden.

His breathing labored, he pulled her tightly to his chest and whispered, "Isabella," softly, reverently.

Isabella cupped her hands to his buttocks, pressing him to her. "Oh, please don't stop, Daniel. You are making me feel so wonderful."

"I know and you don't know how much that pleases me."

"Then why stop?"

"No, Isabella, listen to me. We must. I am not going to finish this here in the garden where servants or any of the guests can stumble upon us. I can't do it."

"Why?"

He squeezed his eyes shut and rested his cheek against the top of her head while he calmed down from the heat, the exhilaration, the out-of-control passion that she ignited in him.

Damn his need for her that stole all his chivalry. Damn the weakness she created inside him.

He set her away from him. The look in her eyes, the expression on her face told him she didn't understand. He had to see that she did.

"Why? Because the only way I can finish what I've started is to back you against the wall and lift your skirts like you were a common harlot on the street. Do you want that?"

Her eyes rounded in shock.

Daniel didn't like talking to her that way, but he had to make her understand the gravity of what they had been doing.

"No. I didn't realize what would come next."

"I didn't think so."

"You were making me feel so wonderful, I didn't want it to stop."

"And I didn't, either."

He couldn't look at her. Instead he focused on her clothing and started rebuttoning her lace-trimmed shift. His fingers felt stiff and swollen as if he had all thumbs.

"I'll do it," she said and turned her back on him to finish arranging her clothing.

"We seem to have fallen into a dangerous pattern of being far too intimate."

"Yes, I think I now understand that some rules shouldn't be broken."

"That's right. We must stop this, Isabella, and stick to solving Throckmorten's murder. If I try to kiss you again, you should slap me."

She turned back to face him with a gasp on her lips. "That's what Auntie Pith told me to do if you should try to kiss me."

"She's obviously a wise woman. You should listen to her."

"I couldn't slap you for something I wanted, Daniel."

Except for her lips she didn't look as if they'd been so passionate. A bit of the lace from her corset was showing, and he tucked it inside her dress.

"You must. Isabella, we can't keep searching for dark corners to have a liaison. I need your help with this. If not we could end up ruining both our lives."

He saw that she took a deep breath and pondered what he'd said.

"No matter what you say to the contrary, I know you will marry someday. A passionate woman like you should be married."

"And of course, you are looking for a proper wife who can be your countess and give you children and nothing else. No love."

It seemed so hollow when she said it like that.

"No passion," she said.

No passion?

Yes, of course he wanted passion if he could find a wife who wanted it. Most titled men preferred that passion come from their mistresses, not their wives. That's not what Daniel wanted.

"I think I understand now, Daniel," she said. "I shall rebuff you should you desire to kiss me again."

Oh, I desire it all right.

"Yes, that is what you must do. And, Isabella, it would help if you gave me the handkerchief so that we would not need to see each other again."

"No, my lord. I couldn't do that. If you insist, I will give up my meetings alone with you, but I will not give up the intrigue."

"All right. I'll go inside first and make sure there's no one about to see you return."

Daniel retreated into the house feeling like the lowest scoundrel. He had been no gentleman. Isabella was not the kind of woman he expected to be drawn to. She was too open-minded. He needed a woman who would obey him and be a proper countess, not a woman who wanted to chase after a murderer.

Daniel opened the door and stepped into the dimly lit hallway. As the light from the oil lamp struck him, so did another light dawn on him.

He'd made one hell of a mistake. He was falling in love with Isabella.

Seventeen

Maybe the most astonishing news is that Lord Colebrooke seems to have eyes for no young lady other than Miss Isabella Winslowe. The two of them seemed to take an unusually long time over the buffet table at a soiree last night. Rumor has it that if they had spent any longer in the refreshment room they would have had to apply for a special license to wed!

—Lord Truefitt, *Society's Daily Column*

DANIEL LAID THE TITTLE-TATTLE SHEET ASIDE AND picked up his cup of tea. "Rubbish. All of it."

"For sure?" Chilton asked, looking at him from across the large dining room table as they lingered over their morning meal. "You looked rather smitten by Miss Winslowe when I saw you with her in the refreshment room last night."

Chilton was handsomely and expertly dressed for the day in a loden green jacket and gold striped waistcoat while Daniel had remained more relaxed with his collar and neckcloth loose. He saw no need to finish his dressing until just before he planned to go out.

Daniel pushed aside the remains of his eggs, cheese, and toast. "Not you, too. Miss Winslowe and I would never suit. She's too—" Daniel stopped abruptly.

Why wouldn't they suit? The lady was headstrong, but he didn't mind that. Her free thinking and adventurous attitude didn't bother him, either, but those weren't the things an earl needed in a wife. He needed a woman who wanted to make a home and have children. Isabella wanted her Wallflowers Society, intrigue, and mischief.

"Too what?" Chilton asked.

Daniel picked up his cup and sipped his coffee. "Too perplexing," he finally said. And she was.

"Perplexing? Is that the best you can come up with? Damnation, Danny, every woman is perplexing. Name me one who isn't."

No, not like Isabella. He could also add that she was intelligent and capable and not easily frightened, but he didn't want to share that with his friend.

Daniel glanced over his cup at Chilton's stricken features and chuckled.

"Perhaps I meant to say I need a wife who will be submissive and obedient, and those are two things Miss Winslowe will never be."

"You think this because she wouldn't relinquish her handkerchief to you?"

Daniel remembered how clever Isabella had been concerning the handkerchief, but he had to be careful. Thoughts of last night would lead him to remember how delicious she felt in his arms, and he had to forget those things about her.

"Just take my word for it that she would not make me a good wife, and leave it at that."

"Ah, yes, I guess an earl would need a wife to be submissive to him. Well, if you want a wife like that, there are plenty to choose from."

Somehow a wife like that didn't sound so appealing when Chilton said it.

"Who else have you pursued?" his friend asked.

"No one, but I plan to remedy that starting today. I will take Lady Katherine Spearmont riding in the park this afternoon and escort Miss Alice Eldridge tomorrow afternoon. And I have decided to dance with at least a dozen different ladies tonight."

"Will Miss Winslowe understand that?"

"Yes, she and I have a perfect understanding of each other."

"That's a rather bold statement."

"I wouldn't have said it if I didn't believe it to be true. I'm turning my attention to finding a husband for Gretchen, myself a wife, and I want to get better acquainted with other titled gentlemen in Town."

"That is after all why you returned to London, isn't it?"

"Yes."

"It appears you've settled into the house here in St. James without any trouble."

"All has gone well. I prefer the house in Mayfair, but this house is big enough."

"How is Gretchen?"

"Good. Thomas Wright is calling on her today, and I'm hoping that she will decide that he will make her an excellent husband."

Daniel watched Chilton closely. It seemed a bit far-fetched, but Daniel couldn't help but wonder if

Gretchen was the lady Isabella said Chilton watched but never approached. His friend's expression didn't change, giving no indication he harbored any unrequited feelings for Gretchen.

Perhaps he should just come clean and ask Chilton what he was doing in Throckmorten's house. They had been close friends for years, but Daniel was hesitant to pry into Chilton's private affairs.

Daniel sipped his coffee again. "How long have we been friends now, Chilton, fifteen years?"

"Longer."

"Have you ever lied to me?"

Chilton's eyes narrowed as he popped a piece of toast into his mouth and chewed.

Finally he answered. "Probably. Yes. But what kind of question is that to ask your best friend?"

"I need the truth from you about something important, Chilton."

Chilton cleared his throat and pushed his empty plate aside. "This sounds serious."

"It is."

"Then ask me."

"Why were you visiting Throckmorten the day before his death?"

Chilton's eyes widened. "You saw me leave his house, didn't you?"

"No, but your card was there." Daniel didn't want to say he'd seen the card when he hadn't.

"So you were there, too."

"Yes."

Chilton remained cautious. "When we were riding, I asked if you had seen him and you said no."

"I didn't," Daniel said. "He wasn't home when I got there. Your card was lying in a crystal dish along with a few others."

Chilton shifted uncomfortably in his chair and then wiped his mouth with his napkin. "All right, so I went to see him, too. He wasn't home when I got there, either. His man didn't know when he would return."

"Why did you visit him?"

"You ask a lot, my friend."

"I really need to know."

"Why?" Chilton asked.

"It has to do with Gretchen."

Chilton's eyes narrowed and his expression turned grim. "Why? Tell me more? Did he accost her or hurt her?"

"I don't think so, but she did arrange to meet him secretly."

"Are you sure he didn't harm her?"

"Quite sure. It was really a very short meeting between them, but I'm doing my best to see that bit of information doesn't get out."

"How does this involve me?"

Daniel rose from his chair and picked up the coffeepot from the sideboard and replenished their cups, then sat back down. "I'm trying to find out who might have had reason to kill Throckmorten."

"There should be plenty of those," Chilton muttered.

"Are you one of them, Chilton?"

Chilton's eyes turned cold and he remained very still as he said, "Yes."

Daniel sucked in a deep breath. He didn't want to ask but had to: "Did you?"

"No, but I can't say I was sorry that someone did the deed. In my opinion it was long overdue."

"What was your problem with him?"

Chilton pick up his cup and took a sip. "You don't need to know the reason. My dealings with the man can't help you."

"You don't know that."

Chilton set his cup down and chuckled derisively. He pushed his chair back from the table and made himself more comfortable in the chair.

"Oh, what the hell, I might as well tell you everything. I probably would have long ago had you not been gone for over a year."

Daniel waited patiently.

"I was seeing a married woman."

"When?"

"Over a year ago. We knew we were taking a great risk, but we took it anyway."

Daniel could relate to that.

"Unfortunately, one afternoon Throckmorten saw me leaving the house where she and I always met. He waited around and saw her leave. When he paid me a visit to tell me he knew about us, naturally I asked him not to say anything. He was more than happy to be discreet."

"Was he?"

"Oh, yes. For a price. I've been paying the devil for his silence for over a year."

"Damn. That was vulgar of him."

"Yes."

"Do you still see her?"

"No. It's been over since he saw us. I couldn't take the chance on anyone else seeing us. I couldn't do that to her. I realized the damage it would cause her wasn't worth the pleasure we shared."

"I'm sorry the dead bastard did that to you."

"At least now you know why I'm not saddened by his death. I do hope he suffered a bit before he drew his last breath."

Daniel believed Chilton, but if he didn't kill Throckmorten, who did?

Daniel noticed his valet standing just inside the doorway of the dining room.

"Yes, Parker."

"I'm sorry to disturb you, my lord, but Lord Gleningwold is here. He says he needs to speak to you right away."

He and Chilton looked at each other, but both remained silent.

"Very well, ask him to join us."

The short, rotund earl walked in with a smile on his ruddy face. The man was noted for his outlandish mode of dressing, and today proved no exception. He wore a bright red jacket that was styled similar to a military uniform with large gold buttons and fringe. His waistcoat was deep purple with wide pink stripes. Daniel had no doubt the man enjoyed the attention his attire always received.

Daniel and Chilton greeted the man warmly, and pleasantries were exchanged.

"We were just finishing. Would you like to join us?" Daniel asked him.

Lord Gleningwold looked over at the sideboard and saw the eggs, sliced pork, and toast. "Don't mind if I do."

While he helped himself to a serving of food,

Daniel motioned for Parker to pour the man a cup of coffee. Lord Gleningwold took a seat beside Daniel.

The men talked about the Lord Mayor and Parliament while the elder man polished off his eggs. He generously smothered the bread in his plate with cooked figs before biting into it with relish.

When he pushed his empty plate aside, Daniel said, "What can I do for you?"

"Oh, this." He reached into his jacket pocket and pulled out a lady's white glove.

Daniel's brows drew together in a frown. Somehow he knew it belonged to Gretchen but said, "I don't understand."

"It has initials in it, and they are the same as your sister's. Would you mind checking with her and seeing if it belongs to her?"

Did ladies have to put their initials in everything they owned?

"Yes, of course. If not, maybe she will know who it belongs to. How did you happen to come by it?"

"It was found in my garden. I assume she lost it at my party the other night. I can't think of another time she's been there recently."

"Yes, it could be hers. She walked in the garden with me and Miss Winslowe. I don't remember what she was wearing, but it's possible she lost it out of her reticule while searching for a handkerchief or dance card."

"Most likely. You didn't by any chance see anyone else when you were in the garden, did you?"

He tried to keep his voice nonchalant. "Yes, as it happens, we saw Lord and Lady Stonehurst and spent a few moments talking to them. Why?"

"Oh, it seems Mr. Throckmorten's brother is checking into his death. It appears the poor bloke was stabbed with a paper knife that came from my home."

"Really?" Daniel said, feigning surprise. "How do they know that?"

"Well, the damned thing has *my* initials on it. My wife puts them on everything. We suspect that someone followed him into the garden with the intentions of doing him harm and picked up the knife from my desk on the way out to kill him."

"But he was found in the Thames," Daniel argued to be safe.

"Obviously someone either killed him in my garden and moved him, or met him later and killed him with the stolen knife."

"I'll be sure to ask Gretchen if she saw anything unusual while we were in the garden."

"Do that. I've assured Mr. Throckmorten's brother that I had nothing to do with his murder. But he was calling on your sister, wasn't he?"

Daniel remained calm. "Throckmorten? No, he never called on her. I believe they had a dance or two, but that was all."

Lord Gleningwold planted his beefy palms on the table to help rise out of his chair. The cups rattled as he shook the table.

"Well, let me know what you find out from your sister. I'll need the glove back if it isn't hers."

"Of course."

"Don't bother to see me to the door. Finish your coffee. I'll see myself out."

Daniel motioned for Parker to follow Lord

Gleningwold to the front door. When he was sure the man had left the house, he turned to Chilton and said, "I've got to find out who killed that man before anyone else comes looking for Gretchen."

Daniel picked up the glove and walked out.

❧

Isabella looked at the group of ladies sitting in her parlor drinking their tea and chattering among themselves. Every one of them was special in their own way. It was difficult to think there might be a murderer among them.

Two of the ladies present had the first and last initials that were on the handkerchief she found in Lord Gleningwold's garden: Amanda Wright and Abigail Waterstone. Either girl would have been susceptible to Mr. Throckmorten's charms as easily as Gretchen had been.

What a nasty man he was to prey on the affections of unfortunate young ladies. It was no wonder someone wanted to kill him.

She needed to find out which of those ladies' middle initial was *L*. Perhaps neither would match, and she could move on to those outside her acquaintances. There were several married and widowed ladies who could have fallen prey to Mr. Throckmorten who had the same initials as those on the handkerchief.

Isabella would have liked to have time to think about Daniel and their time together, but perhaps it was just as well that she didn't. Whenever he crossed her mind, she forced herself to think of solving Mr. Throckmorten's murder, not kisses and caresses from Daniel.

The ladies would be leaving soon. Isabella needed to commence her plan.

She walked over to where a small writing desk stood near a window. "Ladies," she called for their attention and waited until they quieted and looked at her before she continued.

"I'm afraid it's time for you to go, but before you do, I have a request. I have a sheet of vellum and a quill on this table. As you pick up your coat and gloves, would you be so kind as to write your full name for me as you pass?"

"What for?" Lady Lynette asked.

"Auntie Pith and I are making a small gift for each of you, and I want to personalize them. If you would give me all three of your names."

"I have four names," one of the ladies said.

"It doesn't matter how many names you have. I would like for you to list them all."

The girls started lining up to write their names. "Isabella," Lady Lynette asked, "Is it true you are going to marry Lord Colebrooke?"

Isabella stared at her for a moment. "Merciful heavens! No, no, it isn't."

"So the tittle-tattle that's going around is wrong."

"As you know, Lynette, not everything that's written in the scandal sheets is correct."

"That's good, because Lady Katherine Spearmont told me Lord Colebrooke was taking her for a ride in the park today."

Isabella was not prepared for the pain that stabbed her heart upon hearing this information. She put on a brave smile. "I'm glad to hear it, Lynette. Maybe that will put to rest any notion that the earl and I are making a match. Now, come sign the paper."

Isabella turned away and took a deep, steadying breath. What was wrong with her? Why did it make her feel so dreadful to hear that Daniel was seeing another lady? She wondered if he would kiss Lady Katherine as he'd kissed her.

But of course he would. That's what men did. And why did that thought feel as if it were ripping open her chest? She had settled her mind long ago that she didn't want to marry. And even if she did, she knew there was no hope for her and Daniel. They were constantly at odds over things.

Suddenly it struck Isabella what the problem was. It was unthinkable, it was disastrous. It couldn't be, could it?

Isabella Winslowe was jealous of another woman.

Eighteen

DANIEL WALKED INTO WHITE'S AND WENT STRAIGHT into the taproom and asked for a glass of port. If Miss Alice Eldridge had batted her eyelashes at him one more time, he would have swatted at them like an insect!

He didn't know how anyone could talk so long without saying anything of value. What the devil did he care how well she could stitch a pillow or how many offers of marriage she'd already received?

One thing was certain, she wouldn't be receiving an offer from him. If he married her, he'd end up sending her to the country to live out her days while he stayed in Town and spent his nights in the arms of a mistress.

"That's not what I want out of a marriage," Daniel mumbled to himself.

He picked up his glass of dark red wine and took a generous sip, letting the strong drink settle on his tongue before swallowing. Why had every young lady he'd talked to, danced with, or ridden in the park with over the past three days fallen short when he compared them to Isabella?

Most of the ladies he'd called on were beautiful. Some of them had lovely, shapely bodies that would stir any man's fantasy, and still others had the right temperament to be a good wife. The problem was that not one had tempted him to kiss them as Isabella had.

Damn what he was feeling.

Why had she gotten under his skin like a hound after a fox? No matter which way he turned, he couldn't shake her.

It was maddening.

Isabella filled his waking thoughts and his dreaming nights. She was flirtatious and receptive. She was intelligent and knowledgeable. She was playful and provoking. But were those the kinds of attributes he needed in a wife? He hadn't thought so but lately he'd begun to doubt his earlier beliefs.

If wives were supposed to be like Miss Alice Eldridge and Miss Joanne Langley or even the more beautiful Lady Katherine, he was beginning to think he'd just as soon stay a bachelor. He was on the verge of saying to hell with marriage and let Bradford's son take over the title when the time came.

Daniel shook his head to clear it, and then rubbed his eyes with the pads of his fingers. There was no doubt that Isabella had distracted him since the first day he met her. He could safely say she'd turned his life upside down. And even though he'd tried, he'd been powerless to stop her.

Taking his glass in hand, he quit the taproom and walked over to the billiards room, hoping to find Bradford. He could usually be found playing a game of billiards or cards late in the afternoon. Daniel leaned a hip against the door frame as his eyes searched the crowded room for his cousin.

Daniel pushed the noise of chatter, laughing, and the loud smacking of balls together to the back of his mind. He had gone to Bradford's house three days ago to see him but had been told that his cousin had gone to Kent. He was expected back today. And Daniel knew his cousin well enough to know that if he had indeed returned today, he'd be in White's by the afternoon.

Daniel had wanted to talk to him since Lord Gleningwold had left that damned glove lying on the dining-room table. If he didn't find him at White's, Daniel would go to his home and wait for him to return if necessary.

Even though Daniel had hired a runner to look into Throckmorten's murder, he felt an eager restlessness that he needed to do more. Lord Gleningwold had a reason for bringing that glove over. He was making it clear he didn't intend to let Throckmorten's murder be blamed on anyone from his household even though the knife had come from his house.

Daniel was even more determined to see Gretchen wed. He didn't want to go through another Season wondering if she was meeting secretly with anyone. He'd talked with her about Tom Wright and Sir Harry Pepperfield. Either man would make her a fine husband.

A hand clamped on Daniel's shoulder and he jerked around.

Bradford chuckled with relish as Daniel faced him. "Easy there, old chap. I didn't mean to startle you," he said, a wide grin on his lips.

The only reason Daniel held his temper was that he had been looking for Bradford.

"I didn't hear you come up with all the noise coming from the tables."

Bradford shrugged his shoulders. "It looked to me as if you were in deep thought."

"You never could see very well."

"I guess it runs in the family. You jumped just like a man with a guilty conscience. Do you have one?"

"No. Do you?" Daniel asked, looking him over carefully.

Bradford was impeccably dressed in the latest fashion of waistcoat and neckcloth, as usual. And, for this first time since Daniel had been home, Bradford's eyes weren't shot with blood. The puffiness and dark circles were gone, too. For once he wasn't half-foxed.

"Not me. Guilt is something I don't have any use for. That's something only respectable men have to worry with. I heard you were looking for me while I was out of town."

Daniel said, "That's right. I was just about to check the wager book. Come with me and I'll buy you a drink."

Bradford eyed him warily. "You buy me a drink? That's never happened before."

"You should take me up on it. It may never happen again."

"If you're buying, I'm drinking. Let's go."

After checking on their wagers and settling then-bets, Daniel and Bradford made their way into the taproom and sat down at a table. Bradford was served a tankard of ale, and he took a generous swallow.

Not wanting to get right to the point and put Bradford on the defensive, Daniel first took the time to ask about Bradford's son and the latest trouble the Lord Mayor was in with some members of Parliament.

After a few minutes he finally said to Bradford, "Have you heard the latest about Throckmorten's murder?"

Bradford nodded. "Yes. Remember I was with you when Chilton told us he'd been stabbed."

Daniel watched his cousin's face closely for any sign that might give Daniel reason to suspect him of the murder.

"There's been more about it since you've been out of Town."

"What?"

"They discovered that the knife came from Lord Gleningwold's house."

"You don't say? I read the *Times*. I must have missed it."

"I'm not sure it's hit the streets yet. Lord Gleningwold told me. He confirmed it was the knife he used to cut the wax from letters."

"How would a footpad have gotten hold of Gleningwold's paper knife?"

"That's one of the unanswered questions."

A frown drew Bradford's brows together. "Is Gleningwold suspected of killing Throckmorten?"

"No, I don't think so."

"Wait a minute. Throckmorten was at Gleningwold's party. Now that I think about it, that was the last time I saw him."

Daniel continued to study Bradford's face as he talked. If he had anything to do with Throckmorten's death, he was a good actor. He showed no signs of knowing anything Daniel was telling him. He didn't appear nervous or even uncomfortable talking about this, and his hand was completely steady as he picked up the heavy tankard to take a drink.

Bradford sat back in his chair and started looking at Daniel's face as closely as Daniel searched his. "Are you telling me the authorities think someone who was at Gleningwold's party took the knife and stabbed Throckmorten and dumped his body in the river?"

"I'm sure that must be one of the assumptions, yes."

"That was very clever of the murderer, wasn't it? Using a weapon from another man's house."

Daniel nodded. Bradford picked up his ale and drank. Again, his hand was steady. This conversation wasn't bothering him at all. Was that because he was completely innocent or because he didn't give a damn about the man's death and, as he had stated earlier, felt no guilt?

"Were you good friends with Throckmorten?"

Bradford set his tankard back down. "We got along well together, if that's what you want to know. We covered each other's back in games, lent each other money. Yes, you could say we were good friends."

"Did you owe him any money when he died?"

Bradford looked quietly at him for so long Daniel didn't think he was going to answer the question.

Finally his face relaxed and he said, "Yes. I owed him a lot of money when he died, but he knew he would get every dime of it back. I always pay my debts."

"I'm sure you do."

"And I sure as hell wouldn't kill a friend over a few hundred pounds."

"I didn't think you had," Daniel said and picked up his glass of port, feeling confident that his cousin had nothing to do with Throckmorten's death.

"Why are you so interested in Throckmorten?" Bradford asked.

Daniel said, "I was just thinking what a shame it was that someone killed him."

*

The afternoon sky was a wide expanse of pale blue streaked with wispy white clouds. Bright sunshine fell on Isabella. Knowing it wasn't the fashionable thing to do, she'd taken off her bonnet and lifted her face up to the bright sky to feel the warming rays of the sun on her skin.

She sat on a bench in the back garden pretending to read a book of poetry, but the only thing that had seen the pages was the glare of the sun. The book was a good cover for her. She certainly couldn't tell Auntie Pith that she was thinking about Daniel and how handsome he'd been last night dancing with Lady Katherine. Nor could she tell her aunt how much she wished she had been the woman in Daniel's arms.

Isabella had caught Daniel's eye a few times throughout the evening, but they hadn't spoken to each other. That's the way Daniel had wanted it. He had told her he would send word to her when he was ready to talk to her about Mr. Throckmorten's murder, but so far there had been only silence from him.

Isabella's throat tightened when she remembered how positively happy Daniel and Lady Katherine looked as they joined hands and followed the steps of the quadrille. She had seen them together at more than one party over the past three days, and she knew they had gone for another ride in the park again yesterday afternoon.

She hated herself for doing it, but she couldn't help but wonder if he had kissed Lady Katherine or any of the ladies he'd called on the way he had kissed her. The very idea of Daniel kissing the duke's daughter with such uncontrollable passion made Isabella's stomach twist into tight knots.

Suddenly the sun had her hot.

Isabella picked up her book and fanned with it. She must get hold of herself and be practical about this. Of all the ladies Isabella had seen Daniel dance with, Lady Katherine would be the best choice for him. She would be the perfect wife, a fine lady wife indeed.

The duke's daughter was beautiful and proper to a fault. She would know how to manage a large house and all the servants. She'd know how to give elegant parties. She would be quiet and dutiful, and never open her mouth to question his authority on anything. And the very ladylike Lady Katherine would probably faint if she ever saw a dead body.

Yes, Daniel would be very happy with a wife like the prim Lady Katherine.

Isabella had gone home with that horrible sinking feeling in her stomach that made her lonely, the way she had felt when she was growing up, living in the country with her parents. She never had that feeling when she was with Daniel.

She remembered how quiet the house always was, and Isabella knew she never wanted to live like that again. She wanted to be with people who were talking and laughing. She wanted to hear the sounds of the streets of London.

Maybe Daniel had been right when he said she needed a husband. She had loved it when he held her in his arms and kissed her so fervently. She hated to think she might never experience those wonderful sensations again. But she also had her doubts that anyone other than Daniel could make her feel that way.

Perhaps Daniel and Auntie Pith knew her better than she knew herself. Maybe she wasn't meant to be a spinster like her aunt, but on the other hand, she knew she would never be a quiet, retiring wife, either. If she decided to marry, it would have to be to a man who would allow her some independence to be the woman she'd become.

Isabella took a deep sighing breath and looked down at the book in her lap. She wouldn't think about Daniel any more today. It made her too melancholy, and she didn't like feeling that way. She would concentrate on Mr. Throckmorten's murderer. Now, that was worth pondering.

The back door to the house opened, and Isabella looked behind her. Auntie Pith and Daniel were walking down the steps. There was a big I-told-you-so smile on her aunt's lips. Isabella rose from the bench, holding tightly to the book. Her heart started beating faster and her stomach quaked.

"Isabella, dear, look who is here. It's Lord Colebrooke to see you."

Isabella's heart felt as light as butterfly wings, her melancholy disappeared. So much for deciding she wouldn't think about him any more. Daniel was positively dashing in his dark blue morning coat, biscuit-colored waistcoat, and perfectly tied snow-white neckcloth. A gentle breeze blew just enough of his dark hair away from his forehead to be attractive. She couldn't help but smile when she looked at him. Just seeing him filled her with happiness. But she wasn't going to let him know that.

"Lord Colebrooke, I'm surprised to see you."

But delighted.

"Good afternoon, Miss Winslowe."

Isabella purposefully put a questioning expression on her face. "Did I forget you were coming by today, my lord?"

He gave her an enchanting half smile as his gaze swept up and down her face. "No, Miss Winslowe, I'm afraid I stopped by on the off chance you might be available to see me."

"And she is," Auntie Pith spoke for Isabella. "Isn't that right? You don't mind if he interrupts your reading, do you, dearest?"

"Of course not, Auntie. Could we offer you refreshment, my lord?"

"No, thank you, but perhaps, with your aunt's permission, we could take a walk around the garden."

"What a perfect gentleman you are to ask for permission," Isabella said in an overly sweet tone.

Daniel cleared his throat. "I do try to obey the rules sometimes, Miss Winslowe."

"Yes, I'm familiar with how hard you try to obey them, my lord."

"Oh, botheration, Isabella," Auntie Pith said,

clearly annoyed and clearly not understanding the tête-à-tête going on between the two. "Certainly she can take a stroll with you, Lord Colebrooke."

Daniel bowed to her aunt and said, "Thank you."

"I'll just sit here on the bench and read from Isabella's poetry book." She reached and took the book from Isabella's hand and replaced it with Isabella's bonnet. "Put this back on, dearie. You don't want the sun on your face. Now, you two go ahead and enjoy looking at the flowers. Take your time. It's not late and we have no reason to rush."

As they turned away from Auntie Pith and started their stroll, Daniel asked, "Did you enjoy the parties you attended last night?"

"Immensely, my lord," Isabella said as she placed her bonnet on her head but didn't bother to tie the ribbons. "I don't know when I've enjoyed myself more. I danced until my feet hurt."

"I noticed."

"Really?" she asked, throwing a doubtful glance his way.

"Yes."

"How could you? When I saw you, you were on the dance floor with the beautiful Lady Katherine, looking dreamily into her eyes."

He looked over at her with raised eyebrows. "Dreamily? What kind of word is that?"

"The kind that puts sparkles in your eyes and sweet words upon your lips. The kind that charms and enchants every young lady you meet."

Daniel laughed. "You exaggerate, Miss Winslowe."

"Do I?" she questioned.

"Yes. Careful, Miss Winslowe, I think I detect a note of jealousy in your tone."

Isabella huffed. "You most certainly do not, sir. I am merely making pointless conversation until we get far enough away that Auntie Pith can't hear what we say to each other."

"Ah, I should have known you would have a good reason for making such bold statements."

London had been blessed with several days of sunshine, and Isabella was quite comfortable in her long-sleeved dress of bone-white lawn and matching lightweight pelisse. The spring had been so cold there were few flowers in bloom, but the shrubs and yew were full of new growth.

"I assume your dancing with Lady Katherine twice last night put a stop to anyone thinking we were about to announce our engagement."

"I haven't heard the latest tittle-tattle, but I would assume so, yes."

"Good," Isabella said, realizing she didn't like his answer.

She turned back to look at her aunt and had no doubt that her aunt was pretending to read the poetry book as surely as Isabella had been pretending to read it before Daniel arrived.

"Do you think we are far enough away that she can't hear us?" Isabella asked.

Daniel glanced back to Auntie Pith, and then nodded. "I think we're safe."

"Do you plan to ask Lady Katherine to marry you?"

He looked confused for a moment but finally said, "That's not what I came here to talk about."

"Did you kiss her the way you kissed me?"

Daniel coughed and cleared his throat. "Isabella, you can't ask me anything like that."

"Why not?"

"Because it's not the proper thing to ask for one reason, and the other is that it simply isn't any of your business what goes on between other people."

"But I only wanted to know if you shared with her the same passionate—"

"Isabella," he interrupted her. "I will not tell you anything about Lady Katherine or any other lady I happen to be with, just as I wouldn't tell anyone about anything you and I shared."

Isabella looked away from him for a moment before looking directly into his eyes again. "Yes. I suppose you are right. Keeping quiet about such intimate things is the proper thing to do."

"Most definitely."

"In that case, I suppose it wouldn't be proper for me to tell you anything about how Sir William Smith kisses."

Nineteen

THE SKIN AROUND DANIEL'S EYES CRINKLED AS HIS brows drew together in a deep frown. She was sure it was the first time she'd seen him angry. "You didn't let him kiss you, did you?"

Isabella folded her arms across her chest and lifted her chin as she spoke. "According to you, sir, we are not supposed to discuss things like that so I will remain quiet on the subject."

"Yes," he said tightly. "I think it's best that you don't tell me anything about it."

"All right," she said lightly. "Shall we proceed to the subject of poor Mr. Throckmorten?"

"Yes, that's a much safer topic. I need to know if you have discovered who the handkerchief belongs to."

"Why have you waited three days to come and ask me about it?"

"I've been busy."

"Oh, yes, I know. You've been very busy riding in the park with Miss Joanne Langley and taking Miss Alice Eldridge to Ganther's for ices."

"I have spent my time far more wisely than that, Isabella."

"Really?"

"Yes, I made some discreet inquiries to find out which Bow Street runner to solicit because I wanted the best. I've met with him twice to make sure he knows exactly what I want from him. I made another visit to Throckmorten's house and returned his journal without your help and without getting caught."

Her eyes lit with surprise. "I'm impressed."

"Frankly, so was I."

"How did you do it?"

"I watched the house and waited until I was sure the butler had gone out. I slipped in the back door and put it back where I'd found it."

Isabella smiled. "You are a man of many talents, Lord Colebrooke."

"That is one talent I don't want to use again."

He glanced over at her. "I've also talked with Chilton and Bradford and feel quite comfortable neither of them had anything to do with Throckmorten's death."

"If you believe they are innocent, I'll accept your instincts about them. I must say that you have been busy. You did all that and still you had time to escort Lady Katherine to the opera."

The frown Daniel had worn since she'd mentioned Sir William Smith faded from his forehead, and his dark eyes and his face relaxed.

He smiled at her. "Isabella, if you keep this up, I will be convinced you are jealous of Lady Katherine."

And all the other young ladies you dance with, smile at, and speak to!

That was the problem, she realized. As much as she hated to admit it, she *was* jealous. But she would never admit that to Daniel.

Instead she said, "Jealous? Don't be absurd."

Daniel locked his hands together behind his back as they continued their slow stroll of the perimeter of the garden. "Am I, Isabella?" he questioned.

"Completely," she stated firmly, knowing there wasn't a shred of truth in what she said. "I'm no more jealous of Lady Katherine than you are of Sir William. I'm merely trying to point out that Gretchen is still in jeopardy, and we must continue our search to find the killer."

"I know. That's why I had a long talk with my best friend and my cousin. But as I said, I'm convinced they had nothing to do with Throckmorten's death."

"If you are confident of that, then I will be too. Did Mr. Cummerford by chance tell you why he went to Mr. Throckmorten's house?"

"Yes, but unfortunately I'm not at liberty to tell you Chilton's personal story."

"Of course, I understand. Can you tell me if the reason has anything to do with the lady he watches?"

Daniel looked over at her. "This lady you see him watching, is there anything unusual about her?"

"No. She's lovely, friendly, and... married."

"You are very astute, Isabella."

"Thank you, my lord. I believe you've told me that before."

"I'll have to warn Chilton that he needs to be more careful."

"And what makes you believe there is no reason to suspect Mr. Turnbury?"

"I spoke with Bradford this afternoon, and I don't think he killed the man, either."

"Does he have a secret in his life, too?" she asked.

"I'm sure he has many, but I'm not privy to any of them. It was more that he acted so calm when we talked about the man and how he spoke about him. I think he considered Throckmorten a true friend and is sorry the man is dead."

"Oh, dear, it appears our list of suspects is growing shorter."

"Yes, but right now there's another more pressing matter that concerns me."

"And that is?"

"Lord Gleningwold came to my house and delivered something he found in his garden."

"What?"

"A glove that belonged to Gretchen."

Isabella stopped. "Oh, merciful heavens, how did she lose a glove in his garden? I don't understand, Daniel. We would have noticed if she hadn't been wearing one of her gloves that night."

"I questioned her about it. She wasn't wearing that glove. It was from an extra pair she had in her reticule. She said she keeps extras in case one gets soiled while she's eating. She thinks she must have dropped it when she was looking for her handkerchief. Thankfully, she didn't drop that, too."

"Daniel, do you think Lord Gleningwold suspects Gretchen?"

"I'll have to make sure he doesn't. The paper knife found in Throckmorten's chest had Lord Gleningwold's crest on it. Whoever stabbed him took the knife from Gleningwold's house."

"This is not good news."

"No. It was much better when everyone suspected a footpad had accosted him on the streets and done the evil deed. I'm hoping Lord Gleningwold is not putting two and two together and coming up with Gretchen. I told him she was in the garden with us and that we talked to Lord Stonehurst and his lady wife. He has to know that several of his guests walked through his gardens that night."

"But how many of them left something behind."

They started walking again. "I'm not aware of anyone other than Gretchen and the owner of the handkerchief you found. Speaking of which, what did you find out about the handkerchief?"

"If we don't count the married ladies and the widows who attended Lord Gleningwold's party, we have one young lady with the exact initials as the ones on the handkerchief."

"And she is?"

"Amanda Leanne Wright."

Daniel frowned. "Are you sure?"

"I had her write her complete name for me."

"She's so shy she won't even hold her head up when she speaks to you."

"I know. She is in my Reading Society, and I've been trying to get her to hold her head up and talk more. There are other ladies with the first initial of *A* and last of *W* that I can check on and find out if their middle initial is *L*, but all of them are either married or widowed. Before I do that, there's something else we need to consider."

"I know," Daniel said. "Amanda's brother was also at Lord Gleningwold's party."

"And he could have helped her remove the body from the garden."

Daniel nodded as he raked his hand down his chin. "But what possible motive could she have had to stab him?" he whispered angrily.

"Maybe Mr. Throckmorten was secretly courting her as he had been Gretchen. Perhaps he had promised to offer for her and decided not to. There are many reasons a woman can be upset with a man."

"But enough to kill him?"

"Oh, yes," Isabella said with a sweet smile. "Perhaps she was jealous."

Daniel looked at her with such a grim expression on his face that she had to laugh.

"Do you find this funny, Isabella?"

She tried to wipe the smile off her face. "No, of course not," she admitted, before realizing he was holding back a smile, too. It pleased her that he had seen the humor in her comment even if he wouldn't admit it.

"There is also the possibility that her brother killed Mr. Throckmorten. Perhaps Mr. Throckmorten was accosting Amanda and her brother stabbed him to save her."

"With a knife he just happened to pick up in the house before he went out into the garden?"

"That does seem a bit too convenient, doesn't it?" she admitted.

"He owed Throckmorten money, but compared to most men's debts, it was a small sum."

"Men have been killed over small sums before."

"I don't like even thinking about the possibility that Miss Wright or Tom might be mixed up in this in any way at all."

"Because you wanted him to offer for Gretchen's hand?"

"Because I consider him a good man. I merely hinted to him if he'd like to call on Gretchen I wouldn't object. And he has called on her. I can't say she's smitten, but that might happen."

"Yes, but I've also seen her watching Sir Harry Pepperfield."

"Watching him? Really? I know they've danced, and he called on her yesterday."

"What about Mr. Cummerford? She simply glows whenever he is around."

"Mmm. She's always adored Chilton. But she looks at him as another brother."

"You think so?"

"I'm sure of it."

The back door opened and Isabella watched Mrs. Dawson hand a letter to Auntie Pith, but Isabella didn't let that distract her from what she and Daniel were discussing.

"I tried talking to Amanda yesterday when she was here for our Reading Society. I mentioned Mr. Throckmorten's name, but she didn't say anything. She just excused herself."

"That's very different from the way Bradford and Chilton acted. They were quite comfortable talking about the man."

"What about the other men who are listed in Mr. Throckmorten's journal who were at Lord Gleningwold's party?"

"I'm letting the runner I hired check into the backgrounds of those men."

"Mmm."

"That sounds dangerous, Isabella."

"What?" she asked.

"Mmm. Usually means that you are up to something I don't want to be involved in."

"No. No." She shook her head. "No, but I was just thinking."

"I knew it. If you were thinking, that means you want to do something you shouldn't be doing."

"Nonsense."

"Isabella?"

She stopped as they neared her aunt. "Well, look how much we've already discovered by doing things we shouldn't be doing."

"And look at the risks we've taken to accomplish them."

"And not once have we gotten caught."

"Our luck is bound to run out."

She looked into his eyes. She truly loved being with him, talking to him, arguing her point with him. Did that mean she loved him? And what could she do about it if she did?

Softly she said, "I'm not unhappy about anything we've done, are you?"

His eyes seemed to float across her face as if he were memorizing it. "No, I can't say I am."

"So, do you want to hear my idea?"

He took a deep breath. "I might as well," he finally said.

"I think you should invite Mr. Wright, Amanda, and me over to your house for tea."

"Isabella, I can't invite you for tea. A bachelor asking a young lady for tea would be scandalous."

"You must keep your voice down." Isabella looked

over at her aunt, who looked as if she might actually be reading the letter that she'd received.

"It's dangerous, too. Do you realize I can hardly keep my hands off you as it is? If you were in my home, there's no telling what I might do."

Isabella knew Daniel was trying to frighten her, but his words had just the opposite effect. Her breathing increased rapidly, and she felt this wanting anticipation low in her stomach.

"Do you want to kiss me, Daniel?"

"Hell, yes, Isabella." Daniel looked away from her for a moment and then back again at her face. "You don't have to ask. You know I do. I'm glad your aunt is sitting out here with us so for once I can behave like a proper gentleman."

"But I love it when you are a rogue." Isabella smiled as warmth spread down her chest to her stomach and curled low and hot in her abdomen. "I'm glad you want to kiss me."

"I'm not. It's difficult enough as it is to restrain myself without you continuing to remind me how much I want to take you in my arms and—"

He didn't finish his sentence. He didn't need to. Isabella knew what he meant.

"We should go back to what we were discussing."

"Yes. I was saying it will be perfectly fine for me to be at your house with Amanda and Mr. Wright there. I assume you have a housekeeper, and your manservant will be there as well. And of course, I'll bring my maid. We'll make it work, Daniel."

"Maybe it would if I invite Gretchen and Aunt Mattie or if we had it at the house in Mayfair."

"Well, you could invite your aunt and sister, but I feel if there are too many people there, Mr. Wright and Amanda won't feel free to open up and talk to us about Mr. Throckmorten. I think it is best that we leave it as just the four of us."

"Even if I agreed to this, what could we say to them? We can't come right out and ask them if they had anything to do with killing the poor man."

"Of course not."

"But if we managed to gain their trust, one of them might open up to us. What we really want to do is eliminate them as suspects, as you have Mr. Cummerford and Mr. Turnbury."

"Why do I find it so hard to say no to you?"

Isabella smiled at him.

"All right, I'll be in touch later in the week."

Isabella and her aunt walked into the house with Daniel, where he was handed his hat, cloak, and gloves before taking his leave.

As soon as the door closed behind Daniel, Auntie Pith turned to Isabella and said, "Come sit in the parlor with me, Isabella. Mrs. Dawson will be bringing us in a cup of tea."

"All right, Auntie. A cup of tea sounds marvelous right now." She was so happy she would be seeing Daniel again.

After her aunt had settled herself in an upholstered wing chair and Isabella on the settee, her aunt smiled and said, "I told you Lord Colebrooke would be back to call on you, didn't I?"

"Yes, but, Auntie, you know he continues to see other young ladies as well."

Auntie Pith sighed and folded her hands in her lap. "But he always comes back to you. There is a reason for that, my dear."

Yes, there is a reason, but it's not what you think.

Isabella remained quiet because Mrs. Dawson walked in and placed the tea tray on the table between them. Auntie Pith dismissed the housekeeper and poured the steaming tea into delicate china cups with large yellow flowers painted on them.

She handed a cup to Isabella, and she sipped the hot liquid. There was nothing more soothing than a cup of tea after a rousing discussion with Daniel. Every conversation with him was stimulating and far more invigorating that any tonic she had ever taken.

"I have some news I think you will be happy about, Isabella," her aunt said as she relaxed with her cup in her hand.

"What's that, Auntie?" she asked, half listening.

"Did you happen to notice that I received a letter while you were talking to Lord Colebrooke?"

"Yes." Isabella sipped her tea again.

"It was from your father."

Isabella's hand stilled in midair. "And what did he say this time, Auntie? Is his son worse? Is his wife with child again? What excuse does he have now for not returning to London?"

"Actually, he has none. His letter states he will be here within the month."

Isabella's cup rattled as she placed it in the saucer. "You jest."

Auntie laughed softly. "No, my dear, I do not.

What you have hoped for is coming true. Your father is coming for you."

"To stay for the remainder of the Season?"

"Well, he didn't say those exact words, but I'm sure he is. He has been waiting for his son to be well enough to travel, and that has happened."

"Oh. It is wonderful to hear that his son is well. I'm glad about that."

"Why don't you seem happy?" Concerned, Auntie Pith placed the teacup on the table in front of her. "I thought you would be thrilled to see him again."

"I am. I will. I'm shocked. I just never thought it would happen." Isabella hesitated as a pressing weight settled on her chest. "You don't think he will want me to go back to the country with him, do you?"

"Well, I don't know. He didn't say anything about his plans, but no, I don't think so. I know what he wants is for you to wed."

"But you're not sure that he doesn't plan to take me with him?"

"Well, I can't be sure, Isabella. I haven't talked to him, but I would think he'd want to spend some time with you since he's been gone so long. And perhaps the country would be better for his son."

Leave Daniel? Leave London? The tea roiled in her stomach. She couldn't bear the thought of leaving either. What would she do? She wasn't twenty-one yet. Could she deny her father and stay with her aunt? Isabella set her cup on the tray and rose from the settee.

"I didn't expect this news to upset you."

She looked down at her aunt. "No, it hasn't upset

me," she fibbed. "If you don't mind, I just want to be alone and think about what this means."

Isabella walked to her room, closed the door, and leaned against it. If her father took her to the country, Daniel could be married before she returned. Suddenly tears filled her eyes, and that made her angry. She never cried and she wouldn't allow herself such an indulgence now.

She took a deep breath.

She would deny herself the tears and would make some plans.

Twenty

"You look surprised to see me."

"Somewhat," Daniel said as he walked into the parlor of his town house where Chilton waited for him in one of the wing chairs. "This really isn't a good time for you to stop by."

Chilton rose from the chair and looked around the room as if he expected to see what kept the moment from being a good time. "You're busy?" he asked.

Daniel hedged. "I will be soon."

"Oh, well, no problem. What I have to say won't take long."

Daniel hoped not. He was expecting Isabella and Thomas and Amanda Wright within a matter of minutes. Daniel didn't want to explain their visit to Chilton. It would be difficult enough if any members of the *ton* got wind of this afternoon tea.

He was playing with fire again, but it seemed that was all he had done since he first met Isabella. The strange thing to him was that he really didn't mind. The more time he spent with her, the more he wanted to spend time with her.

"Can we talk about it later, Chilton? I'm in a bit of a rush to get some things done."

Chilton eyed him warily. "Are you all right? You seem restless."

"No, no. I'm fine."

"Good, because this really is important, it's about Gretchen."

Daniel tensed. Was it possible Chilton heard something about Gretchen and Throckmorten? "All right. Tell me."

"May I sit down?"

No. There's no time.

Daniel said, "Of course."

Chilton took one of the wing chairs in front of the settee and Daniel took the other. He tried to relax into the chair but found himself trying several different positions, unable to sit still while he waited for Chilton to speak.

"Are you sure you're all right?" Chilton glanced around the room again as if he expected to see someone or something that looked out of place. "You're acting rather strangely."

"Yes, I'm sure I'm fine," Daniel said, trying to keep his exasperation out of his voice. "What have you heard about Gretchen?"

"Heard? Nothing. Why? Is something wrong with her?"

"No. I thought you must have heard—Never mind about that. What did you want to say?"

"I really think I need a splash of brandy, Daniel."

"Is it that bad?"

"What?" Chilton asked.

"What you have to tell me about Gretchen."

"I don't think it's bad at all, but I have no idea what you will think. Offering me a brandy is usually the first thing you do when I come over, and the one time I really need it, you don't."

There's no time.

Holding on to his temper and his patience, Daniel rose and strode over to the sideboard. He took the top off the decanter and poured a spatter of brandy in a glass, barely covering the bottom. He didn't have time for his friend to kick back and relax with the fine brandy.

Daniel handed him the glass. "Just tell me what you have to say."

Chilton took the glass and looked at the undersized amount in the glass and then back at Daniel. Daniel remained quiet and took his seat and pretended not to notice.

Chilton downed the contents in one swallow and placed the glass on the barrel-shaped table that stood between the chairs.

Suddenly he rose from the chair and said, "I think I'd rather stand."

"Fine, we'll stand," Daniel said.

What he had to say must be really bad, Daniel thought. His stomach clenched. Why didn't Chilton just spit it out? Rising, he faced his friend and said, "Chilton, you are the one who is acting strange. Get on with the reason you came over here."

"I want to ask for Gretchen's hand."

"To do what?" Daniel quizzed him.

"To marry her."

Daniel's breathing halted in his throat, and he took

a step back. "Marry Gretchen? What do you mean, you want to marry her? I don't have time for this foolishness today, Chilton."

"This is no game. I'm asking for Gretchen's hand in marriage."

Daniel looked at his friend as if he'd lost his mind. Chilton was handsome, from a titled family, and he had a generous yearly income from his father that more than took care of his needs, and he looked serious.

"Why?"

"Damnation, Daniel, why do you think? She'll make me a good wife. You know I've always been quite fond of her."

"I know that," he said quickly. He was just too stunned to know what to say. "You've always treated her like a sister—not a wife."

"I've had no reason to treat her like a wife. She's just turned old enough to marry. Daniel, I know you must be thinking I haven't given this any thought."

"Well… I haven't had time to think anything, but yes that would cross my mind."

"I've been considering this since the first party of the Season. It was the first time I saw Gretchen as a woman, not as your little sister. She's become a charming and lovely young lady."

Daniel had noticed how lovely Gretchen was, but he'd never expected Chilton to be interested in her. He had been pushing Tom Wright and Harry Pepperfield, and he had considered a dozen other men who might be suitable for Gretchen. He had never once considered his best friend married to his sister.

"I don't know what to say."

"How about something appropriate."

There's no time.

But Daniel had to ask one more question. "What about the married lady you were involved with?"

"That's not what I had in mind, but it's a fair question. I told you it's been over between us for a year. I only continued to pay Throckmorten to protect her. I've been thinking about Gretchen since before you returned. I just hadn't made a decision. It's taken a while, but I've finally decided I need to get on with my life. I need to marry, and I can't think of anyone I would rather marry than Gretchen."

He'd been thinking about marrying Gretchen for weeks? "But what about love?"

Chilton smiled. "But you see, Daniel, I do love Gretchen. Maybe not with an all-consuming passion, but I know her, and I like who she is. I want to make her happy."

What more could Daniel ask for in a husband for his sister than that the man wanted to make her happy?

"I would like to call on her tomorrow and make my intentions known. I wanted to go with your permission and your blessings."

Daniel reached out and grabbed Chilton and hugged him, clapping him on the back several times before letting go of his friend. Daniel needed time to think this through, and time was what he didn't have right now.

"You sly fox! Of course, you have my permission and my blessings."

He put his arm around Chilton's shoulder and started walking with him to the door. "This is the best news I've had since returning home. Why don't we meet at White's later tonight after the parties and we'll share a bottle?"

"All right. I would like to know how you think Gretchen will react."

"No reason to worry about that. I know Gretchen will be pleased to have you call on her." Daniel stopped in the foyer and picked up Chilton's hat, cloak, and gloves and gave them to him.

"You really think so?"

He opened the front door and ushered him out. "I'm certain she's secretly loved you for years, Chilton, but she never thought she had a chance because of her poor sight."

"That's never bothered me. I've always told her to wear the spectacles so she can see where she's going."

Daniel clapped him on the shoulder again. "I'm really pleased about this, Chilton. I'll see you later in the evening."

Daniel felt relief that he was leaving, but he also felt happiness. Imagine his best friend wanting to marry Gretchen. Nothing would please Daniel more.

He watched Chilton bound into his carriage like a man well-pleased with his mission. Now he had more reason than ever to get the problem of Throckmorten's death cleared up as soon as possible.

As Chilton's carriage drove away, the Wrights' carriage pulled to a stop at the curb.

❧

The cakes and sandwiches were delicious and the blend of tea was rich and flavorful. Isabella was impressed with how well the afternoon had progressed.

She and Daniel sat in chairs that stood opposite the dark green brocade settee that held Thomas and Amanda Wright. The parlor was small and cozy. A fire burned in the fireplace and took the bite out of a day that was dreary with gray skies and a cool wind.

The conversation between the four had remained constant primarily because of Daniel talking to Mr. Wright about horses, Parliament, and their latest wagers at White's. Isabella had managed to keep a nervous-acting Amanda's interest by talking about books they'd read, embroidery, and the latest fashion.

But soon the cups were empty, and the conversations were winding down. It was time to broach the intended subject for the afternoon.

Isabella looked at Daniel, and he gave her a nod. She put her teacup aside. It was time to begin.

"Amanda, I have something you lost." From her pocket, Isabella pulled out the handkerchief that she found near where they had found Mr. Throckmorten's body.

Amanda's eyes lit with unconcealed surprise. She looked at her brother and gave him a smile of relief before taking the handkerchief.

"I'm so happy to have it back. It's the handkerchief my grandmother gave me." Relief washed down her face as she hugged it to her breast. "Thank you, Isabella."

"So it is yours?"

"Oh, yes. I didn't realize I'd left it at your house. I've been so worried." She looked back to her brother. "I—I thought I had lost it somewhere else."

"I didn't find it at my house, Amanda," Isabella said. "Where did you think you had lost it?"

"It doesn't matter now where she thought she lost it," Tom said, inserting himself into the conversation. "I know she's happy to have it back."

"It does matter, Tom," Daniel said, speaking up for the first time.

Mr. Wright swallowed hard. Amanda jerked her head around to her brother again. "That's right. I don't know where I lost it, do I, Tom?"

"No." Tom took hold of his sister's hand and squeezed it. "She had no idea where it could be when she told me it was missing."

He rose from the settee and pulled Amanda with him. Isabella and Daniel rose, too.

"I think you know exactly where she lost it," Isabella said. "And it's time you tell the authorities."

Anger flared in Mr. Wright's eyes. "That's an absurd statement, Miss Winslowe."

"Is it, Tom?" Daniel asked, taking a step closer to Isabella. "We don't think so. We believe Amanda knows exactly what happened to Throckmorten."

Amanda clutched the front of her brother's coat. Her eyes were wild with fear. "Tell them no, Tom, tell them I don't know what happened."

Mr. Wright took hold of her shoulders and gently shook her. "Amanda, calm down. Everything will be all right." He looked up at Daniel. "I must take her home. She doesn't know what she's saying."

"Tom, you need to let her tell us what happened to Boswell Throckmorten."

"Mr. Throckmorten?" Mr. Wright's eyes widened

and his gaze jumped from Isabella to Daniel. "Why did you mention him? We… I don't know what you mean. I have no idea how he was killed."

"We think you do," Isabella said. "We want to help you and Amanda, but you must tell us everything."

"We don't know what you're talking about. Now, excuse me. I have to take Amanda home."

Daniel blocked his way. "No. I can't let you leave until you tell us the truth about what happened in Lord Gleningwold's garden."

"What is this?" Anger twisted his face and his voice rose. "You had us over here on the pretext that you wanted to talk to me about your sister. And now all you want to do is make accusations. We won't stand here and be insulted."

Daniel remained firm. "We know Amanda was in Lord Gleningwold's garden with Throckmorten. Her handkerchief was found near his body. If you don't tell us what happened so we can help you, I'll have to go to the authorities, and you won't have my help."

Isabella looked into Amanda's frightened eyes. "You and your brother are going to need a good word from the Earl of Colebrooke."

"It was my fault," Amanda said, with tears streaming down her cheeks. "Tom was only trying to protect me."

"Amanda, be quiet."

"No. I can't. I won't." She jerked away from her brother. "It's my fault Mr. Throckmorten is dead. I stabbed him."

"Amanda, don't do this." He turned to Daniel. "That's not true. What she said is not true. She didn't stab him, I did."

"Let me tell them what happened," she said.

Mr. Wright turned angrily on his sister. "No. You don't have to do this. No one knows what happened."

"I do. I know that your life will be ruined if I don't tell the truth."

"My life be damned, Amanda. I don't care about it. It's you who must be safe."

"Tom," Daniel said calmly but firmly. "Let Amanda say what she wants to."

"I'm her guardian. It's my job to protect her even if it's from herself."

"I know that, and you have. But in this matter you must let her talk."

Tom took a loud sighing breath and lowered his head.

Amanda began, "Mr. Throckmorten asked me to dance two evenings in a row. I couldn't believe someone so handsome was interested in me. When he asked me to meet him secretly, I accepted because I thought he was going to announce that he loved me. I let him kiss me, but he never mentioned love or marriage. And he never asked me to dance again."

"Amanda, you don't have to do this. Please don't do this," her brother said again.

She paid him no mind but continued as if he hadn't spoken to her. "I saw him walking around Lord Gleningwold's party looking so debonair and smiling at everyone. I started following him. That's when I overheard him telling another gentleman that it was time to pay up his wager. I listened and realized that he had made a bet with the other man that he could get kisses from all the ladies who attended Miss Winslowe's Wallflowers Society."

Isabella gasped.

Amanda continued. "He was getting money for every one of us he kissed. I was horrified. I was sick to my stomach."

Isabella was sick to her stomach, too, just hearing what that awful man had done. He'd made a sport of coaxing young ladies into kissing him for money. No doubt Gretchen was one of his conquests.

Daniel moved closer to her. She felt his warmth and it comforted her.

Mr. Wright lowered his head and slowly shook it. "That's enough, Amanda."

Amanda turned to her brother. "No, I want to tell it all. I wanted to make him pay for treating us so badly. I looked down at the table beside me and there was a paper knife. I wanted to stab him in front of everyone so they would know what a horrible man he was. But he walked away before I could. I watched him stop and speak to Gretchen, and then I followed him out into the garden."

"That's where I come in," Mr. Wright said, picking up the story. "A friend told me he saw Amanda walk into the garden alone. I hurried after her and found her struggling with Throckmorten. At first I thought he was accosting her, but then I realized they were fighting over a knife."

"Sweet mercies!" Isabella whispered.

"I pushed her aside and took up her fight. I only wanted to take the knife from him, but he kept stabbing it toward my chest. I turned the knife away from me, and it just seemed to sink down into his chest. I didn't mean to kill him. I just saw him and Amanda struggling with the knife."

"I believe you," Daniel said.

"We were trying to decide what to do when we heard Gretchen calling his name. There was no time to do anything other than hide behind a large shrub. We were still there when you and Miss Winslowe joined her."

"How did you get his body out of the garden?" Daniel asked.

"When the three of you left, I picked him up and pulled his coat around the knife and dragged him out a side gate to my carriage. All the footmen were huddled around a fire laughing and talking. I don't think anyone saw me."

"I'm the one who wanted to hurt him," Amanda said. "Not Tom. He thought Mr. Throckmorten was trying to kill me with the knife. He can't be blamed for this."

"It will be up to the authorities to decide that, but it sounds as if it was an accident to me."

"It was, my lord," Mr. Wright said earnestly. "I didn't mean to kill him. I didn't want to hurt him at all. All I saw was my sister struggling with a man who had a knife. I only wanted to save her."

"You must tell the authorities what happened."

"I can't. There is no one else to take care of Amanda but me. Don't make me do this."

"I'll speak to them on your behalf. I'm sure they will listen to a kind word from me. And in return for my assistance, I want your word that you will never breathe a word about Gretchen following Throckmorten into that garden."

"I would never bring her name into this. You have it. Thank you, my lord."

Daniel nodded. "Now take your sister home. I'll speak on your behalf tomorrow."

Tom looked back at him. "I suppose this ends my intentions toward Gretchen."

"Yes," Daniel said without hesitation.

He went to the doorway and called to his servant. He told him to show Mr. and Miss Wright out.

After they left, he turned to Isabella. They smiled at each other. The crises were over. Mr. Throckmorten's murder was solved. Daniel had saved Gretchen's reputation. Isabella felt as if a weight had been lifted off her shoulders.

Now Isabella could concentrate on Daniel, and she had made her plans and knew exactly what she wanted to do.

She said, "Can you believe how close we came to figuring out exactly what happened?"

"We were very close, but we didn't figure out the wager about kissing the girls in your Reading Society."

"Thank you for not calling them Wallflowers. They are not. I'm appalled they were ever called that. All of them are special young ladies to me."

"You're right, Isabella. They are. And I think it's wonderful you help them."

"I never thought my association with them might lead someone to do what Mr. Throckmorten did. What a tragedy that it led to his death."

"Your group of ladies had nothing to do with that. It was Throckmorten's own illicit games for money that got him killed."

Isabella looked at Daniel standing so tall and so powerful beside her. She had a great desire to be circled in his embrace and to rest her head against his strong shoulder.

Over the last few days she had become acutely aware of how deeply Daniel had affected her life. She loved arguing with him, kissing him, and laughing with him. She had even found excitement in being jealous of him. She loved the way he tried to be so honorable and how she had thwarted him at every turn. There wasn't anything about him she didn't love.

Yes, love. She loved him.

That was very easy to admit to herself, but how could she make such a confession to Daniel? She had thought about it and decided the best way to let him know that she loved him was to show him.

And the way to do that was to give herself to him. She had no doubts that she had fallen in love with him, no doubts about what she wanted to do. No doubts she would be doing the right thing.

If her father returned and insisted she return to the country with him, this could be her only chance to be with Daniel. She was not going to spend the rest of her life thinking about having missed this opportunity. Daniel was too important to her.

"You've been here a long time," Daniel said. "We should get your maid and send you on your way."

She stood very close to him. "In a few minutes. I want a little time alone with you."

Daniel's eyes searched hers. "That's not a good idea, Isabella."

"Why?"

"Must you always challenge me?"

She smiled, feeling calm and wonderful inside. "Yes."

"All right, then. Because when we are alone together, we do things we shouldn't do."

"I know. That's exactly what I have in mind."

Her heart was overflowing with love for him. She knew he wanted to save her from himself, but that's not what she wanted.

Isabella wanted Daniel.

Daniel was too much of a gentleman to come to her so she had to go to him. She understood his reluctance and she appreciated it. He prided himself on doing what was right in all areas of his life.

"Isabella, we'll talk later. Now go out that door."

She turned and walked to the parlor door, but instead of walking out it, she closed it and turned the key to lock it before facing Daniel again.

"What are you doing?" he asked.

Slowly she started walking toward him. Her maid waited outside with her carriage. Daniel's servants were in the house. Isabella chose to go against all she had been taught for one afternoon of Daniel's loving.

"Why did I ask that? You obviously don't know what you are doing or you wouldn't be doing it."

She knew he was trying to make light of the moment, trying to turn her mind away from what she knew she wanted.

Isabella stopped in front of him and said, "You're wrong, Daniel. I know exactly what I'm doing. I want to kiss you."

She saw by the look in his eyes that he studied over his answer before saying, "No. Kisses between us lead places I don't think you want to go."

"You're wrong. I do want to go. And I want you to take me."

Twenty-one

"As much as I would like to accommodate you, Isabella, I can't."

His voice sounded serious. His eyes flashed a warning for her not to tread further with this subject, but confident in how she felt and what she wanted, Isabella ignored him and said, "Tell me that you don't want me to stay here with you."

"I can't because that's not true. I ache for you. You know that."

She took a step closer to him. "Then why deny me? Why deny what we both want?"

"Because there are some rules I can't be persuaded to break, and making love to a proper young lady is one of them."

Isabella reached up and gently pulled on his neckcloth. The bow unraveled in her hands. "And what about my wishes? Don't they matter?"

"Yes. I've taken them under advisement and come to the conclusion you don't realize how serious it will be if you stay here any longer."

She placed her palm on the side of his face. She felt

the faint stubble of beard on his skin. Her heart filled with love and desire. She leaned over and kissed him, softly, briefly on the lips but long enough to send a bolt of longing striking through her like searing heat.

Daniel drew a ragged breath, and she saw in his eyes that he wanted her as much as she wanted him.

"You've broken rules for me before," she said softly. "Do you regret that?"

"I don't regret anything we've done."

"Then indulge me one last time."

He placed his fingertips under her chin and tilted her head back a little farther. "Maybe there is one way I could be persuaded to again, but when a gentleman makes love to a proper young lady, breaking that rule comes with a price."

Wanting ran hot inside Isabella. "I will pay any price for an hour in your arms."

His hands slid around her waist, and he pulled her to him. He looked deeply into her eyes. "Are you sure?"

Isabella's heart pounded, but she didn't hesitate as she said, "Yes."

"You are so tempting, Isabella." His voice was a little husky and a little demanding. "More so than any other woman I've met. Let me have your word."

Isabella knew that young ladies who had liaisons with men were ostracized from Society. She would be giving up a lot if that should be what he asked of her, but the way she was feeling right now, she knew she had to take the chance he wouldn't ask anything so devastating of her.

The first time he'd kissed her, a flame of desire had ignited inside her. She had been waiting for this time with him. She loved Daniel enough to give up whatever he asked of her.

"I promise."

Daniel's mouth came down ravishingly on hers in a searing kiss that had been waiting much too long to be delivered. His lips were warm, soft, and moved possessively, demandingly across hers as his arms circled her back and pulled her tightly against his chest.

Isabella parted her lips and accepted his tongue in answer to his burning ardor. His caressing tongue thrust forward into the depths of her mouth, torturing her again and again. Isabella gasped with surprise, with pleasure at the tingling feeling that ran through her. She'd been hungry for the taste of him, and he was being generous.

She put her eagerness and her heart into the kiss. She slid her arms around his neck as she settled into the blazing heat of his embrace. This is what she'd been waiting for.

The hot, potent kiss fueled her already burgeoning desire to experience all he could show her. The warmth of his arms, the passion of his kiss, created an undeniable yearning inside her to demand his loving.

He smelled of soap, clean and fresh. He tasted of flavorful tea and sweet cakes. She felt his strength in his arms and his hands as he caressed her back and shoulders. She delighted in the faint tremor of passion she felt in his body. She knew that he wanted to touch her as much as she wanted him to. That filled her with happiness and a strange sense of comfort.

"Isabella," he whispered as his lips left hers and he dotted her face with quick, moist kisses, "you have too much control over me."

"No, Daniel, you make me work for every indulgence you make."

Daniel moved his hands to the front of her dress and unbuttoned her pelisse. He stripped it from her shoulders and let it drop to the floor. Isabella's hands found the ends of his neckcloth and she pulled it from around his neck along with his collar, letting them both drop to the floor around their feet.

Daniel looked down at the small settee in front of the tea table. Suddenly he turned and looked behind him at the larger Sheraton settee that stood against the back wall in a small alcove that was framed by green velvet draperies. He reached down and hooked one arm behind her knees and lifted her into his arms, as if she weighed no more than a quill. With long fluid steps he strode to the secluded settee and laid her down on it.

He sat beside her and quickly took off his Hessians before turning back to her. He let his fingertips glide softly across her cheek, down her neck, over her collarbone to the swell of her breasts which showed from beneath the neckline of her dress. She trembled with delicious chills of longing.

"I like the way you look at me," she said.

"I love to look at you. You are so beautiful, Isabella."

She smiled up at him. "I'm glad my appearance pleases you."

He gazed deeply, passionately into her eyes. "You please me."

With warm confident hands he slipped her dress off her shoulders. He worked with the bodice and her corset until he freed her breasts for his view, for his touch. He grazed her nipples with his palms, and Isabella felt them harden at his touch. An ache started low in her abdomen.

"Your breasts are soft and firm, perfect in size and beauty."

Isabella didn't know what to say other than "Thank you."

He cupped them and lifted them up one in each hand and caught her nipples between his thumb and forefinger and rubbed them with the lightest pressure. The ache between her legs grew more insistent.

The feelings his touch created inside her were so wonderful she found herself saying aloud, "Don't let this end."

"No, Isabella, it's just beginning," Daniel whispered as he dipped his head and covered one rosy peak with his mouth.

He sucked and flicked one tip with his tongue as his hands massaged the fullness of her breasts. Isabella lifted her chest up to him. Her arms went around the back of his head. Her hands played in the thickness of his hair as she gently held him to her bosom. He suckled first one breast and then the other, thrilling her with sensations that took her breath away.

"Daniel, I know you've kissed me like this before, but I don't think it's ever felt this good."

He raised his head and gave her the sweetest smile. His lips were moist, full, and manly. "That's because this is more relaxing than a wet, dark garden."

"Much," she answered. "I can hardly catch my breath."

Daniel rose and pulled his shirt over his head and thrust it aside. Isabella gasped at how powerful he looked. She never imagined he was so muscular through his chest, shoulders, and arms. His wide chest tapered at the waistband of his black trousers. His stomach was flat and ribbed with muscles.

She laid her palm flat on the bulging swell of his chest and softly let her hand glide from one side to the other, and then up and down from his throat to his waist.

Isabella looked up at him with awe. "You look so powerful and so beautiful."

Taking hold of her hand, Daniel kissed the back of the palm, and then the inside. He smiled down at her again with sparkling eyes. "You are the only beautiful one in this room."

"I'm glad I'm here with you like this, Daniel."

"Me, too."

He bent over her and kissed her softly on each breast before catching her lips with his again. Isabella slid her arms around the widest part of his back. Her hands couldn't be still. She loved the feel of his hard body, his muscles rippling beneath her palms as she kneaded and caressed the firm, naked skin.

Daniel let his kisses slip from her lips to the crook of her neck. She heard him breathe in deeply as if he were trying to take her inside him. Her lower stomach muscles contracted with a need she didn't understand, but somehow she knew she wanted to feel his weight on top of her.

She moaned and squirmed beneath his gentle yet fervent touch and kisses until she finally dragged her mouth away from his and said, "Lay with me, Daniel."

Daniel answered with a desperate, "Yes, Isabella, yes." He stretched out beside her half on top of her and half on the settee. "I've wanted you like I've wanted no other woman." He pushed his lower body alongside her thigh. "Feel what you do to me."

Isabella felt the hardness of his manhood press tightly against her and it seemed natural to lift her bottom to try and get closer to him.

"I feel something very stiff. Is that good?" she asked.

"That's very good," he answered.

Her awareness of what they were doing increased. Excitement and anticipation built inside her.

When she felt the warm bare skin of his chest against her hard nipples, Isabella gasped with a pleasure she'd never experienced before.

Resting on one elbow, Daniel looked down into her eyes and said, "I'll stop anytime you say. If it hurts too bad just let me know."

She nodded, but couldn't imagine that anything would make her want to stop. All she could think was that she wanted more and more and more. She was too eager to experience all he had to show her.

Her heart beat faster, her stomach contracted fiercely. She knew something even more wonderful than what she was feeling at that moment was going to happen. She sensed it all over her body and she couldn't wait. She closed her eyes and concentrated on all the luscious sensations spiraling through her as Daniel continued to caress and kiss her.

"Oh, Daniel, I love the way your skin feels beneath my hands. It's so smooth and your muscles are so firm. I love the way your body fits next to mine." She let her hand rub down his chest to his waistband.

His lips caught hers again in a bruising kiss as his chest flattened against her breasts. He lifted the rest of his body on top of her. With a few quick motions he shoved her dress up and her drawers down. He parted her legs with his knee before letting his weight settle softly and slowly between them.

Isabella gasped again. Her heart beat so fast she was afraid she was going to lose her breath. A rising hunger like nothing she had ever known spread deep inside her.

It felt so natural for him to be on top of her. She lifted her bottom again and Daniel pressed his hardness against her softness while his lips ravaged hers.

She heard him moan as he dragged his lips away from her, and he asked on a shaky breath, "Am I going too fast?"

"No. I feel hot and out of breath, as if I've been running and—"

"Yes?"

"I feel as if something is missing inside me."

"Good, that's the way you're supposed to feel."

While he continued to kiss her madly, he put his hand between their bodies, and she knew by his movements that he was unbuttoning his trousers. She felt him shoving them down, and she moved her hands to his hips and helped him push them past his knees.

He started to lower himself to her again, but she stopped him by pressing her palm to his chest. "May I see you?"

She felt a tremble in the arm that held his weight off her. "Are you sure you want to?"

She nodded.

Daniel pushed backward and held his body up and away from her by holding on to the back of the settee.

Isabella looked at his pulsating shaft. It was beautiful. She reached out and touched its satiny length and its rigid hardness with her hands. She heard him moan with pleasure. She looked at his face. His eyes were closed. The expression on his face was so intense, for a moment she thought he might be in pain.

"Does it hurt?" she whispered.

His eyes opened and he looked down at her and smiled. "Oh, yes, it's killing me. But no, it doesn't hurt like you're thinking. Have you seen and touched enough, my beautiful, inquisitive Isabella?"

"I like the way it feels," she said, cupping him with both hands.

"I like it, too, but I've had all I can bear."

Isabella shivered with anticipation and nodded.

When he settled back between her legs, she felt the length of his body and the length of his long, hard shaft pushing against her.

Into her mouth he whispered, "Oh, Isabella, what you do to me is so powerful. I'm filled with wanting you."

"I feel it, too, my lord. I feel as if something has been building inside me and it's about to explode."

"Oh, yes, Isabella, it is. I'll see to it."

He dipped his head lower and sucked her breast into his mouth again, harder than he had before, but it didn't hurt. He laved and nibbled first one and then the other. His savage treatment only made her lift her buttocks and press tighter against him.

"Mmm, you taste good," he murmured against her skin. "So sweet and firm. I can't get enough of you."

His hand slipped between them again, and she felt a maddening pressure against her womanhood. It felt right for the force to be there, but it was as if her body wouldn't give in to his demand.

Suddenly his shaft broke through, and she felt a searing pain and just as quick a fullness that took her breath away. Isabella jerked with a whimper of shock, but Daniel held her close to his chest, kissing her forehead, her eyes, her cheeks, and her lips. She gasped at the fullness, the wonder; the unimaginable feeling of being joined with Daniel.

Her arms tightened around his back when he tried to push away from her. "No, don't stop," she begged.

"Are you sure you're all right?" he whispered as his lips traveled to her ear. The warmth of his breath comforted her.

Isabella was so filled with wonderment that she could only nod.

Daniel covered her lips with his and kissed her tenderly as his body started moving slowly, up and down. In and out.

"Join me," he said. "Help me love you."

Isabella did so and lifted her body to meet his. It seemed awkward at first but within moments they were moving together as one. Joy leaped inside her. Daniel loved her. They were making love. Her heart swelled with so much love for him she had to fight back tears of happiness.

Something was building inside her. Daniel kissed her tenderly; his hands massaged her breasts as his fingers rubbed her nipples. Isabella closed her eyes and gloried in the feel of Daniel's mouth on her lips, his hands on her breasts, and his body moving deep inside her.

She clung to him and moved with him until a spiral of sensations came together in an explosion of gratification. She let out a pleasurable cry of completion. Her fingers dug into his buttocks and held him to her for what seemed like a long, long satisfying time.

When her grip on him relaxed, his hips started pumping again and for a few more moments he rocked into her. His breaths came in heavy gasps until she felt his body shudder. His arms slid under her back and he pulled her close, tight, sinking himself as far into her as he could go.

Isabella smiled to herself. For her it was over too quickly. They lay quietly for a few moments with only their breathing breaking the silence.

Isabella felt no shame or regret. What she'd shared with Daniel had exceeded her expectations. The only thing that would have made their time together any better is if she'd been able to tell him she loved him.

Maybe she did regret she couldn't do that. She couldn't have him think in any way that she meant to trap him into marriage by insisting they have this short time together.

"My dearest, Isabella," he whispered into her ear. "You are so perfect for me."

Isabella was breathless, wrung out. She was so satisfied she felt like a pool of hot wax, yet she had never felt better in her life. She was contented. She threw her arms around him and laughed with vigor.

Daniel lifted his head and looked down on her with a curious expression. "Why are you laughing?"

"I'm happy, Daniel," she said. "You have made me very happy."

"Me, too."

"I mean it, Daniel."

"So do I."

Isabella inhaled. She was filled with an over-whelming satisfaction, and all she could do was lie in Daniel's arms and smile.

"It was more wonderful that I thought it would be."

He braced himself with one elbow. "It was just as heavenly as it has been in my dreams."

"You dreamed about what we just did?"

"Many times."

"I love the way it makes me feel when you kiss me and touch me." She ran her hand over his smooth, muscular chest. "I love the way your skin feels against mine. I love the way you feel inside me when you are big and—"

Daniel took hold of her hand and stopped her. "That's enough about that for now. We must straighten our clothes before your maid comes looking for you."

A deep pain of loss struck Isabella, and she tried to push it away. She had known this time had to end, but she didn't want it to. She had to find the strength to accept it. She took a deep breath and shored up her courage. She didn't want to be sad for what she wouldn't have with Daniel. She wanted to be glad for what she'd shared with him just now.

Daniel rolled off her and helped her to rise from the settee. He turned his back to her and started rebut-toning his trousers.

Isabella pulled her sleeves back up on her shoulder and started arranging her corset, wondering where she would get the courage to tell him good-bye.

It was heartbreaking to know their time together had been so short. She wanted to stay here with him forever, but she knew that wasn't to be.

She pulled up the bodice of her clothing. "Thank you for spending this time with me, Daniel, and for showing me what happens between a man and a woman when they come together."

Daniel swore as he spun around, almost falling over as he tried to shove his foot into his boot. A scowl curled his beautiful lips. "Don't say things like that, Isabella, and don't thank me."

"But I do."

He picked up his other boot. "What just happened between us was more than just a man and a woman coming together."

A glimmer of hope fluttered to life inside her. "It was for me. It was very special."

"It was special for me, too."

She bent down and picked up her pelisse. "I hadn't told you, but my father is coming home."

Daniel halted his movements, his boot half on. "He is? When?"

She slipped her arm into her sleeve.

"His letter said by the end of the month."

"That must make you happy."

"I want to see him, but…"

"But what? He's been gone years, hasn't he?"

"Yes, but I fear he will insist I go back to the country to live again. I knew by the time I turned twenty-one and could return to London on my own, you would already be married. That's why this time alone with you was so important to me."

Daniel finished pulling on his boot and started stuffing his shirttail into his trousers. "It is true, I will be married by the time you turn twenty-one."

A jagged pain splintered inside her.

Twenty-two

A LUMP SWELLED IN ISABELLA'S THROAT AT DANIEL'S pronouncement, but she didn't look up at him. She couldn't. She had known he was looking to marry from the first day they met. How could she have known then that the news he'd delivered would devastate her.

Isabella concentrated on the buttons on her pelisse as she calmly asked, "Who did you decide to marry? Lady Katherine?"

"No."

"Alice Eldridge?" she asked, realizing her fingers were so trembly by his news that she couldn't get her pelisse fastened.

"Oh, no, not her," he said as he grabbed his neck-cloth and collar from the floor.

Isabella looked up at him. "Miss Joanne Langley? Really, Daniel, I don't think she would be the best choice for you."

A questioning expression eased across his face. "Is that so? Why?" he asked as he fitted his collar and neckcloth around his neck.

"Well, she doesn't smile very often and her laugh is rather shrill."

"Oh, you noticed that?"

"Of course and I think you would get tired of that as the years go by. And she is rather short, and I do believe her shoulders slump a bit."

"Without doubt."

"So maybe you should consider someone else."

She looked up at him. He continued to tie his neckcloth. She loved him so much, but she had to remain strong and not let him know.

She wanted to smile at him, but found that she was just too sad. Her heart ached because she knew how desperately she was going to miss him.

"Perhaps it's best you don't tell me who you will marry."

"Would you rather read about it in the Society column?"

Prolonging it would be a good idea. She might break down in front of him and beg him not to marry anyone. "Yes. Yes, that would be better. Do not tell me. Most likely I will be in the country by the time you marry, and there will be no need for me to know."

He finished tying his neckcloth into a bow and walked over to her. He pushed a loose strand of hair behind her ear. His touch was warm, comforting, yet she felt hollow inside. She would miss him greatly.

Isabella took a deep breath. "Do I look presentable? Does anything appear out of place?"

"You look beautiful. There's only one thing left to do before you leave."

"And what is that?"

"You must pay the price for what just happened between us."

The lump in her throat grew bigger. She felt as if she would choke, but somewhere inside herself she found the courage to say, "I promised. Whatever you wish me to do, I accept that. What is it?"

Suddenly she closed her eyes and squeezed them tightly, as if that could make his punishment bearable.

"Open your eyes, Isabella."

"No, I can't. Just tell me what I must do."

"All right. You must marry me."

She heard his husky, whispered voice, but she couldn't have heard him correctly. She opened first one eye and then the other. He was standing so close to her, smiling so sweetly at her.

She moistened her lips. "I think you are going to have to say that again. I didn't understand what you said."

He bent his head close to hers. "You heard me correctly. You cannot deny me. You must marry me as soon as I can make the arrangements."

Isabella's heart leaped for joy. He wanted her to marry him? But did he feel she had trapped him? No, she couldn't do that to him. That's not what she planned.

She smiled and lovingly touched his cheek with her palm. "Daniel, I'm not going to do that to you. I couldn't. I know what I asked of you was selfish, but I have no desire to leg-shackle you. I only wanted to have the memory of being with you when I go to the country with my father. Do not worry. No one will ever know what happened between us."

"The only reason I agreed to touch you this afternoon is because I knew I was going to marry you."

He pulled her into his arms. "Isabella, I love you and I want you to be my wife."

For the second time that afternoon he had left her breathless. "You love me? Daniel, do you love me?"

"As insane as it sounds, yes!"

Isabella laughed and threw her arms around his neck and kissed him with all the passion she was feeling. His kiss was demanding yet cherishing, and she loved it. She felt as if her heart was going to beat out of her chest, she was so happy.

"I'm thrilled, Daniel. I love you so much. I knew you desired me, but I can't believe you love me, too."

"I do. How could I not fall in love with such a tempting mischief-maker?"

Daniel started to kiss her again, but Isabella stopped him with a hand to his chest. "Daniel, there's something you should know. I don't think I could ever be a conventional wife."

"Thank God. If they are all like the ladies I've been calling on, I don't think I could live with one."

Isabella laughed and Daniel joined her as they hugged. "Daniel, I'm so glad you fell in love with me."

"So I am. You make me happy, Isabella. I enjoy being with you. You are a challenge and unpredictable, and I know I don't want to live without you."

She smiled up at him. "That's exactly the way I feel about you, and yes, yes, yes, I will marry you."

He caressed her cheek with the back of his hand. "It's about time you said yes."

"I didn't want to appear too eager."

"There's one other matter we need to clear up."

"What is that?"

"Did you really let Sir William Smith kiss you?"

She smiled at him. "Of course not. Daniel, you are the only man who has ever kissed my lips."

"And I intend to keep it that way. I'll speak to your aunt and tell her we want to be ready to marry as soon as your father arrives. If he gets here by the end of the month, he can attend the wedding. If not, he'll have to bless us after we've wed. I refuse to wait more than two weeks to have you as my bride and in my bed."

Isabella reached up and kissed him on the cheek. "Two weeks. That is such a long time. I will have to slip over here and see you before then."

Daniel smiled. "Isabella, don't start that. We will wait until we are married."

Her hand slipped to the buttons on his trousers.

He chuckled and hugged her up close. "Maybe not." He set her away from him. "Now, you will ride home with your maid, and I'll follow in my carriage. I want to speak to your aunt about us immediately. This is unbelievable. I've settled Gretchen's future and mine in the same day."

"But how did you settle Gretchen's future? You can't possibly still consider Mr. Wright a suitable match for your sister."

"No. Someone infinitely better has come along and asked for Gretchen's hand."

"Oh, how wonderful! Who?"

"Chilton."

Isabella gasped with delight. "Your best friend. Daniel, that's wonderful for you and for Gretchen. I feel sure they will be happy together."

Daniel smiled. "Me, too. They know each other

well, and I couldn't have been more surprised when he told me his intentions. I know Gretchen will agree. I think she's always loved him."

"This will give such hope to all the ladies in my Reading Society."

"I'm glad you have them over. I hope you'll continue after we're married."

"Of course I will." Her heart felt as if it was bursting with love. "Thank you, Daniel, for knowing that I want to continue my work with them."

He smiled and kissed her again. "Chilton will be in my family and you will be my wife. There's nothing more I could want."

"And all I want is you."

"Come here, my tempting Isabella." He pulled her to him and kissed her softly, tenderly and lovingly.

Isabella thrilled to his touch.

Dear Reader,

I hope you enjoyed Isabella and Daniel's story. This was one of my favorite books to write. I had such fun with all the quirky ladies in the Wallflower Society. It took some careful planning to make sure the missing dead body didn't take away from the lightheartedness of the story. But most of all, as always, I loved developing the romance in the Regency time period with all its strict Society rules. It's a challenge for me to see just how many rules I can let my hero and heroine get away with breaking before they find their happily-ever-after.

Please visit my website at www.ameliagrey .com to see a complete list of all my books. Many are still available from your favorite local or online bookstore.

I love to hear from my readers. Please contact me at ameliagrey@comcast.net.

Happy Reading,
Amelia Grey

One

Anger can be an expensive luxury.
—*Italian Proverb*

IVERSON BRENTWOOD WAS OUT FOR BLOOD.

It hadn't taken him long to locate the address of the person he was looking for. His body tense, he lifted the collar of his greatcoat and stepped down from the comfort of his dry, warm carriage and into the chilling spring rain. Settling his hat lower on his forehead, with keen purpose, his boots splashing the puddles, he walked toward the front door of the elegant house in Mayfair. Banks of cold fog drifted in from the Thames and swirled in the dreary late afternoon air. The one bright spot was a lone light that shone from a front-room window of the place he sought.

Droplets of water fell from the brim of his hat as he stepped under the overhang of the stoop. Unclenching his tight fist, Iverson lifted the heavy door knocker and rapped it quickly a couple of times. The clang seemed to rattle the windowpanes in the house and reverberate down the quiet street. He waited impatiently in the fading light of day as the seconds ticked by, and then rapidly struck the brass plate a few more times.

It was hell being a twin, or so Iverson had thought until he arrived in London and found out hell was actually realizing the man he always thought was his father wasn't. The easiest thing for him and his brother to do would have been to sail back to Baltimore on the first ship. Instead, he and Matson had decided to keep with their original plan and move to London, and prove to their older brother and the gossipmongers that they weren't going to hide from anything. And the questioning glances and whispers about their parentage had settled down, until today.

A tall, buxom woman wearing servants' attire jerked open the door. Her thin, graying brows scrunched together in an irritated line across her forehead, as did her lips on her flat, pinched face. She looked him up and down with peculiar, deep-set brown eyes and then sniffed with annoyance.

"Ye didn't have to hit the knocker so hard. I'm slow, not deaf, ye know."

Iverson had never been taken to task by a servant and was momentarily surprised by the woman's insolent manner. He was in no mood to be hauled over the coals by a peevish maid. But before he could gather his wits and put her in her place, she snapped her large hands to her ample hips, glared at him once again, and said, "What can I do for ye?"

The woman clearly wanted him to know she had better things to do with her time than bother with him. Her surly attitude made him even angrier with her employer. It shouldn't surprise him that the scoundrel he was after had such a disrespectful servant in his employ. Iverson should have expected it.

Refusing to let go of his temper until he faced his intended prey, Iverson held his offensive retort in check and remained in what he considered a civil attitude. "I'm Mr. Iverson Brentwood here to see Sir Phillip Crisp."

The servant rolled her eyes beneath puffy lids and lifted her rounded chin as if to dismiss him. "I'm afraid that's not possible."

"And why isn't that possible?" he asked, his ire growing stronger.

"He isn't here." She extended her hand, palm up, and added, "I'll be happy to take your card and give it to him when he—"

"That won't be necessary," Iverson answered, assuming this woman's brusque attitude was merely a ruse to keep people away from Sir Phillip. Iverson wasn't going to be duped that easily and certainly not by a churlish servant who didn't know her place. He swept off his dripping hat and laid it in her outstretched hand. "I'll stay until the man returns." He then stepped past her and entered the well-appointed, dimly lit vestibule, unbuttoning his damp greatcoat as he went.

Sharp disapproval flashed across her face. "What are ye doing? Ye can't just come in here without an invitation."

Iverson had no quarrel with the woman, but he was tired of her disagreeable manner. He gritted his teeth, scowled, and said, "On the contrary, madam, I can, and I just did." He draped his wet coat across her extended arm. "I intend to see Sir Phillip before I leave this house today."

"But I don't know when he's returning," she barked, clearly outraged.

Her shrill voice grated on Iverson's ears, but if he had to endure the noise of the banshee in order to get to Sir Phillip, so be it. Anger burned in his chest, and he would not be put off so easily.

"That won't be a problem," Iverson said, peeling his well-fitted leather gloves from his hands and plopping them on top of his hat. "I'll wait. No doubt he'll be here by supper time, or for sure bedtime."

"Excuse me, sir."

At the sound of the softly spoken feminine voice, Iverson turned and saw one of the loveliest ladies he'd ever beheld. She was tall, graceful, and beautiful. Thick and shiny chestnut-colored hair was attractively arranged on top of her head, leaving nothing to distract from the lovely shape of her face, the slender column of her neck, or her gently rounded shoulders. She was dressed in a modest, pale-lilac gown that suited her ivory coloring perfectly. The high waist of her frock fit snugly under the fullness of her breasts, causing Iverson to take a second glance. There was a distinctly wholesome quality about her that immediately caught his eye, and Iverson was instantly drawn to her.

His hot anger toward Sir Phillip Crisp started cooling. She stopped a short distance from him, but he saw no fear in her delicate features—in fact, just the opposite was true. She seemed confident, very much in command of herself and unruffled by the situation she was confronting. With deliberate concentration, he watched her and couldn't help but wonder about her connection to Sir Phillip: daughter, sister, mistress, or wife?

She looked suspiciously at him and said, "I must ask who you are and why you are frightening Mrs. Wardyworth."

There was a slight tilt to her head and lift to her shoulders that immediately let him know she was challenging him. Her bright green eyes blazed with more questions than she had asked. The firm set to her gorgeous lips insisted he state his case without delay or face her judgment.

Iverson knew the polite thing was to introduce himself, but for the life of him, the only thing that came to mind was to say, "Frightening her?" He glanced around to the peevish servant smugly watching him. "No man, woman, or beast could frighten her. I doubt Napoleon's army in their heyday could have terrified this ill-mannered harpy."

"Did ye hear what he called me, missy?"

Keeping her imperious demeanor, the young lady turned to the woman and calmly said, "Yes, Mrs. Wardyworth, I heard."

"The bugaboo insisted on coming inside. Brushed right past me as if I weren't standing right in the doorway, he did."

Iverson couldn't believe his ears. Had the servant called him a bugaboo right in front of her mistress?

"I understand. I'll handle this now. Why don't you have Nancy make you a cup of tea?"

Mrs. Wardyworth sniffed again. "I think I'll do that. Would ye like for her to make a cup for ye, too?"

"That would be lovely."

Mrs. Wardyworth smiled sweetly at the lady and then looked down at Iverson's coat, hat, and gloves in her hands as if she didn't have the faintest idea what to do with them.

"Let me take those from you," the young woman said and lifted the damp things from the servant and laid them on a nearby table.

"Thank you, missy," she said. "You always know exactly what to do."

Mrs. Wardyworth glowered at Iverson as she turned and lumbered down the corridor. He had never seen a servant be so openly rife with impudence to a guest and not be thoroughly chastised by her employer.

Iverson grunted a laugh that rumbled softly in his throat as he slowly shook his head. He looked at the poised·lady before him and said, "I've heard of pampering the help, but I don't believe I've ever witnessed it in such dramatic fashion until just now."

Her eyes narrowed, and she looked at him intently. "Then you are by far a richer man for having seen how a few kind words can brighten a person's day and lift their spirits."

Iverson was near speechless again. Not only was the servant surly, now he was being chastised by this unflappable, overly self-confident lady. What kind of household did Sir Phillip have?

"Is that so?" Iverson quipped, not wanting to be scolded by such a delectable-looking female. "Then please tell me why my pockets don't feel any heavier."

A hint of a smile twitched at one corner of her mouth. "I wasn't referring to money, and you well know it. Now, tell me, what can I do for you, Mr.—?" Her light green gaze slowly swept down his face to settle on his lips.

A flash of awareness tightened his chest and quickened his lower body as she looked at his mouth, letting her attention linger there for much longer than necessary. "Brentwood," he said and swallowed hard. He wasn't sure he liked being attracted to her. "Mr. Iverson Brentwood."

Her gaze flew back up to his eyes in a brief moment of panic, and he would have sworn he saw her swallow hard, too. No doubt she had read or at least heard about the rubbish that blasted poet, Sir Phillip, had written about Iverson and his twin brother's arrival in London. And if that had been all the man had written, Iverson might have been inclined to overlook it or even laugh it off, as Matson had suggested they do, but there was no way he could let pass the slur it cast on his mother.

That had Iverson fighting mad. His mother was no longer alive to defend herself, and he wouldn't let anyone besmirch her memory and get away with it.

Iverson had a feeling Sir Phillip would be as easy to control as Lord Waldo Rockcliffe. Shortly after Iverson arrived in London, the Duke of Rockcliffe's youngest brother had the gall to ask him why he and his brother looked so much like Sir Randolph Gibson, given he wasn't their father. The answer Iverson gave him was a quick punch that left him with a black eye for a few days. Lord Waldo had never mentioned the subject again, and neither had anyone else. That one unplanned cuff had put a stop to much of the churning gossip, until today, with the publication of the parody *A Tale of Three Gentlemen*.

It wasn't that Iverson had enjoyed or wanted to hit

Lord Waldo. In fact, it was distasteful to him. It was a gut reaction. Only later did Iverson realize if he had let Lord Waldo get away with asking such a personal question, others would follow suit, and before long, his family would have been the laughingstock of London. Once again, his honor dictated he quell anyone else's tendency to ask probing questions or write unforgiving humor about his parentage.

Iverson was determined to put the rumors, gossip, and ill-mannered remarks back in the closet where they belonged by scaring the devil out of Sir Phillip. Everyone had to know there would be a price to pay for making comments or writing about something that was none of their concern.

"I see you recognize my name," he said, his simmering anger at Sir Phillip rising again.

"It would be difficult not to."

"No doubt because you read Sir Phillip's claptrap in *The Daily Herald* today?"

Her delicately arched brows raised a fraction. Her shoulders lifted ever so slightly before she pinned him with an intense stare. "Mr. Brentwood, I heard your name shortly after you arrived in London last fall, as did anyone who stepped inside a ladies' parlor, a gentleman's club, or the gaming hells near the wharf. Surely I don't have to tell you that by now the name Brentwood has been whispered in every taproom and manor house in London."

Iverson's breath caught in his throat. She was absolutely stunning when her feathers were ruffled, and he had obviously done that by denigrating Sir Phillip's writings. He'd never met a young lady who was so bold. He didn't mind that she hadn't pulled her punch or shied away from the cold, hard truth, but instead threw an insult right back into his face. She certainly had backbone and wasn't afraid to let him know it. That made her extremely attractive to him. He had never cared for the timid, retiring wallflower. He didn't know that he'd ever met anyone—let alone a lady—who had the nerve or fire to take him on and give him such a face-to-face dressing down.

He chuckled to cover his admiration for her courage and his slight discomfort at the veracity of her words. He gave her a perfunctory nod. "Gossip does travel fast and long, especially when it's salacious."

Assuming she had gotten the better of him, at least for the time being, she relaxed her shoulders. Another hint of a smile played around the corners of her attractive mouth and Iverson found it very inviting. In fact, much to his immediate distraction, there wasn't much about her he didn't find greatly appealing.

"Quite frankly, Mr. Brentwood, I didn't know there was any other kind."

Her admission reminded him that the poet was often in the gossip columns, too. In just the few months Iverson had been in London, he'd known of Sir Phillip's name being linked to a married actress, a widowed countess, and a madame by the name of Shipwith.

"Tell me, who you are?" he asked.

Pride shone in her sparkling eyes, and her feminine chin lifted another notch. "Miss Catalina Crisp. I am Sir Phillip's daughter, and his only child."

Iverson didn't know why, but he felt a sense of relief she wasn't Mrs. Crisp, but he sure as hell wasn't happy this beautiful and enticing young lady was Sir Phillip's offspring. She was, by far, the most intriguing person he'd met since coming to London.

Shortly after his arrival, Iverson had been introduced to her father, and he'd seen the man at several parties during the winter, though surprisingly, his daughter had never been with him. Sir Phillip wasn't at all like the pompous poet Lord Snellingly, who was an irritating fop, demanding attention from everyone and constantly wanting some poor soul to listen to him recite his dreadful poetry. Sir Phillip enjoyed the ladies. He was always talking, laughing, or dancing with a lady. In fact, the few times Iverson had been around him, he didn't think he'd even heard the man mention his poetry. He didn't have to, because his poetry was actually good.

Unlike Keats, who had recently been ridiculed in *The Examiner* as a "complete failure," and by *Blackwood's Magazine* as an "unsettled pretender who had no right to aspire to poetry," Sir Phillip was constantly being lauded and praised for his poetic genius. Iverson certainly had no reason to think the man would ever write a parody about him and his twin brother.

Clearing his throat and his thoughts, Iverson said, "In that case, Miss Crisp, I would like to speak with your father."

"My father is not here."

"Yes, your maid told me he was gone," he muttered under his breath and rubbed the back of his neck in frustration. "And as I told her, I'll wait for him to return."

She gave him an understanding smile. "First, Mrs. Wardyworth is my housekeeper, not my maid. And second, my father has been gone almost a week. If you plan to stay until Papa returns, you will have to take up residence, and I'm afraid I can't allow that, because it would shred my reputation."

"On that point I will agree with you." Iverson took in a deep breath. "So tell me, when is he expected back?"

"Sir, I can't possibly tell you what I don't know."

"And if you don't know," Iverson echoed, "then how can you be certain he won't return tonight?"

"I'm not." She looked thoughtful for a moment before adding, "There are times when my father simply packs his trunks and follows his dreams and his muse. It often keeps him away for days at a time, but whatever road he takes, it eventually leads him back home. Perhaps you could check again in a few days to see if he has returned."

That gathering storm of anger rose in him again. Iverson wanted to see her father now and put a death scare in him so he wouldn't have any desire to print more of that sensational, obnoxious, and completely false drivel about his family.

"No, no, Miss Crisp." Iverson shook his head impatiently. "I'm afraid that answer is not good enough."

She sighed softly, folded her hands together in front of her and pleasantly said, "I don't know where he is, so I don't know what more I can do for you."

A wave of sweet anticipation swept over Iverson, and his lower body hardened. Iverson knew exactly what she could do for him. He had an intense desire to pull her into his arms, press her soft breasts against his chest, and kiss her delectable lips. Impulsively, he took a step toward her with that in mind, but the reality of what he was about to do raced through him like a wild fire through dry brush, and he stopped just as he went to reach for her.

What was he thinking?

Kissing her would be madness.

Iverson was treading on unfamiliar ground here. He'd never been so enchanted by such a strong and determined young lady. She was the daughter of the devilish man he came to turn into mincemeat. The last thing he needed to do was kiss her inviting lips. Iverson had done some rash things in his lifetime, but thankfully, someone was watching over him just now and stopped him from creating even more scandal. It was enough of a thorn in his side that he found her immensely attractive.

Emptying his mind of wayward thoughts, he said, "There is a lot you could do for me, Miss Crisp." He stopped and cleared his throat and his thoughts again. "But I'll not mention what that is, because even though I'm not always a perfect gentleman, as you no doubt have noticed, I'm the last person to want to take the shine off your pristine reputation."

Another knowing smile played on her lips. "I'm sure you have done plenty of that to innocent young ladies in your time."

About the Author

Amelia Grey grew up in a small town in the Florida Panhandle, and has been happily married to her high school sweetheart for more than thirty-five years.

Amelia has won the Booksellers Best Award, Aspen Gold Award, and Award of Excellence writing as Amelia Grey. Writing as Gloria Dale Skinner, she has won the *Romantic Times* Award for Love and Laughter, the Maggie Award, and the *Affaire de Coeur* Award for best historicals.

Her books have been featured in Doubleday and Rhapsody Book Clubs and have sold to many countries in Europe, and in Russia, China, and most recently in Indonesia and Turkey.

Amelia's Rogues' Dynasty Trilogy—*A Duke to Die For*, *A Marquis to Marry*, and *An Earl To Enchant*—also *A Gentleman Never Tells* and *A Gentleman Says "I Do"* are available at your favorite local or online bookstore.

Amelia likes flowers, candlelight, sweet smiles, gentle laughter, and sunshine.

Please visit her at www.ameliagrey.com, www.Facebook.com/AmeliaGreyBooks, or ameliagrey@comcast.net.

A Dash of Scandal

by Amelia Grey

Is she stealing… or just hiding in dark corners…

The Earl of Dunraven is obsessed with catching the thief who stole a priceless heirloom from him. When he keeps running into London newcomer Millicent Blair in places she shouldn't be, his suspicions aren't the only thing aroused…

But Millicent's real secret is a far cry from what the earl thinks—and would horrify him much more if he knew. Yet, every encounter increases the attraction between the powerful earl and the lovely, intelligent, and feisty Miss Blair…

Welcome to the sparkling Regency world of Amelia Grey, where the gossip is fresh and a new scandal is always brewing.

"This is the perfect recipe for a perfect Regency romance novel. A pinch of mystery, a slice of romance, a sliver of gossip, and a dash of scandal. What more could you ask for?"—Royal Reviews

For more Amelia Grey, visit:

www.sourcebooks.com

A Gentleman Never Tells

by Amelia Grey

❧

A stolen kiss from a stranger…

As if from a dream, Lady Gabrielle walked from the mist and into Viscount Brentwood's arms. Within moments, he's embroiled in more scandal than he ever thought possible…

Can sink even a perfect gentleman…

Beautiful, clever, and courageous, Lady Gabrielle needs Brent's help to get out of a seriously bad situation. But the more she gets to know him, the worse she feels about ruining his life…

Enter the unforgettable world of Amelia Grey's sparkling Regency London, where a single encounter may have devastating consequences for a gentleman and a lady…

❧

"A stubborn heroine clashes with an equally determined hero in the latest well-crafted, canine-enhanced addition to Grey's Regency-set Rogues' Dynasty series."—Booklist

"The book is delightful… charming and unforgettable."—Long and Short Review

For more Amelia Grey, visit:

www.sourcebooks.com

The Virtuoso

by Grace Burrowes

--- ❦ ---

A genius with a terrible loss...

Gifted pianist Valentine Windham has little interest in
father's obsession to see his sons married, and instead p
passion into his music. But when Val loses his music,
flees to the country, tormented by what has been rob
from him.

A widow with a heartbreaking secret...

Grieving Ellen Markham's curious new neighbor offe
kindred lonely soul whose desperation is matched onl
his desire, but Ellen's devastating secret could be the
thing that destroys them both.

Together they'll find there's no rescue from the past,
sometimes losing everything can help you find what
need most.

--- ❦ ---